Welcome To Witherleigh
Richard Radcliffe Paranormal Investigations
P.J. REED

RICHARD RADCLIFFE PARANORMAL
INVESTIGATIONS

Welcome To Witherleigh

The Witherleigh Puzzle

To those who wander
Solve this rhyme,
And head backwards
To an older time.

Her blood once blue
Turned cold and white,
A ghostly figure
On a fog bound night.

Between three moors
Across three lanes,
A woman in white
That feels no pain.

There are whispers she
Once did favours,
To reward her
Helpful neighbours.

In North Devon
Her memory stands,
As she silently watches
The empty lands.

CHAPTER ONE

The car jolted unhappily through the mud-splattered lane. At least he hoped it was mud. Black and white cows peered knowingly at him through breaks in the overgrown hedge.

'Well, that's the last time I clean you until we get safely back to London,' Richard muttered, as he slowed to avoid a pair of suicidal pheasants. One stood in the road, frozen in fear, the other ran for its life, and disappeared into the hedgerows. Richard stopped the car and let the pheasant cross safely to rejoin its companion. He saluted the birds and watched as they wandered through the lines of gnarled trees, which flanked each side of the narrow road.

Trees stooped over each side of the road. Their branches joined together above the middle of the lane, like skeletal brown arms twisting into each other, blocking out the late autumn sun. Richard stared at the crowding trees. There were melted faces in the lines of the bark.

He shivered as a feeling of panic surged through his body.

Richard gripped the steering wheel. His knuckles whitened as electrical pulses ran up and down his spine. He swallowed and pinged the band around his wrist. The sharp pain broke through his thoughts. The trees straightened. Their faces became lost in the creases of the bark. Richard twanged the rubber band again. Important things had to be performed twice. He started the car and drove carefully past the sullen trees.

Richard looked at his watch. He had to be at the Witherleigh Day Centre by two. The ladies of the Anglican ministry were putting on a special cream tea and he could not be late.

The cluttered trees gave way to the rugged open fields of the North Devon wildlands. This was a harsh, ancient land. Undulating fields of dark green, broken by rows of hedges and the occasional windswept tree; dejected and alone amid a sea of grass.

Richard felt as if every mile he drove closer to Witherleigh dragged him further back in time. He pinged the rubber band on his wrist.

'The change to a simpler life will be good. It's just what I needed,' he whispered.

Richard drove past a long wooden farm fence. A buzzard sat perched on a fence post. The bird was so still, it looked like a wooden carving of itself. The buzzard flew away disturbed. Richard half-smiled. He had never seen a bird of prey in flight and watched, captivated by the effortless majesty of its wings' slow movement as it soared into the steel grey sky.

A four-wheel drive beeped loudly. Richard swerved back to his side of the lane, the old car's wheels squelching to a halt in the mud, which ran in gulley's along the side of the road. He let out a deep breath and waved an apology at the red-faced driver, who shouted something inaudible, as the Range Rover roared past him.

The little white pills were not good for his concentration

levels. He shook his head. Perhaps down here he could be rid of them.

The lane swung around a corner and opened into a single carriageway. He drove past a row of weather-beaten houses scattered along the road and an abandoned Methodist church, its windows and doors boarded up. At the side of the road, a small sign hidden among the straggling grasses and perennial bushes, welcomed him to Witherleigh. His home for the next liturgical year.

A young man came out of the village newsagents, its window cluttered with brightly coloured flyers. The man stood and watched Richard, his face blank and unwelcoming. Richard almost waved but stopped himself and frowned as he ran his hand through his wild, brown hair instead.

His old vicar had warned him about these isolated Devonian villages. *The people are lovely, warm-hearted, and will do anything for you, once they get over the shock of seeing a newcomer.*

Richard sighed. Nothing could be as bad as the All Saints ministry in London.

He drove past a young family and smiled a greeting as they waited to cross the road. Four faces stared back at him. The youngest child frowned and gripped a weather-beaten Barbie doll by the straggling remains of its once platinum blond hair. Richard felt his stomach sink as if he had just eaten one of his mother's leaden rock cakes. He fixed a friendly smile to his face and parked his car outside the Witherleigh Day Centre. A big homemade sign burst from the window exclaiming, 'Welcome to Witherleigh! Tea and coffee available inside'. Bunting had been strung across the front entrance to the tiny cabin-like

Centre. It fluttered apathetically as a sudden wind howled through the silent village.

Richard whispered, 'I can do this,' two times. Then climbed from his car and walked tentatively over to the centre. A thin, heavily made-up, middle-aged woman blocked the doorway.

'Welcome to our little village,' she smiled, surveying Richard slowly.

Richard blushed and quickly tucked the rumpled white shirt into his jeans and smoothed the crinkles from his faded blue sweatshirt. The corner of the woman's lip curled upwards. She stared down at him and watched his unease with satisfaction.

An awkward silence descended.

Richard swallowed his embarrassment and smiled.

'Thank you for the banner. It's a lovely welcome.' He scanned the room and saw an ancient face watching him from behind the hospital-sized windows. 'I'm Richard Radcliffe, the new Children's, Youth, and Family Worker for the diocese. It's a pleasure to meet you. Mrs… er?'

The woman begrudgingly shook his hand. Her hand felt hard and cold in his. He let her hand drop too quickly to be polite.

'I am Seraphina Ashcroft,' the lady announced.

Richard resisted the urge to wipe his hand on his jeans and smiled at her. 'This village has a delightful character. I hope to get to know everyone very soon. I believe the first children's ministry group is being held tonight?'

'Oh, do not worry about that. It was cancelled, we thought you might be tired from your long journey, what with your problems. Come in and have a cup of tea.' Seraphina swept to one side.

Richard opened his mouth to protest but said nothing. He recognised the presence of his father in the proceedings.

Anything he said would be smoothed away and ignored.

Richard nodded at Seraphina and entered the centre.

A cheerful 'farmer's wife' looking woman bustled over and showed him to a seat on the far side of the centre. Richard smiled a thank you as she thrust a huge mug of steaming tea into his hand. The woman stood over him, her arms folded across her ample chest, as he drank the most uncomfortable mug of tea he had had in his life. He drained the scalding liquid as fast as possible.

An elderly man, who had been seated at the back of the centre, shuffled past him and muttered something inaudible.

'I'm sorry, I didn't quite catch that?' Richard looked up.

'Don't you pay no 'eed to old Snowy he's 'armless but best keep yer distance, 'ee don't like grockles.'

Richard frowned, 'Er… what's a grockle?'

The tea lady gave him a pitying glance. 'That'll be one of your types, a foreigner to these 'ere parts.'

Richard balled his hand into a fist and resisted the urge to touch his rubber band, as an overwhelming feeling of foreboding rushed across his soul. He shivered as the centre door opened and a cold draft blew through the cafe. Richard rose from the table.

'Thank you for the delicious tea but I must get unpacked. The devil finds work for idle hands,' he joked.

The tea woman nodded. 'Aye, that 'ee does,' she replied grimly.

Richard quickly vacated the centre. The pine detergent which perfumed the little cafe clawed at his throat. He coughed and rubbed his stinging eyes. He had smelled the caustic pine smell before in the unit, just before he had been sent to the Devon diocese to recover.

The smell haunted his dreams and it had followed him here.

***

Mrs Bell watched Richard hurry from the centre. The smile fell from her face. She tutted and retrieved the industrial strength bleach cleaner from the back of the centre and proceeded to wipe down the table and chairs where he had sat.

'Well, what do you think of the new youth worker?'

A clear voice called from the doorway. Mrs Bell jumped.

The cleaning spray cluttered to the floor.

Mrs Bell apologized, retrieved the cleaner from the floor, and clutched it to her escaping bosom. 'He's a young'un an' a bit nervy, Mrs Ashcroft.'

Seraphina looked at her with an expression of disgust mixed with an equal portion of contempt. 'Let's try and keep this one for a little longer than the last, shall we, Mrs Bell?'

Mrs Bell stared at the sparkling white tile floor and nodded.

***

Richard jumped back in his car, his biggest luxury possession and wiped the beads of sweat from his forehead. He found meeting new people physically draining, which was a little at odds with his employment, but at least it placated his father slightly.

'My son is not a complete wastrel. He just wasn't bright enough to finish his degree,' Reverend Radcliffe would explain to a sympathetic audience at every opportunity.

Richard fished a dog-eared letter from the back of his jeans. He checked the address for the sixth time that day and typed the coordinates into his phone. A friendly electronic voice activated, and he drove slowly from the village. Richard checked his mirror and smiled as he saw the stout figure of Mrs Bell waving enthusiastically at him. At least somebody in the village seemed pleased to see him.

Half an hour later, he breathed a sigh of relief as an old sign at the top of a pot-holed farm track welcomed him to Home Farm – Home to Happy Holidaymakers.

Grass grew from a one-foot wide garden which had sprouted from the centre of the muddy track. The sheep grazing in the field looked up and watched him in fascination as they chewed noisily. Richard sighed. He doubted any holiday makers - happy or not - had ventured down this track for a very long time.

Richard pulled up outside the decaying farmhouse. Paint had peeled away from the once white window ledges, which had blistered and cracked in the autumn rains.

Formal flower gardens had been laid out in front of the sprawling house. The gardens showed signs of past glory with a few drying, stooped flowers, Richard did not recognise, standing sadly among a carpet of creeping weeds and dirt. He searched for a bell but gave up and tried the door handle. The door swung sullenly on its hinges to reveal an equally dishevelled interior. The sound of high-pitched, operatic notes floated through the house.

'Er… hello, Mr Butler, I'm here about the holiday home. The diocese secretary Mrs Dawkins booked it for me?' Richard enquired politely, half-hoping that by some terrible misfortune, the holiday home was double-booked, and he would have to seek accommodation elsewhere.

The chorus ended in mid-scream. Richard heard a settee creak as the farmer stomped towards the door.

'You the fancy bloke from up London, are you?' He looked Richard up and down, as if he were sizing up a heifer for market.

Richard was slightly taken aback. In his ancient jeans, faded sweatshirt, and untamed brown hair, he had never considered himself to be in any way fancy. He nodded politely. 'I'm Richard Radcliffe, the new North Devon church networks children's and youth leader.'

'Well, I never liked the last one,' the farmer muttered, 'and I don't think you'll do 'right here, neither. I ain't got time to stand 'ere all day chatting. I got milking to do, so you best hurry up and follow me.'

The farmer pulled on a pair of filthy looking wellies and strode across the muck-ridden farmyard. Richard stared miserably at his white trainers, picked up his suitcase, and ran after the huge farmer.

'There she be. Buttercup Cottage.' Farmer Butler swept his arms across the outside of the cottage then tossed Richard the key. 'Don't go worryin' about rent, it's comin' straight from your salary, Reverend Radcliffe said you would cope better if you didn't have money to fuss with.'

Richard bit his lip and swallowed his anger. His father's presence seemed to follow him everywhere.

The farmer nodded a farewell. He whistled for his dogs and marched towards a big grey building lurking by the side of the farmhouse.

Richard stared miserably after the disappearing farmer, then turned to survey Buttercup Cottage - a mould-encrusted caravan, which sat wallowing in the mud, on the edge of the cattle field. The wind howled through the silence. Richard shivered. An oppressive feeling of emptiness seemed to squash him into the field. He unlocked the tiny door and ran inside, away from the silence of the fields.

An earthy stench of mould clawed at his throat and he gagged. Panic flashed through his body and his fingers gripped around the rubber band. 'I will be fine,' he whispered. 'All it needs is airing and a lot of bleach. I can do this.' He opened the little cupboard door, beneath the black-streaked sink. The cupboard shone white with several sprays of industrial strength bleach cleaner.

The rest of the day was spent cleaning, wiping, and emptying the junk left behind by the previous tenant. By the time night fell and the fields turned to black, the inside of the caravan sparkled. Richard ripped the plastic covering off the new mattress, which had been precariously perched on an ancient wooden bedframe, filling one side of the caravan. He peeled off his sweat-stained, mould-smelling clothes, and lay naked on the bed. 'At least the mattress is clean,' he murmured gratefully.

The sound of the cows mooing mournfully across the dark

field lulled him to sleep.

While an object, tied to the back-door porch, caught by the rushing wind, thudded against the side of the caravan.

CHAPTER TWO

An oozing darkness filled Richard's dreams as he watched the world decay. He tried to move but his arms and legs were pinned to the bed. He was trapped. His heart beat faster, sweat poured from his forehead, and panic surged through his brain, as the familiar feeling of impending doom crushed the life from his body.

In the distance, someone began to knock. The sound dragged him from his sleep, and he lay in bed panting as he listened to the early morning wind, as it rattled around his caravan. A breath of black mould had crept across the outside of the window. Richard sighed. He was sure that he had cleaned all the detritus from the caravan yesterday.

Something knocked against the little porch.

Probably a cow.

Richard climbed from his bed and padded across the rough vinyl floor to the tiny kitchen area. The early morning sun shone through the window, illuminating the desolate Devon landscape. Dark shapes in the cow fields nodded and cawed as a scattering of crows ripped their morning breakfast from the mud.

Richard smiled. He felt almost as hungry as his ravenous

neighbours.

The door of the caravan shot open. Farmer Butler strode inside. Richard grabbed a shirt to cover himself, as the farmer stared down at his naked body.

He felt his cheeks glow. Several awkward moments passed.

'Er… hmm… can I help you with something?' Richard stuttered.

'I brought 'ee some fresh milk, not the townie pasteurised stuff, real milk straight from the shippen. Sweet enough to sprout some real hairs on your chest.'

'Thanks… er… that's very thoughtful of you,' Richard replied, as he edged away from the farmer.

Butler placed a dainty, cream-coloured jug on the tiny caravan table, nodded, and left the caravan.

Richard snatched the remainder of his clothes from the caravan floor and quickly threw them on. He peered cautiously through the caravan window and watched with relief as the farmer disappeared among the undulating green fields.

Country people are strange, but strange does not mean bad.

He snapped the rubber band twice. *You must accept one another just as Christ has accepted them,* his father's voice boomed through his thoughts.

'Oh crap! I must be a worse Christian than I thought,' Richard groaned.

He smelt the jug and tentatively took a sip. It tasted like a spoonful of sickly, thick cream. Richard spat the sticky cream into the stained mini-sink, with apologies to Farmer Butler's herd, he preferred his milk from a bottle, not an udder.

Richard upended his rucksack and the contents spilt across

the floor. He grabbed a crumpled bottle of water from the pile and drained it. The tide of sickness abated. This countryside living was going to take a bit of time to get used to.

Richard ate his breakfast in silence and watched as the fields lightened.

After he had tidied away his meagre breakfast, Richard decided to phone his new vicar, Reverend Anderson. Anderson was the vicar of the Church of Saint Anthony, the last remaining church in Witherleigh.

There was no tone. He tried again, then stared at his phone in disbelief. There was no signal.

'Of course, there wouldn't be a signal down here,' he smiled to himself. It was like he was living in a different century.

Richard put on his once white trainers and headed up to the top of the lane. The higher the altitude, the better chance of contact with the outside world, he reasoned as he trudged up the muddy lane.

The view from the top of the lane was spectacular. Dark green fields dipped and rolled in every direction. The greenness was only broken by the thorny hedgerows and ancient trees which stood aloof and untouched in the fields. The bottom fields of the farm ran into a line of trees which formed the border of the woodlands and climbed up the valley side. The only thing that spoilt the ever-lasting elegance of the view was a tall wire fence, which separated the woodlands from the farm. Double lines of barbed wire ran around the top of the fence. A collection of silver objects had been tied to the barbed wire.

Richard squinted at the fence.

The blurred objects cleared and transformed into a

collection of knives, forks, scythes, and scissors that glinted as they twisted in the rising sun.

Probably to keep deer and badgers out from rooting around the crops, Richard reasoned as he ran his hand through his uncombed hair. He scanned the surrounding farmland. There was no fallow land or sign of any crop except grass. A vague feeling of unease shivered through his body. Richard dismissed it instantly.

It could not be happening again.

He pinged the elastic band on his wrist four times and watched the cows as they grazed in the field. A quiet calmness descended.

I just need to keep busy, he thought.

Richard checked his mobile and was relieved to see that two tiny black bars had appeared. He scrolled through his contacts, pressed call, and swallowed. It was not a call he would have chosen to make.

The phone rang for a minute. A stern woman's voice answered.

'Hello, this is Richard… Radcliffe, I am the new youth worker.'

'I know who you are.'

'Can I speak to Reverend Anderson please,' Richard enquired.

'No,' replied the voice. 'He is resting today. He was working all night. You can see him at the church office after service on Sunday.'

'Oh… I've never heard of an all-night church emergency,' Richard answered.

'Most church emergencies happen at night when the darkness falls. You will get used to it. Good day to you.' The phone disconnected.

Richard shoved the phone back in his jean pocket and thought for a moment, as he watched two rooks circle in the morning sky.

If the flock is unwilling, go out and shepherd them in. An image of his father at the church council meeting banging his fist on the oak table stirred in his memory. Besides, he did not want to spend a whole day trapped on the isolated farm with only Farmer Butler for company.

Richard rushed back to his caravan, grabbed his keys, and drove slowly up the pot-holed farm lane. Butler stood with his arms folded as he stared at Richard from under the solitary oak tree, its withered grey branches in stark contrast to the fading green of the fields. Richard waved as he drove past the farmer.

The farmer stared back at him.

***

After an uneventful quarter of an hour's drive, Richard entered Witherleigh.

Saturday had left the little village desolate. Anyone able-bodied enough to leave the village had migrated to the large supermarkets and bright coffee shops of the nearest town, Ashdurton, over an hour's drive away. Only the very young and elderly remained behind.

Richard parked in the tiny market square and searched for signs of life.

The Witherleigh Store's door jingled open and the old man

from the centre shuffled out. He saw Richard from across the empty road and called out in a low, guttural voice. Immediately, the shopkeeper appeared in the doorway, his arms folded, as he shooed the old man along.

The old man walked on, arguing to himself, as he disappeared down a narrow street. Richard nodded to the shopkeeper and crossed the surprisingly full car park which sprawled across the centre of the village.

The first stop on his visit was to drop in at the Witherleigh Day Centre.

The tea had only the briefest relationship with a teabag, consisting mainly of milk and boiling water, and the centre had the atmosphere of a hospital morgue, but at least Mrs Bell was friendly and could introduce him to the other members of the St Anthony's congregation.

The apathetic bunting had been removed but the welcome sign was still propped up against the window. The bottom of the sign had white water marks on it. A faint grey shadow radiated from the lower left-hand corner of the paper, as a rash of mould began to eat away at the gaudy coloured wording.

The wind from the surrounding moors ran around the village and brought with it a dampness which lowered the temperature. Richard shivered. He flattered his wild brown hair with his hand. He had forgotten to brush it again; no wonder people were wary of him.

'I must look like a vagrant,' he groaned, as yet another gust of wind ruffled through his hair.

Richard took a deep breath, and was about to open the centre door, when something blond caught his attention. He turned and stared at the curl of blond hair, which protruded from a drain, at the side of the road. Richard bent down, peered into the drain, and breathed a sigh of relief, as the tiny head of a Barbie doll peered back at him from inside the drain. The doll's face was covered in black grime. However, it could have been some little girl's treasured possession. Richard gently pulled at the doll. Its head was stuck fast in the gap. She had been jammed into the drain with considerable force.

Richard tugged the doll hard. The gutter relinquished its grip on the doll's head, and he tumbled face down onto the road, with the muck-covered doll lying dejectedly in his outstretched hand.

The door of the centre swung open. Mrs Ashcroft appeared in the street. She stared down at Richard. Her immobile face frowning slightly.

Seraphina ignored the doll.

'Good morning, Mr Radcliffe. Lunch is served at midday. However, you may come in now if you wish. Mrs Bell will see to you.'

Mrs Ashcroft walked off down the road, her stilettoed footsteps echoing in the silence of the empty village.

Richard smiled as she passed him. It wasn't the impression he had wanted to make but at least people were beginning to recognise him. He stood up, brushed the dust from his jeans, and entered the warmth of the centre.

'Good morning, Mrs Bell,' he announced in a voice far more confident than he felt. 'One of your delicious cups of tea, please.'

Mrs Bell bustled into the dining room; her face flushed from

23

the heat of the kitchen. Lunch was obviously a busy affair. Richard glanced around the centre. All the seats sparkled white but sat empty. He looked at the white plastic clock, mounted above the door to the kitchen. The monotonous clicks of the second-hand juddered. Time stopped for an instant and then jolted forward one minute. It was eleven-thirty. He was half an hour early for the lunchtime rush.

Mrs Bell stared at the filthy doll in his hand. The welcoming smile froze on her face.

'Sit you down, my lover, one cup of tea coming up. Is there anything else I can get for you? It's pasty and baked potato for lunch an' that'll be ready at twelve, but I'll make an early one just for you. Perhaps you'll want to wash your hands an' your doll before you eat?'

Richard laughed. 'Not mine I'm afraid. I found it in the road.'

Mrs Bell frowned, looking from the doll to Richard but gave him an encouraging smile as she bustled back into the kitchen.

The doll was getting him into all sorts of trouble but the thought of the little girl standing by the side of the road, as she gripped her beloved Barbie tightly, made him smile.

However, he could not give the child her doll back in such a terrible condition, it could cause a cholera outbreak or something and that would definitely be the end of his ecclesiastical career.

He walked across the centre towards a little printed sign stating 'Washroom'. A drop of black viscous mud plopped unnoticed from the doll and landed on the sparkling floor. Once safely inside the washroom, Richard wet a paper towel and carefully wiped the black muck from the doll.

The smile on his face froze.

The doll's face had been destroyed. Its features burnt together to make an expressionless, amorphous plastic blob. Its humanity extinguished. The doll looked more like a grotesque monster than a barbie princess. The arms and legs of the doll were unburnt but had been mutilated. Slashed in a series of parallel cuts. Each cut was barely a couple of millimetres apart and was sharp to touch. Cut with either a fine knife or perhaps one of the scalpel's used in A' Level art classes or by surgeons.

The owner of this doll had something very wrong with them.

This was not the doll of a child. He wrapped the doll in a toilet paper shroud and shoved it to the bottom of the bin. Some of the muck from the doll stained the lines in his palm black, forming an odd pattern… almost like a rune. Gingerly, Richard sniffed his hands. They smelt of a curious mixture of swimming pool chlorine and wet mud, which was odd because the nearest pool was an hour's drive across the fields.

He washed his hands four times, but the caustic smell would not go. He sighed and went to open the washroom door.

The voice of Mrs Ashcroft resonated through the centre. 'And did you see what he was carrying? A filthy doll!'

Someone muttered in agreement.

'His father was right. The boy is obviously quite mad. I do not think he will cause us any problems.'

Mrs Ashcroft's shoes clinked from the centre.

Richard felt his knees give way as he collapsed onto the washroom floor..

CHAPTER THREE

Richard covered his face with his hands. He heard the soft tread of Mrs Bell's flats creep across the centre and pause outside the washroom door. He pinged the band twice and held his breath. The footsteps moved away. Richard let out a sigh of relief and bashed the back of his head against the hard, white wall.

He grabbed the phone from his pocket and scrolled through his contacts. The number of the Nightingale Unit flashed across his screen.

He threw the phone across the room. It skidded to a rest as it clanged against a metallic wastepaper bin. Richard looked up and saw his reflection distorted in the metal. If he rang Dr Berghaus for advice, his father would be notified immediately and this time he might not be able to escape the hospital so easily.

He had not been wrong in London. He had done nothing wrong in Witherleigh, but a hollow feeling in the pit of his stomach warned him that it was happening again. He gritted his teeth and clenched his fists. He could feel his nails cutting into the palms of his hands. This time he would prove them wrong.

Richard stood up, walked over to the shining white sink,

and splashed the icy cold water onto his face. Then he picked up his phone and walked from the bathroom.

Mrs Bell was hovering anxiously around his table. 'Are you alright, my lover. I thought I heard a crash.'

A concerned frown creased her rounded face.

'I'm fine, thank you,' Richard smiled. 'Just dropped my mobile on the floor, fortunately, nothing got broken.'

A confused crack appeared between her faded blue eyes. 'Well, my dear, if you need anything just let me know. Your pasty should be ready by now.'

She disappeared through the kitchen doors.

Richard gazed out through the large window which opened Witherleigh before him in all its empty glory. In the distance, he could see the dark forbidding moor, encircled by primordial woodlands and the browns of fallow fields. Richard could feel God's immortal presence in the countryside. He felt calm and protected.

Below the fields, protruding into his vision like ugly squat cages, sat a terrace of old shops selling a variety of strange sounding goods such as 'Bumblebee Saddle Polish' and 'Ringworm Paste.' Interspersed between the shops were drab little houses lining each side of the road. Partially hidden in the porch of one of little shops, stood Mrs Ashcroft, a mobile phone pressed to the side of her face, as she observed him through the glass.

Richard wondered whether she was reporting back to his father or the 'us' he had heard her mention earlier. Either way he was sure the report would not be a positive one.

Richard clenched his fist. A stabbing pain made him grimace

and he stared at his hand. A series of weeping, red marks cut across his palm. He looked over his shoulder to make sure Mrs Bell was not lurking behind him, and quickly wrapped his palm in the grubby hanky he found in the back pocket of his jeans. A faint trace of blood seeped through the white cloth. Richard felt a familiar wave of foreboding flow over his body.

If the cuts were horizontal, why was the blood on the hanky in the shape of a triangle?

Mrs Bell burst through the kitchen door, her face beaming as she placed a steaming plate of Cornish pasty, the biggest jacket potato he had ever seen, and a landslide of baked beans in front of him.

'Here you are, my lover, that'll see you right for the day.'

Richard waved at Mrs Ashcroft with his good hand and smiled his thanks to Mrs Bell.

Mrs Bell patted his shoulder. 'Eat up now. If you need anything just call out. I'll just be serving the other tables.'

She nodded and disappeared back inside the kitchen.

Richard looked around the centre. The lunchtime rush had begun. An elderly couple sat silently in one corner, staring vacantly at their blank phone screens in order to avoid talking to each other. The man looked up and stared at Richard with the tired expression of someone who had lived too long. Richard flushed and shovelled a forkful of baked beans into his mouth.

The centre door swung open.

A green jacketed farmer and his cow dog strode into the centre. He grabbed a table in the middle of the dining room and yelled, 'Down Spud… Make it quick Mary, that bloody man from organics who don't know a carrot from a turnip is comin' by to take photos of me turnips. It's all about authenticating yer bloody veg now.'

The old man looked up from across his pasty. 'Well, don't let 'ee go on yon top field then. I've seen yon tractor lights past midnight an' I knows what's yer spreading. Organic my arse!'

The farmer glared at the old man. 'I was just muck spreadin.' Ain't no law 'gainst that, Jacko.'

Jacko snorted, 'Aye, but what you mixed in with the dung is about as organic as my dick,' he yelled as his grey-haired wife hid her face further behind her phone.

'Well, you tell organics that, an' I'll tell the social that no one round 'ere as ever seen yon Billy, an' unless 'es been 'iding in yon barn these past twenty year, 'im an' 'is disability payments is gone.' The farmer's voice filled the cramped centre.

''Ee do that an' I'll take me hunting knife and skin 'ee alive.' Jacko put his fork down and stared menacingly at the farmer.

Spud whined and hid behind the farmer's chair.

The farmer muttered something under his breath and took an enormous mouthful of pasty, then dropped the remainder on the floor for Spud.

Mrs Bell appeared and placed a steaming mug of tea in front of the farmer.

'Just eat up and be gone, Arthur, we don't want any trouble here, especially in front of the new young vicar.' Mrs Bell, Arthur, and Jacko stared over at Richard.

Richard opened his mouth to protest the fact that he was in fact a lay worker, but the look on Mrs Bell's face changed his mind. An oppressive silence descended on the centre. Richard ate the rest of his gargantuan lunch as quickly as possible and after paying his bill, escaped the building. Once safely outside the centre Richard frowned. 'There is something very wrong with this village and I am not imagining things... this time,' he whispered.

He pinged his rubber band twice, just to make sure.

Richard shivered as the autumn wind blew through his thin sweatshirt. He looked at his watch. It was two o'clock, the vicar had to be awake by now. He crossed the little village square and headed left past the grandiose village pub, the Bishop's Nod.

The Nod was a large Georgian coaching inn. It stood looking over the little square with an air of quiet arrogance, proud of its position on the Witherleigh main road. It was a beautiful grey brick building with two large red chimneys at either end. The upper floor of the inn was reserved for guest lodgings. A sign stuck to the inn's door stated that there were rooms available, but at sixty pounds a night it was too steep for a lay worker's wage. Richard sighed. He was condemned to sampling the delights of Buttercup Cottage for the foreseeable future.

The lower floor of the Bishop's Nod catered for its day guests. A row of immaculately trimmed hanging baskets swung in harmony as their chains groaned in the afternoon breeze. Outside the inn, a flurry of red parasols, marked a row of abandoned picnic tables. Richard could not resist staring through the white lattice work of the Georgian windows as he passed by. The interior of the pub was dark, but he could see the outlines of people sitting around the tables, enjoying their lunch. The door opened, and a couple spilled out onto the road, laughing as they wandered happily down the street. The delicious smell of spicy curry trailed through the door after them.

Richard walked around to check the menu, which was hung on a hook by the imposing white front door.

The door crashed open and a slender barmaid dashed towards him. She grabbed Richard by the hand and dragged him into the alleyway which ran beside the inn.

The touch of her soft hand in his made, Richard blush violently and he stuttered, 'Er… can I hh-help you… Miss?'

'Are you the new vicar?' she hissed, as she pinned him against the wall of the pub.

Richard felt the cold of the wall against his back, a cooling contrast to the heat of her body.

'Er… well… I'm really only a youth worker but I am new to the parish,' he whispered, as he stared into the girl's searching brown eyes.

The girl flicked a long chestnut ponytail over her slim shoulders.

'Whatever… just get out while you still can,' she said as she looked over her shoulder, towards the entrance of the alley.

'Pardon?' Richard frowned; it was not the conversation he had hoped to have with the attractive barmaid. 'What are you talking about? I've only just got here.'

'Haven't you ever wondered why there is a vacancy at the church? They killed him. They're all in it together, you need to go… now.' She glared at him, as if willing him to run.

Richard sighed.

How was it that the only girls he ever attracted were slightly insane? He squinted at the name tag pinned to her chest, realised he was staring at her chest, and almost screamed.

'Well… Bethany or um… Miss Bond, I will be very careful, but I have a meeting with Reverend Anderson which I can't be late for. Good afternoon,' Richard replied as he crossed his fingers, hoping the small lie would not be held against him.

Bethany opened her mouth to say something but changed her mind. She waved to a couple, in matching dark green jackets, as they walked past the alley.

Richard nodded to Bethany and quickly vacated the alleyway, turned right, and down the main village road until he came to the Church of St Anthony.

The church was a beautiful example of a thousand years of Christianity. Its walls were built from flattened grey handmade bricks.

Three large arched, stained-glass windows ran alongside the nave, watched over by the church tower which dominated the horizon. The tower was the tallest feature in the village and stood guard over the sleeping cemetery.

The perimeter of the cemetery was encircled by a tall black, spiked fence. Richard walked around the fence searching for an entrance. At last, he came to the church gate. It was chained shut. The chain snaked between the railings and the fencepost and was joined together by a large, rusting lock. Richard gave the gate a shake. The chain rattled. A pair of rooks watching from the sweeping branches of an old yew tree, cawed loudly, and flew disturbed into the grey sky.

The wooden door to the church remained firmly closed.

Richard cursed; meeting the elusive Reverend Anderson

was proving a lot harder than he had imagined.

Richard thought for a moment and shook his head; of course, the Reverend would be at the manse not the church, after a hard night of ministering. Richard skirted around the edge of the church until he saw a sign saying, 'The Vicarage'. Underneath someone had written in a row of neat black capital letters, 'Visits by Appointment only'.

Richard patted the folded letter in his jeans; he would definitely be welcome. He had a signed letter to prove it.

He walked down the pathway. It was ill-used and overgrown. The Reverend obviously did not have many guests. A small copse had grown on either side of the path. The falling afternoon sun filtered through their naked branches and cast black lace shadows across the path. The path itself was barely visible under its crunchy covering of fallen leaves, which glowed in vivid shades of red and brown.

Richard picked a red leaf from the path. It was smooth but cold. He threw it into the air. The leaf flew in circles on the gusting wind which carried it high into the clouds.

'Arise, shine, and enjoy your freedom,' Richard whispered.

He walked down the pathway and the smile faded on his lips. The autumnal rains had soaked the ground and turned the narrow pathway into a hidden quagmire. Its smooth chestnut brown surface was a façade. His feet sunk slowly into the sticky mud. He sighed and continued to squelch his way down the track.

The crowded path opened out and Richard spied the outline of a grey brick building between the mass of trees. A heavy trail of grey smoke hung in the sky; at least someone was home.

He trudged towards the smoke.

A figure darted out from behind a naked oak tree. Instantly, Richard recognised the figure as Snowy, the rather dirty, elderly man from the centre. He felt his stomach sink. He really did not have the time or energy to deal with more odd villagers.

"Av 'ee see 'er?' Snowy demanded as his pale blue eyes scanned the trees.

'Er, seen who?' Richard asked turning around and checking the foliage for the unknown person.

'Me wife, Martha, she didn't come 'ome from selling 'er cheese at the market yesterday. She must've missed the Temperley bus an' the next one won't be coming 'til next week.'

'Er… Snowy isn't it? Calm down, everything is going to be fine. We will contact the police. I'm sure they will be able to find her.'

Richard fished his mobile from his pocket and flicked his screen open. Then groaned. A tiny 'no service' sign appeared in the top right-hand side of the screen. 'Is there ever any service in Devon?' he muttered. He put the phone back in his pocket.

'Don't worry, I'm going to the manse. We can use the landline from there to phone the police station.'

Snowy looked wildly around him, staring suspiciously into the rippling trees.

'But I need to find me Martha now.' He turned and ran back into the trees.

Richard swore and shook his head. His father's words echoed inside his brain, *respect your elders, their grey hair shows their suffering and wisdom.*

'I would if they weren't so bloody odd,' Richard retorted, as he trudged as fast as he could towards the smoking building.

CHAPTER FOUR

The manse was bigger than it had first appeared. It was a tall frowning building that seemed to look down upon its surroundings with an air of disappointment. The ground floor consisted of two overlarge, white-framed windows which stood each side of the white-columned doorway. A large ivy had crept across the front of the house, its dark green leaves flickering just below the empty sash windows of the second floor.

Richard ran up the stone steps and hammered on the front door. He stood back as he scanned the windows for signs of occupation. A sudden movement caught his eye. He squinted up at the grey tiled roof as a dark shadow crossed the left skylight. Richard opened the gold letter box and shouted through the gap, 'Reverend Anderson! Please open the door. One of your parishioners is in trouble. I know you're in here!'

The door remained firmly closed.

Richard cursed under his breath and ran his hand through his hair. Perhaps the manse had a better signal. He grabbed the mobile from his back pocket and dialled 999. The mobile remained stubbornly silent. Richard pinged his elastic band twice. He would have to go back to the village square - he had seen an old cream phone hanging languidly on the wall of the community centre. Richard turned to leave then paused as he heard the great white door swing slowly open.

Reverend Anderson's grey, stubbled face appeared around the door, 'There is no need to swear this close to the house of the Lord. In my day, young curates did not blaspheme.'

The Reverend looked down at Richard's mud-drenched footwear and shook his head disapprovingly. 'And in my day, they were well-dressed and clean too.'

Richard blushed and stared at his feet. 'But I'm not a vicar or a curate. I am just the new youth worker.'

'What!' shouted the Reverend.

'I'm not ordained. I'm just the new youth worker.' Richard stared at the hawkish features of the aging vicar.

'But I was promised another curate. Your father said you had attended the seminary.'

Richard nodded. 'Yes, but unfortunately I had to leave.'

'Ah yes,' Anderson said as he stroked his grey stubble, 'Now I remember... you had to leave without a degree as you could not cope with the pressure and started seeing ungodly things.'

The vicar turned and bellowed over his shoulder, 'Mrs. White!' His voice reverberated through the silent hallway. 'It's Reverend Radcliffe's boy, you know, the one who went mad.'

Mrs White appeared from behind a door in the hallway. She looked at Richard's shoes in disgust. 'Well, if you want to come in, you had best take off your trainers and socks too by the look of them. I'll get the plastic sheeting in case you mark the upholstery.'

She tutted and retreated down the corridor.

Richard's naturally pale face drained of all colour and he felt winded, as if he had been punched in the stomach. He swallowed and stuttered, 'W-we don't have time for this. I met an old man called… er… Snowy something, in the woods just outside here, he was extremely distressed as his wife Martha is missing.'

The Reverend's piercing grey eyes widened for an instant and then narrowed as he stared at Richard.

'Remove your footwear and follow me,' he ordered.

Richard groaned inwardly.

He unlaced his sodden trainers and stuffed his equally wet socks inside them, and followed the Reverend into a darkly furnished study, which appeared to have been last decorated in the reign of Queen Victoria. The smell of old books and open fires lingered on the stale air. He shivered as the cold of the room penetrated his thin sweatshirt. The red brick fireplace stood unlit. Its mantlepiece empty. The Reverend had either no family or no family he wanted to be reminded of. Plastic sheeting had been placed carefully over a high-backed dark leather armchair. The Reverend beckoned him to sit.

Richard sighed as he remembered his father's final piece of advice as he prepared to leave London. *Do not be hasty in judgement or action. Nothing can ever be rushed in the countryside.* Richard sat on the plastic covering which squeaked suspiciously under his weight and waited.

Reverend Anderson loomed over him. 'You need to stop this nonsense, immediately, boy.'

'But what about Martha?' Richard frowned up at the Reverend.

Reverend Anderson tutted as Mrs White entered the room with a sandwich-laden tray, signalling the arrival of afternoon tea.

'I see Mrs Bell has been filling your head with nonsense.' His two grey eyes seemed to pierce through Richard.

Richard opened his mouth to protest but the Reverend waggled a perfectly manicured finger towards his face.

'Martha Snow died over twenty years ago,' the Reverend said firmly.

Richard gasped.

Obviously, poor Snowy had never recovered from the tragedy. At his age, his grief could even have been exacerbated by some form of dementia. It was clear, however, that he desperately needed some sort of medical assistance.

'I'm sorry. I didn't realise… even so, Snowy looked in a very disturbed state. I have seen him in the village just wandering around and talking to himself. We need to find him and get him some help.'

The Reverend glanced over to Mrs White. She clutched the tiny silver cross which hung on the end of her necklace and stared at Richard.

Anderson cleared his throat and spoke in a slow, clear manner as if addressing a child. 'Snowy is beyond even God's help now. He died twenty years ago. Hanged himself in Elfsworthy Woods and was found swinging on an ash branch. His clothes still dripping with Martha's blood. Snowy slit her throat after she returned home late from selling her cheese at Temperley farmers' market. He thought she had made him a cuckold but instead she made him a murderer.'

Richard felt the room darken.

'But he can't be dead. I spoke to him about ten minutes ago.'

The Reverend shook his head. 'No, you did not see him. Mrs Bell must have filled your head with village ghost stories. She should know better, with your predilection to mental illness… but then she is touched by the devil herself.'

Richard raised a delicate brown eyebrow.

'I have seen her reading the word of the devil. He puts coded messages in horoscopes, you know. The weak are easily taken.'

Richard's opened his mouth to protest but changed his mind and stayed silent. He closed his eyes, blocking the crow-like vicar from his vision. It was all happening again but this time he had a witness. Mrs Bell had seen Snowy at the centre. He felt as if a leaden weight had lifted from his heart and smiled with relief. His father would have to believe him now.

Mrs White handed him a cup of tea. The vicar watched Richard, his face a mixture of disgust and pity, as he sipped from the delicately painted Old Country Rose teacup.

'Were they buried together, then?' Richard asked.

The Reverend's teacup chinked heavily against its saucer.

He shook his head.

'Martha is here, buried beside her parents. Snowy died unrepentant and a sinner. He did not deserve a Christian burial.'

Richard frowned and took another sip of tea.

'He remained where he had ended. The wood had more use for his sinful, jealous body than the village.'

Anderson leant over in his chair, his fingernails digging into

Richard's knee. 'Do not allow yourself to be seduced by the devil. Any more of this wicked talk and I will have to inform your father.'

Richard bit his lip. He took a few deep breaths to try to calm his heart, which seemed to be beating out of his chest. He felt an overpowering urge to ping his band, but two intense grey eyes were watching him, scanning him for signs of weakness. He had to find Mrs Bell. She had seen Snowy; with her testament, he could prove that he was not imagining things.

Richard stood up and made for the door.

Mrs White barred his way.

'But you haven't finished your tea,' she said accusingly, following him into the hallway.

Richard shook his head. He stuffed his mud-caked socks into his pocket and slipped on his equally muddy trainers. 'I'm s-so sorry, but I have to leave now.'

He ran from the manse.

***

Mrs White shut the solid white front door and shook her head.

'He didn't even finish his cup of tea and I served it in the best Royal Worcester china.'

The Reverend put his hand on her arm. 'Don't fret, Mrs White. It's just another sign of his affliction.'

Mrs White looked up into his careworn face. 'What do you mean, Reverend?'

He patted her arm. 'Well, Mrs White, anyone who will not take afternoon tea is obviously as mad as a brush.'

Mrs White nodded, amazed as always at the Reverend's

insight, and slowly closed the manse's door. 'Do you want me to get the chocolate digestives, Reverend?'

Anderson nodded; his eyes fixed on her silver cross which still hung between her tightly enclosed breasts. She tucked the chain safely back between them and the Reverend smiled. She glowed under his ecclesiastical gaze. Reverend Anderson was the most pious man she had ever met.

***

Richard ran along the lane.

His feet splashed through the mud, which splattered against his clothes, but he did not care. There was something wrong with the manse. He could feel it in the cold draught that blew through the building. It was the same oppressive feeling of being watched, that permeated through the village.

There was something very wrong with Witherleigh.

The tall trees loomed over him as the lane cut through the crowded copse. Sounds of rustling leaves and snapping twigs made Richard turn around. Snowy burst through the bushes.

'Have you seen me Martha? She 'asn't come 'ome from market yet. She might 'ave got injured in the woods, can 'ee come an' help me look for 'er?' Snowy's faded blue eyes scoured the woods for signs of Martha.

'Go away! You are dead, Snowy!' Richard crossed his arms and planted his feet firmly in the mud.

Snowy's head twisted round, one hundred and eighty degrees towards Richard. A thin smile curled one end of his lips upwards.

Richard managed to free a sinking foot from the muds

tenacious hold and took a step backwards. The mud squelched, and he almost toppled over. Snowy laughed. His face greyed and his lips faded. Blood began to run down his right arm and drip down onto the mud. Richard shivered as the temperature dropped. A dark red stain appeared on the front of Snowy's fawn, check shirt.

'She was wearing that make-up stuff an' done up like a painted trollop. No wonder the men were all sniffin' around 'er like a bitch on 'eat, I sees it with me own eyes. 'Er talkin' to folks at the market.' Snowy's eyes dissolved into empty black sockets, and grey skin slipped from his bleached bones.

He lunged towards Richard.

Richard twisted to the left; his feet trapped by the black mud.

'I deserved better!' Snowy screamed into Richard's face and vanished.

Richard spun around searching the undergrowth but there was no sign of Snowy anywhere. He breathed out slowly, his tense body deflating. Richard could feel his heart pounding against his ribs as a wave of fear washed over his shaking body. He held his breath for four seconds and pinged his band. The elastic snapped against his skin and flew into the undergrowth.

Richard swore, pulled his feet from the mud, and waded down the rest of the path. If he stayed away from the trees, Snowy would not be able to contact him.

Eventually, the manse lane filtered back onto the main road. Richard scurried along, hoping to blend in with the empty street. He needed to go home, if going back to the ancient caravan could be classed as home. Richard crossed the road and into the market square. He breathed a sigh of relief as he took the car keys from his sock-filled pocket.

'Oh, look everyone, it's the new vicar. 'Ee's the one that plays with dolls.' A rotund young farmer strolled out from a gang of scruffy teenagers hanging around the public lavatories of the square. The teenager walked into Richard, his shoulder banging into Richard's chest.

Richard did not move.

'Are you mad?' laughed a red-headed girl wearing a thigh-high mini-skirt and red high heels.

Richard looked from her to the rest of the gang, his face closed, and he growled, 'No, I'm not mad. But I've just come out of a psychiatric care facility and I'm seeing things again.'

The laughter stopped. The girl tottered back to the safety of the public toilets. The rotund farmer exchanged worried glances with his mates, who had shuffled behind him, and put his hands in the air. 'No offence mate, we be only 'avin' a laugh.'

The young farmers quickly reformed on the opposite side of the toilet block.

Richard grinned to himself and jumped into his car. *Then you will know the truth, and the truth will set you free.'* For once, his father's teachings had actually been useful.

CHAPTER FIVE

Someone was banging on the tiny back porch of the caravan. It was a rhythmic, slow thud which pierced his dreams. Richard groaned, struggled out from the tiny single bed, and padded across the cold lino. Cautiously, he opened the back door. The wind caught the door and it banged against the caravan wall. His home juddered. The china, stacked up against the side of his draining board, clinked together, and a yellowing photograph of the farm fell from its hook; its glass splintering across the floor. Richard took a deep breath. It was not the way he had wanted to start the Sabbath.

Richard peered through the doorway. It was empty except for a row of three hessian bags, tied to the roughly sawn porch frame, swinging slowly in the wind. One of them must have been the cause of the knocking. He unhooked the bags, brought them inside the caravan, and dumped them onto the tiny kitchen table.

The bags smelt putrid, like rotten eggs left to fester.

Richard opened one of the sacks and poured the contents out. A pile of black feathers exploded across the room and the scrawny, balding body of a dead crow flopped onto the table. Tiny pale maggots wormed their way through holes in its skin

45

and fell wriggling onto the table.

Beads of sweat glistened on his forehead, his stomach churned, and he gagged as the smell of death permeated through the caravan. 'Keep calm,' he whispered as a surge of panic flooded through his body. His hands shook as he picked up the decaying crow and the two remaining bags, ran to the open door, and threw them onto the muddy field. He stood in the doorway for a moment breathing in the chilled air, trying to purge the stench from his lungs.

A large Friesian cow paused mid-chew and stared at him suspiciously, then turned, and nodded to her companions. The rest of the herd looked up from their breakfast, mooed at him in chorus, and proceeded to follow a big moody-looking brown cow to the scattered trees, which lined the far side of the field.

Richard watched the cows depart to a safe distance. They sensed something unnatural and being sensible creatures wanted nothing to do with the sacks.

Richard took a kitchen knife from inside the caravan and then squatted down in the field as he slit open the second bag. A goat's head stared back at him. He felt his heart miss a beat and then clatter against his ribs. Richard said a quick prayer and sliced open the third bag, hoping for no more decaying animal parts.

Bundles of tiny brown leaves, tied together with black string, tumbled onto the mud, crumbling into delicate paper-thin flakes as they fell. A familiar smell filled the air. Fresh grass with a hint of pepper.

At least it smells better than the other bags, Richard

thought, as he inhaled the dried parsley.

'Mornin', young vicar.' Farmer Butler's voice boomed through the silence. The big farmer stared down at the collection of dead objects at Richard's feet. His dogs whined and slunk backwards, cowering behind their master.

'Ah… making crow pie, are you? It tastes like chicken, so I've been told. Never touch 'em meself though. Hundreds of 'em flockin' in them woods, watchin' you. They'll know if you eat their own,' the farmer said grimly, shaking his head.

'Oh, I see. Er… thanks for the warning. So, did you hang these bags here?' Richard asked, taking the jug of sickly milk from the farmer.

'I can't say that I did.' The farmer thrust his hands deeply into his pockets and stood watching Richard as he tried to shove the strange collection of trophies back into one of the hessian bags.

Richard turned scarlet under his gaze and prayed the farmer would leave. After an awkward pause, the farmer yelled, 'Rupert, Henry, come to heel. We got cows to tend, be seeing you, young vicar.' The farmer nodded, swore at Rupert for attempting to bite Henry and marched off into the mud.

Richard scratched his head. Perhaps these were harmless bags of food left by well-meaning parishioners? He closed his eyes wishing it was true. However, he could not shake off the feeling that the trophies had been touched by something unhealthy. He looked across the beautiful, dark green rolling fields. A gust of wind almost knocked him from his feet, and he shivered. How could something so natural and beautiful contain something that made his flesh crawl? He shook the thoughts from his head. One dead bird does not a coven make. He smiled ruefully to himself. Dr Berghaus would say it was merely a manifestation of paranoia and hand out some more pills, but then, he had never seen the creatures that should not be there.

The autumnal sun blazed orange across the fields. Richard took his Sunday suit from the miniature wardrobe, looked at his wristwatch and swore. He would be late for morning service. Richard threw on his white shirt and black jacket as he hopped unsteadily into his trouser legs. Then he upended his rucksack. A bulging white envelope stamped with the Nightingale Unit green heading plopped onto the bed. Richard ripped open the envelope. A selection of multi-coloured rubber bands fell across his bed. He stood for a minute, his fingers tracing over the bands. Their presence was slowly taking over his entire life. He hated them but they helped refocus his mind when the tide of panic began to take control. The doctors had said it was a form of post-traumatic stress after London, but it had been lurking in his body like an insidious shadow ever since he was a child and had realised the monsters that haunted his dreams were real.

Richard slipped a yellow rubber band onto his wrist. He ran from the caravan, shoved his Sunday tie and white socks into his jacket pocket, and leapt into his car.

***

The Church of St Anthony stood proudly against the background of green fields. Its bells chimed and sang across the little village. Outside the church, a small line of villagers filed through the wrought iron gates and up the narrow pathway to the church. High-pitched happy voices trickled through the church doors as a pair of church wardens welcomed the faithful into the house of God.

Richard sat in his car and watched the line of people lessen as he slipped on his tie. He decided not to put on the inappropriately themed Christmas socks he had hastily grabbed in his rush to leave the caravan. Carefully, folding them back into a ball and hiding them in his jacket pocket. He was certain that no one in the congregation would be looking at his feet. Richard ran his fingers through his hair and pushed a flopping mass of curls from his tired, bright blue eyes. He breathed deeply, pinged his band twice, and vacated the safety of his little car.

The last of the tail of people stood huddled underneath the Gothic arch of the church's entrance porch and murmured to each other as he approached. Richard nodded and smiled as he passed by. He was not surprised by their lack of welcome.

He shook the ancient church warden's hand and stated, 'Good morning, my name is Richard…'

'I knows who 'ee is. The vicar wants to see 'ee now. Follow me.'

Richard's heart sunk. He followed as the elderly warden shuffled down a small corridor on the left-hand aisle, parallel to the nave, and into a little room hidden away from the main church.

The warden knocked twice.

'Open!' Reverend Anderson commanded.

'The new youth worker is 'ere for 'ee, Reverend.' The

church warden signalled for Richard to enter, then nodded to the vicar, and quietly shut the door. His dragging footsteps formed a baseline to the church chatter.

'Ah good to see you again, Richard. You made it at last. I was beginning to wonder if you were coming. I have a sermon to preach in a few minutes.' He said pointedly looking at the gold Rolex on his wrist. 'So, I will come straight to the point.'

The vicar motioned for Richard to sit on an ancient wooden chair and turned to readjust his stole in the huge guilt-edged, full-length mirror which dominated the room.

Richard scanned the dressing room. It was roughly the size of a large cupboard. Windowless, it was lit by a single bulb which hung limply in the centre of low ceiling. The bulb flickered as it glowed, throwing dark shadows against the magnolia walls.

Directly opposite him, stood the golden mirror. Silk flowers, cut-out paper hearts, letters, and notelets emblazoned with words of thanks proudly surrounded the mirror.

Anderson watched Richard through the reflection and beamed. 'Just some trinkets from my thankful flock.'

The Reverend finished his adjustments and turned, staring down at Richard.

'Well, my boy. I hope you are settling into our little village. The people here don't see many outsiders, so it will take them some time to get used to you. Why I remember it took me almost a month before I got my first dinner invitation, when I was transferred here from Ashdurton.' He looked Richard up and down. 'It will probably take you a bit longer, though,' the vicar decided as he sprayed his smartly flicked grey hair in place.

Richard opened his mouth to respond. Anderson raised his hand. 'I can appreciate how difficult it is adjusting to countryside life, especially since you have just been let out of a mental asylum.'

Richard flushed and opened his mouth to protest. The vicar ignored him.

'I have spoken to Reverend Radcliffe and he agrees with me. It's best if you do not take up the position of Children's, Youth, and Family Worker just yet. No one wants you near their children. You can understand that, surely?'

Richard felt his heart constrict.

The vicar continued. 'However, every cloud has a silver lining, as they say. We need an odd job man to clean the church and do general repairs. You can stay and do that if you want too.'

Richard felt his heart rip in two.

The Reverend frowned at Richard, a look of concern crossing his pointed features. 'Don't worry about the money, it's exactly the same - minimum wage. You must trust me, Richard, this is the best solution. You will have somewhere to stay, you will be doing God's work, and you won't scare any of the villagers. After the service, when everyone has left, you can begin by cleaning the church. Don't forget to lock the church up once you have finished.' Reverend Anderson turned to face the mirror again as he slapped some *Creed Aventus* Eau De Parfum onto his cheeks. Anderson sighed. 'Yes, I know it's a ridiculously expensive brand but what can I do? It was a gift from the Ashcrofts last Christmas? Anyway, I am sure you want to take your seat in the pews now. I'm reading from John, it's always a seat filler.'

Richard had been dismissed.

He stumbled from the room, sought the darkest end of the corridor, and slid to the floor, his back against the cold wall. He drew his knees to his chest as he hid his face in folded arms. The coldness of the stone penetrated through his thin black jacket.

Stilettoed footsteps pierced the silence of the shadows. Richard recognised the sound and looked up just in time to see Mrs Ashcroft bang on the door of the mirrored room and promptly march inside, without waiting for a response.

'Have you spoken to the boy yet, Reverend?' she demanded.

'Yes, Seraphina.' Anderson's voice boomed across the corridor. 'I have, and he has agreed to stay on as caretaker as you so cleverly suggested last night.'

The footsteps moved further into the room and a chair creaked.

'I will inform his father tonight. Reverend Radcliffe will not mind what his son does as long as he stays away from London. A man in his position cannot possibly have an insane son going around accusing people of being possessed and seeing ghosts everywhere. It puts the church in a very bad light. It's not the Dark Ages anymore. The Anglican church is a church of charity, forgiveness, and tolerance.'

'Most definitely,' Mrs Ashcroft added. 'Look at the community centre. We are always looking after the poor and needy, at great expense to the church, and at even greater personal sacrifice.'

'You are right as always. The whole village is indebted

to you and your charitable works. Indeed, you are a shining example to the Christian community,' the Reverend replied.

Seraphina laughed softly, revelling in the vicar's compliment.

'Also, if his son's antics come to light, it might affect his position on the God TV network. Most clergy would kill for an opportunity like that.'

Mrs Ashcroft's foot tapped against the stone floor. 'What about the money?'

'As long as the boy stays down here, away from the press, the Reverend will send a monthly donation to the church. After all, we need it for the new church organ.'

'But I thought that was being repaired with the bequest from Mrs Bates' will last year?' Seraphina queried, her voice growing higher, more piercing.

'Hmm… unfortunately, it was not quite enough,' the Reverend answered apologetically.

The organ roared to life and an army of discordant notes descended down the corridor.

'Ah, my flock calls. After you, my dear.' Reverend Anderson opened the door wide to let Seraphina through.

'You are always such a gentleman, Godfrey,' she commented, as she walked through the doorway and headed towards the nave, her severe yellow bun sailing down the corridor. It reminded Richard of a shark's dorsal fin.

Richard waited until they were out of sight and followed them into the main church. The congregation shuffled and stood in unison; their gaze fixed on Anderson as he crossed to his ornately carved lectern.

Richard made his way to the back of the church and

slipped into an empty pew. Instantly, a tiny grey-haired woman appeared and handed him a little white booklet. He stared vacantly at the order of service as his brain cycled through his options. Going home was impossible; if he suddenly appeared on his parents' doorstep he would be instantly removed and sent to the Nightingale Unit again. He could try to find a job elsewhere, but his finances were crippled with two years of student debt, and his CV included an involuntary stay in a psychiatric unit. He really had no other options.

He was trapped in Witherleigh.

Richard cursed under his breath and glared at the silent congregation who sat lost in their prayers.

'Mind if I sit down by 'ee. I'm waitin' for me wife, Martha, that woman would be late for 'er own funeral.'

Richard let out a sigh and hissed under his breath, 'Oh, go away, Snowy, you're dead.'

Snowy turned to face him. His faded blue eyes drained to black. 'Well, give me a proper Christian burial then,' and he vanished.

'That's not a very nice thing to say, especially not at church!' Two attractive brown eyes glared down at him.

'Oh God! Sorry! I wasn't talking to you,' Richard exclaimed in horror.

Bethany raised a finely carved eyebrow. 'Well, who else were you talking to then?'

Richard went scarlet. 'Um, I was just thinking out loud,' he whispered as Reverend Anderson started the service.

Richard bent in his seat as he joined the rest of the congregation in prayer.

Loud footsteps echoed through the still church. He glanced sideways as a man in an overlarge shiny blue suit and black shoestring tie slid into the end of his pew. The man turned and winked at Richard, then bent forward in prayer, a fussy mass of brown hair flopping across his face.

The flock rustled through their hymn books and stood. Richard jumped up and fumbled through the pages of his hymnal desperately searching for the first hymn.

Bethany tutted and nudged his arm, shoving her book under his nose. Richard whispered his thanks and attempted to sing 'All Things Bright and Beautiful', but all he could focus on was the musky scent of her perfume and the warmth of her body next to his.

CHAPTER SIX

The congregation stood for the final time. The organ music pounded against the walls of the ancient church as the green wall hangings declaring the word of God, swayed to the organ's beat. Reverend Anderson walked down the aisle and smiled benevolently to his flock as he passed them by. After an appropriate pause, the congregation burst into a cacophony of chatter, intermingled with a shuffling of feet, as the herd stampeded towards the open church doors and the prospect of Sunday lunch.

Bethany thrust her hymn book into Richard's lap and disappeared into the crowd.

The man sitting at the end of the pew, turned to Richard and smiled. 'That was a good one. The Reverend is renowned throughout the diocese for not mincing his words and he is right. The church provides for the poor and needy so those with spare pennies must support the church. It is Christianity in action.'

Richard nodded. With the decline in the funding of the mental health services and the surge in families in crisis, he was all too familiar with the financial pressures on the church. He had heard it every day of his life.

'Oh sorry, am I preaching again? I do apologize, force of habit… I'm John Sparke, curate to the North Devon diocese. This time next year I'm going to get my very own church,' he said glowing happily, as he thrust out a hand for Richard to shake.

They shook hands, probably for longer than necessary. Richard could never work out the optimum shaking time, so he ended up gripping the proffered hand awkwardly for a count of ten before he relinquished it, in order to make sure he did not seem submissive.

His father could not stand weak offspring.

Richard stared at the curate. Was Reverend Sparke actually the missing curate? He did not seem that missing. Quickly, Richard assessed the curate. Apart from the big hair and unusual choice of suits, he seemed relaxed and almost happy.

'Hello, I'm Richard Radcliffe, I appear to be the new church caretaker. Have you been here long? Have you noticed anything… er… different about this parish?'

Reverend Sparke grinned, 'Ah! You're down from London, I take it? The accent gives you away instantly, I'm afraid, old man. Yes, the locals are a little quiet to begin with, but once they get to know you, you will find them extremely welcoming and warm people. This afternoon I have been invited for a delicious Sunday roast at Armitage Hall with the Ashcroft's, which is the reason I've got the best suit on.' He stroked the shiny blue material lovingly. The Reverend stood up and checked his wristwatch, a huge digital monster.

'Well, good to meet you, Richard. I must dash, I really don't want to be late. It's a frightfully good spread and I'm starving.

I'm sure you will get the royal summons to the manor soon.' He winked and sauntered off down the aisle.

Richard smiled. He doubted he would ever receive such an invitation, but it was good to meet a fellow newcomer to the village.

Slowly, the church emptied.

Richard sighed. It was time for him to begin his new career – from top seminary college student to caretaker in only two years, his career was definitely on a vertical path of achievement. It was just as the Dean of Jesus College had prophesized when he won the Brennan award for academic excellence in his first year at Oxford University. Unfortunately, the vertical path had headed in the wrong direction.

Richard dismissed the balding Dean from his thoughts and stood. The forgotten hymn book lying open on his lap, crashed to the floor, and disappeared under the pew in front. Richard cursed and dived under the pew to retrieve the wayward book. Reverend Anderson kept a spotless church and Richard was in no doubt that he would be unimpressed, if he found hymnals strewn across the floor.

Stilettoed footsteps resounded through the silent church. Richard recognised them instantly and tried to squeeze the rest of his gangly body beneath the pew.

Mrs Ashcroft walked past him; her face set into as much of a scowl as monthly injections of Botox would allow. Mrs Bell hurried behind her. Richard twisted his neck around the side of the pew and watched as they approached the altar. To the left of the altar stood the medieval font. Richard could just see the font's stout oaken legs. Each leg was carved with the robed body of what appeared to be a saint.

'Get the holy water, Mrs Bell,' Seraphina commanded.

Mrs Bell uncovered the font and dipped an ancient green bottle into the water. Then she passed the bottle to Mrs Ashcroft who corked the top and placed it carefully into her oversized leather handbag, emblazoned with the letters 'D & G' in thick gold.

'Come on, we need to get Snowy sealed into the afterdeath before that interfering boy tells his father. We don't want outsiders poking their nose into private village affairs,' Mrs Ashcroft said as she stalked out of the church.

Richard watched them leave the church with the vials of stolen holy water.

 The women had both seen Snowy and they were going to exorcise his soul. It was not something he had expected from the middle-aged ladies of the community centre. He was not starting to see things again. Snowy's ghost was real. Richard breathed a sigh of relief and then frowned.

There was something very wrong with Witherleigh.

 Richard pinged his elastic band eight times, his wrist reddened. The pain jolted him into action.

Richard managed to unwind himself from the pew and threw the hymn book onto the small collection table. A piece of white paper sailed slowly through the air and landed a foot away from him. He bent down, scooped the paper from the stone slab floor, and scratched his head as he read the note. 'Where have the curates gone?' He frowned and shoved the note in his pocket, then went to the storeroom in search of the vacuum cleaner. Bethany was paranoid, probably even madder than he was, but she smelt so nice.

Two hours later the wooden church pews shone. The delicate scent of lavender permeated the musty dankness of the church. A low hanging sun peered through the stained glass windows, illuminating the brightly coloured image of the Archangel Michael standing over a fallen angel, his spear tip pointing downwards towards the angel's heart. Michael had been lucky. He had seen demons and probably ghosts too, but he had never been accused of having paranoid delusions.

The sun hid behind a cloud. The image of Michael flickered and disappeared. A gentle breeze blew through the church, playing with the tapestry wall hangings, and rustling through the order of service sheets, neatly stacked on the little wooden table, tucked behind the last pew.

The air in the church felt electrified as if charged by some unseen force. Richard shivered as an electrical pulse ran up and down his spine. It was a sensation he had felt before.

Richard turned and ran from the church.

Once outside the church, he locked the big oaken doors and tested the ring-shaped door handles twice, before he was satisfied that they were locked. Quickly, he ran up the path and snaked the padlocks through the black spiked fence.

Now he knew why Reverend Anderson had been so insistent about locking up the church after he had finished the cleaning. There was something malevolent lurking in the shadows of the church.

Richard stood for a moment and stared through the iron posts, his eyes searching through the arched church windows, but the stained glass shielded the interior of the church from any external gaze. Richard squinted into the smaller oblong window nearest the door. Two tiny, amber lights seemed to be moving through the darkened church.

Richard gripped the black railing, the cold almost freezing his hands to the metal, as the dancing lights sent a chill through his body.

Something wicked was trapped in Witherleigh.

The church bell chimed.

He heard the voice of his father booming down from the pulpit, *'Put on the whole armour of God, that you may be able to stand against the schemes of the devil, Ephesians 6:11.'*

Richard dismissed the voice. When he had told his father, he was indeed fighting the devil, he had been locked away. It was only then that he had realised that God had chosen only a special few to fight his battles, and that to make his warriors stronger he had given them the gift of suffering.

However, he was not strong enough to fight a demon alone.

He needed an ally. He thought of Mrs Ashcroft and an image of her scowling face loomed into his memories. He dismissed the thought. He was not that desperate yet.

Richard paused for a moment and stood listening to the silent village, its population seeming to have blended back into the countryside. The main street was devoid of life. He looked up and down the empty road.

A little girl stood watching him from across the village square. The girl waved and disappeared down the narrow street which ran adjacent to the market, her long black pigtails waving through the air as she ran. Richard watched her go and smiled.

Protecting the innocent was worth the sacrifices he had made.

He crossed over the road and walked over to the centre. Mrs Bell had seen the ghost of Snowy. She shared his secret burden and he suspected that she also made a very good Sunday roast. His stomach grumbled expectantly. Then his heart dropped. The café was deserted.

He pulled on the door handle. It was locked. Propped up against the glass, half-covering his drooping welcome sign, was a small notice sellotaped to the window, it read 'Closed due to official church business.' An insidious black mould had crept over both. Richard groaned. He should have known. Mrs Ashcroft seemed the type of woman who demanded instant gratification. Poor Snowy was probably being dispatched back to the other side and being told, in the strictest terms not to come back.

I wonder what she wears in bed.

The random thought strolled across his mind. Richard gasped in horror and pinged his rubber band four times.

Snowy had been killed in the woods by the vicarage. They would have to summon his spirit from there. Richard crossed over the market square and scurried down the road towards the vicarage. The smell of roast vegetables hung in a mouth-watering cloud around the Bishops Nod and his stomach rumbled hopefully. However, he passed the inviting warmth of the pub's open door and turned down the little lane. The overnight rain had not improved the condition of the path, which now consisted of three inches of churned red, oozing mud. His once white trainers disappeared in a sea of brown.

Richard made a mental note to purchase some wellie boots from the store as soon as he could.

Richard trudged onwards until he reached the copse of trees which lurked in the shadows just before the manse. He crouched behind an empty oak tree and watched.

Snowy stood motionless, trapped under a naked rowan tree. His feet were lost under a pile of shiny red leaves. Grey shadows crossed his face. His eyes were circled with bands of black which accentuated the amber glow of his eyes.

He was passing over.

Richard edged towards the rowan, trying to blend into the fading greenery. Any outside interference and the passing would be stopped.

Mrs Ashcroft stepped out from the shadows of the tree and hung something on its bare trunk. Richard squinted through the undergrowth. It was a cross made from two sticks. Thick, red wool was woven between the sticks, forming a diamond, or spirit trap. Any lost spirit wandering nearby would be sucked into the trap.

'Do not struggle, Mr Snow. Accept your fate like a man,' she commanded.

'But I don't wants to leave. Me an' me Martha belongs together,' Snowy cried.

'Well, you should have thought about that before you killed her.'

Mrs Ashcroft flicked the spirit trap, and it began to turn.

The trees that crowded around the rowan rushed backwards and disappeared as the world turned grey. A sudden, frozen wind howled and ran around the tree, picking up handfuls of fallen leaves and carrying them away in lopsided spirals. The woollen trap expanded rapidly, until it was the size of a man. Snowy tried to struggle but the force of the spirit trap kept him tied to the spot.

The centre of the trap, where the twigs crossed, erupted into black flames which ate a hollow black doorway in the air. The fire roared and reached forwards, catching Snowy by his old green anorak, and dragging him into the flames. Snowy screamed in terror. The skin on his face and hands bubbled and melted. A yellow gas rolled through the lane leaving behind the pungent smell of rotten eggs.

The flames vanished. The spirit trap retracted back to its original size. Mrs Ashcroft untied the string and slipped it back into the pocket of her Green Barbour jacket.

'Come on, Mrs Bell. We need to destroy his remains before he breaks through again,' Mrs Ashcroft commanded.

Mrs Bell nodded and began to dig.

CHAPTER SEVEN

Richard stood up and backed silently through the undergrowth, shocked at the sight of Snowy's torment, and Mrs Ashcroft's callous disposal of his soul.

Snowy had been offered no chance to repent his crime and would be serving the rest of days walking amongst the burning fires of the *Abyss*. Richard shook his head. Everyone deserved a chance of redemption; being an avid churchgoer Mrs Ashcroft must have known that. A vague feeling of uneasiness fluttered in his chest. He would have to talk to Reverend Anderson. His heart felt heavy as he trudged back to the manse. Perhaps if he spoke to the Reverend on his own, without the presence of the formidable Mrs White, he would be told the truth about Witherleigh. The Reverend could not be as oblivious to the events in Witherleigh, as he appeared to be. Anderson had to feel the sinister presence which lingered in the village streets, or why would he insist on the church remaining locked or be out all night on ministering business? It had to be a cover. Richard shook his head. He had let outward appearances cloud his judgment. He needed to do better, to think unclouded.

Richard reached into his battered blue rucksack and pulled out a small plastic prescription bottle. The Clozaril 50mg pills jingled a welcome to him. He unscrewed the white plastic top and poured the pills into his hand. Just seeing them made him feel safer, more in control, but it was a false control. It numbed his feelings and quietened his thoughts, but evil was still out there. The pills just hid the evil from his thoughts but no amount of pills could hide him from the dark creatures of the world. They would always find him. Richard opened his hand and let the pills trickle through his fingers. They fell across the ground, lying there enticing him.

Richard stamped them into the mud.

'I will face my demons head on,' he muttered as he placed the empty pill bottle back in his bag and carefully circumnavigated the sea of stinging nettles which had spawned beneath the trees.

Finally, he broke through the clawing, brown undergrowth and jumped down from the bank onto the squelching pathway.

The afternoon sun was falling, casting shadows across the front of the manse. Richard could see Mrs White moving across the window, the contours of her body highlighted in the darkness, by the electric lights. She stopped walking and peered through the window.

Richard ducked out of sight and found himself entangled in a climbing rose. Its fragile brown petals crumbled under his touch. A thick stem grabbed his trousers, as its thorns raked his leg. He grimaced and crept backwards, away from the rose's thorny embrace.

'Hello!' A loud voice with a distinctly upper-class accent burst through the silence.

Richard flinched and turned to follow the sound.

Reverend Sparke waved from a small wooden bench in the front garden opposite him and grinned. 'Well, fancy seeing you here, old man!'

Richard crossed the neat grass square and sat next to the smiling curate.

'What are you doing here?' Richard enquired. 'Have you come to see the Reverend too?'

'Oh! Heavens no! This afternoon I have been invited for a delicious Sunday roast at Armitage Hall with the Ashcroft's. I'm just waiting for the afternoon bus. It takes you to the top of the lane. I can't cycle there in my best suit or I'd end up looking like Worzel Gummidge! No doubt the new Mrs Ashcroft would have a few words to say if I dripped mud across her Persian rugs. They were a wedding gift from her mother, don't you know.' He grinned as he lovingly stroked the shiny blue suit.

Richard stared at the curate. The fading afternoon light made his face glow iridescently through the shadows. Richard looked down at his mud-splattered clothing and then across to the immaculately dressed curate. His suit was pristine, untouched by the autumn Devon mud. A tingling sensation rose through Richard's spine.

'You're dead, aren't you, Reverend Sparke?' Richard whispered.

'I have been wondering about that myself. Lately, all I seem to do is wait for this damn bus,' the curate replied solemnly.

'What year is it?' Richard asked.

'Er… 1980,' the curate replied hopefully.

'Well, you've been waiting for that bus for a very long time.

Welcome to the twenty-first century.'

'Oh hell!' said the curate. 'So, I never did get my own church?'

Richard shook his head.

John Sparke vanished.

***

Mrs White finished the last of the washing-up. The china tea set could not be trusted to the heavy handedness of the parish dishwasher, which could not distinguish an Old Country Rose cup from a Tesco's own brand. The parish tea set had served visitors to the manse for over one hundred years. In her reign as housekeeper not one chip had appeared in a single piece of bone china. If she had known the young man had mental health issues, she would have kept the Royal Worcester firmly under lock and key, displayed in the imposing, and impregnable, oak dresser which dominated the expansive Victorian kitchen.

She massaged the china dry with a bleached white tea towel and carefully put each one back in its assigned place, then locked the dresser and slipped the key back under a china flowerpot on the left-hand side of the sparkling window. Satisfied that no one could assault her china, she glanced through the window. Her faded blue eyes were drawn to a hunched dark shape seated on the Christian meditation bench, its animated gestures casting flickering shadows across the sleeping evening lawn. Mrs White tutted and shook her head. She folded the tea towel over the wooden drying rail and went to find the Reverend.

Reverend Anderson's deep voice resonated through the hallway. She followed its sound to the closed study door, knocked and walked in.

'Everything will be fine, my dear. I will pop over later tonight after Mrs White's most delicious Sunday roast.'

Mrs White beamed under the compliment.

'Goodbye Mrs Bailey, I will see you soon.'

He placed the receiver on the cradle of the ancient black telephone stand and smiled at Mrs White. 'That was poor Mrs Bailey. Life has not been easy to her with three young daughters and an absent husband. I will have to minister to her tonight.'

Mrs White nodded solemnly.

'How long will you be?' she asked.

The vicar rubbed the greying bristles on his chin thoughtfully for a second and replied, 'I will be there for as long as she requires. A shepherd must tend to the needs of his flock. I will go straight after dinner; please do not wait up for me. I might be very late back, and I would hate to make you stay up late too.'

Mrs White nodded. 'You are so kind Reverend, always thinking of others first.'

Anderson smiled and sipped on a large glass of Chateau Certan de May Pomerol.

'Oh yes, and just so you know. That Radcliffe boy is sitting on the meditation bench talking to himself.'

The Reverend peered through the window. 'If it gives him comfort in his time of need, let him stay and be content.'

'Very good, Reverend.' Mrs White smiled sweetly. 'Food will be served shortly.'

'Excellent,' the Reverend smiled and laid his hand on her shoulder.

Mrs White could feel his warmth through the strong cotton print of her floral Sunday dress. Her stomach somersaulted, as a feeling of moral goodliness surged through her body.

The smell of boiled cabbage wafted through the study doorway and she raced to the kitchen. A woman on a mission. If the poor vicar was going to be up all night tending to Mrs Bailey, a slightly hysterical, young blond woman, who needed far more than her fair share of religious and moral guidance, then she would ensure the poor man would not go to the woman on an empty stomach.

***

Richard turned to see the grim face of Mrs White glaring at him from an upper window. He looked at the illuminated hands of his watch. Somehow time had jumped forward to eight o'clock or perhaps he had sat for too long and let the time slip away from him. Sometimes he lost time, or time lost him. It was too late to visit the Reverend now. He stood up and waved goodbye to Mrs White. She did not respond in kind. Richard smiled; he often had that effect on people.

Slowly, he trudged back down the pathway.

There was one person who seemed to know a lot about the missing curates. An image of Bethany flashed into his brain. He blushed and hurried on through the mud.

Richard followed the path as it wound around an ancient oak, whose empty branches stretched across the pathway.

The falling dusk carried in a touch of frost which covered the oak with a cloak of ice, that sparkled in the light of the ascending moon.

The darkening countryside flickered to greyscale.

'Oh crap!' Richard whispered.

***

Several dark figures appeared beneath the branches of the oak. One was holding a flaming torch, while the other two wrestled with a dark shape on the grass. A fourth man stood, illuminated by the light of a flickering lantern, as he looped a thick rope over the lowest hanging branch of the tree.

'An' 'ee can hang there 'til 'ee rots, you murderin' scum!' one of the men hissed at the thrashing figure, his voice muffled by a thick grey scarf.

Richard dropped to his knees and crawled behind a browning rhododendron.

'I'm sorry. I didn't mean to hit 'er so 'ard. I don't know me own strength sometimes,' Snowy whimpered, his huge bloodshot eyes pleading with the standing man.

'Aye, 'ee will be sorry soon enough when you go to hell. You're a badden like your pa, the evil sod, an' now you're goin' down to join him.'

'Get him up!' the well-dressed standing man ordered.

Snowy was dragged to his feet. The standing man put the noose around Snowy's neck and secured it.

Snowy kicked out at his captors, his hobnail boots cracking against their shins. One of the men screamed and rolled backwards into the undergrowth.

The standing man laughed. The rope jerked taut and Snowy stood erect. The man signalled to his two uninjured companions. They pulled on the rope. Snowy shot high into the air, his neck cracking with the force of the ascent.

'Well, that were a lot easier done than said,' a short, muscular man stated, as he wrapped the end of the rope around the trunk of the oak tree.

'Aye,' said the third. 'But 'ee won't be up there long mind you, what with the rooks an' all.'

'This is the death of all sinners, it is the agony of the damned,' the standing man announced. 'Now go home. All of you.'

'Yes Mr Ashcroft, sir,' the men replied, nodding in deference to their master.

The short man bent down as he helped the injured man from the clawing brambles, and they disappeared into the night.

Richard walked over to Snowy, his corpse swinging in the night breeze and looked at his watch. Five hours had passed since Snowy had been exorcised.

The dead did not stay underground for long in Witherleigh.

The icy scene flickered and Snowy's corpse vanished.

***

Richard hurried past the oak tree. In the dusk, the trees seemed taller, looming down upon him like silent spectres, tall black shadows against the navy sky. Their roots coiling as they crept along the ground. The low bushes snagged against his jacket. An owl hooted a warning, but it was too late, Richard tripped over a root and fell headfirst into the mud. He lay there for a moment and listened. In front of him, from somewhere beyond the overgrown path, he heard a door slam shut and people shout their goodbyes to one another, over the sounds of clinking glasses and laughter.

Richard breathed a sigh of relief. He extricated himself from the mud and jogged down a sloping bank towards the happy sounds. Finally re-joining the main road once more. The streetlights cast an amber glow over his mud-splattered clothes. Richard sighed and turned into the little alley adjacent to the Nod. He could not go into the pub in such a condition, or he would be shipped back to London instantly.

Richard sat by the dustbins, his knees drawn up to his chest, resting his head in his arms, as he listened to the sounds of people having fun. His stomach rumbled as occasional gusts of roast beef wafted through the back-kitchen windows.

After what seemed hours, he heard the faint tapping of pointed stilettos on paving stones. He sprung to his feet, his back against the inn wall, and waited.

Bethany muttered something under her breath as she opened the gaping black mouth of the hungry bin and tossed in the latest offering.

'Evening!' Richard whispered over her shoulder.

Bethany let out a scream which died on her lips as Richard sheepishly appeared from the shadows.

'Oh God! I'm so sorry! I didn't mean to frighten you,' he stammered in horror as Bethany glared at him.

'You didn't frighten me. You surprised me, that's all!' she hissed. 'Why are you still here?'

Richard glanced shyly in her direction. Several strands of chestnut brown hair had escaped the rigid confines of her ponytail and all traces of make-up had disappeared. She looked beautiful.

'I need to talk to you about the missing curates. Was Reverend Sparke one of them?'

Bethany frowned. 'Reverend Sparke disappeared over forty years ago but the diocese claimed he relocated. He was never reported missing.'

'Hmm...' Richard ran his hand through his messy brown hair. 'Was he the first?'

Bethany snorted. 'Of course not, I've researched back to the 1600s and from that date onwards at least eight curates, ministering in the Witherleigh area, have disappeared without trace. Probably more, but the old records are sketchy.'

Richard raised an eyebrow. 'Really? And no one apart from you has ever noticed?'

Bethany looked like she was about to hit him. Richard hastily retreated further into the alley.

'Of course, they noticed. From the 1600s to the 1700s all the missing curates were 'victims' of the great pestilence. Then after the fire that partially destroyed St Anthony's in 1711, the curates were relocated to St Pauls Church in Temperley and the vanishings stopped. It's only since the creation of the Moor Ministries in the 1880s that the church forgot about the disappearances, and the curates came back to Witherleigh. It didn't take long for the vanishings to start up again though.

Richard Dicken was the first to go missing. There was only one other disappearance in the nineteenth century. Then four curates went missing in the twentieth century - James Goodebody, John Sparke, John Bell, and Ezekiel Bond. That's about one curate disappearing every twenty years. You see a pattern? The time between vanishings is getting narrower. The last one to go missing was about a decade ago. An Oxbridge curate named Harry Hood. He was last seen in 2010, and now a decade has past, and I think they are going to come for you!'

She poked a finger into Richard's chest. He blushed and felt a volt of electricity surge through his body.

'Hmm, that's all very interesting… er… Bethany, but how do you know all this?' Richard asked.

'What do you mean? Just because I work in a bar, it doesn't mean I'm stupid y'know! I have a degree in medieval studies from Cambridge,' she snapped.

Richard blushed. 'I'm so sorry. I didn't mean to imply...' he stuttered.

'Well, don't be, I'm just messing with you. I googled it, and besides, Reverend Bond was my father,'

'Shit!' Richard whispered. 'I'm so sorry. What happened?'

'They said he had a nervous breakdown and ran off. I didn't believe it. Not for a minute. Mum got herself divorced and then remarried young Nigel, the garageman. Her way of coping, I guess. But me, I knew he would never leave us, so as soon as I could, I left the delights of Kent and came down here to the third world. Been looking for him ever since. They're all in it y'know, and I'm not being paranoid. You have to believe me.' Her brown eyes flashed defiantly at Richard, daring him not to believe her.

A memory hit Richard so hard that he stumbled backwards into the wall.

***

'You have to believe me, Father,' he screamed as the two burly nurses dragged him into the closed ward of the Nightingale Unit and pinned him onto the bed, while a slightly more feminine nurse in a white dress shot a needleful of Haldol into his arm.

His last memory before the six-month drug-induced haze, was of the concerned face of his father as he stared down at him, shaking his head sadly, as he turned to the moustached nurse and announced, '*He was adopted, you know. You just cannot change bad DNA, even with the best of upbringings.*'

The nurse had nodded, and Reverend Radcliffe turned and walked from the ward.

***

'Are you OK?' Bethany's voice cut across his thoughts.

'Yes, I was just thinking,' he muttered.

'Well, you looked like you had zoned out. Sorry if I scared you, but this shit is real and you're next. Unless we stop them.'

Richard ran his hands through his flopping hair. He knew nothing about the history of disappearances, but he knew John Sparke was real and dead. Therefore, Bethany might just be telling the truth.

He nodded. 'I do believe you, Miss Bond, but how do all the ghosts and other evil entities fit into all this?'

Bethany stared at him for a full minute.

Richard smiled uncomfortably at her.

'What other evil entities? Oh hell,' she groaned. 'You really are a nutter, aren't you?'

'That's what everyone tells me. But I prefer to believe the voices in my head,' Richard replied.

Bethany looked like she was about to run back into the pub.

'It's alright. I was only joking!' Richard said and forced a smile across his face.

Bethany frowned at him and looked at her watch. 'Well, I got to go anyway, people will be going dry.'

Richard watched her run back to the pub and shook his head. He certainly had a way with women.

The clock tower chimed, its happy peals sounding through the village. The pub door swung open as another couple tottered out into the main street, their raised voices and laughter blended with the cheerful chimes of the church bells. The couple walked arm in arm, through the village square, in a haze of amber streetlights. The car blinked happily to see them and the man, obviously a gentleman, opened the passenger door and helped the lady into her seat.

Richard squinted through the darkness at the couple and gasped. Quickly, he stepped back into the shadow of the alley as Mrs Ashcroft looked up from her car seat, her cold blue eyes scanning the darkness. The tall man, he assumed to be Mr Ashcroft, started the car, and the Range Rover roared into the night.

John Sparke had died the day he had been invited to the Ashcrofts. Mrs Ashcroft had tried to exorcise Snowy and banish him into the *Abyss*. It was odd behaviour for an expensively dressed lady of the manor. He frowned and ran his hand through his hair, pushing the untidy waves from his eyes.

He was certain that Mrs Ashcroft knew more about the occult than most modern, self-confessed, joss stick wielding wiccans. He needed to investigate Mrs Ashcroft further. A lunch invite would have presented the ideal situation, but he doubted one would be forthcoming. Such investigations would have to wait until tomorrow, however.

He unlocked his car and headed back to the delights of Home Farm.

'I must remember to wear boxers tonight,' he muttered, as a bleak farm light winked at him through the darkness.

CHAPTER EIGHT

The caravan door creaked open and there was a squidging sound, as a pair of muddy wellington boots strode across the floor. A gust of swirling wind blew through the caravan, rearranging the papers strewn across the cluttered table. Richard felt a massive urge to pull the duvet over his head and pretend he was invisible. Unfortunately, it had seldom worked as a child and he did not think the magic of the duvet would save him now. He pulled the duvet up to his chin and opened his eyes.

Farmer Butler stood over his bed holding a dainty, floral patterned cream jug.

''Ere 'ee go, fresh out of Daisy-Bell's udders not two hours ago. I thought it best not to wake 'ee though, it being milkin' time at six an' 'ee still bein' asleep an' all. I popped in earlier to check on 'ee,' Farmer Butler smiled, proud at his superior level of guest care.

Richard sat up and checked under the duvet.

'Oh shit, I forgot the boxers,' he groaned, as he grabbed hold of the duvet, making sure it remained firmly in place over his lap.

'Er… thanks,' Richard smiled up at the farmer. He took the

jug and positioned it on top of the duvet, protecting his lap.

Farmer Butler stood watching him for a minute. 'Don't 'ee want to put it in the fridge. It'll go bad in this heat?'

Richard looked at the frost crystals which had spread across the windows of the caravan. 'I think it will be fine for a minute while I finish my morning prayers.'

He closed his eyes and started chanting through every prayer he knew.

'Oh aye,' the farmer muttered, 'I best be off then. Enjoy your milk – it's extra creamy today.'

The caravan door closed shut. Richard opened his eyes and breathed a sigh of relief. He smelled the jug suspiciously and indeed it did smell extra creamy. Daisy-Bell may have excelled herself this morning, but he still preferred his milk well pasteurised and from a carton.

Richard looked at his wristwatch. It was almost nine. He was going to be late for church cleaning duties, but after witnessing the events of Sunday night, he had no wish to set foot in that church again.

He sighed and threw on the clothes, piled up at the foot of his tiny bed. Then padded across the cold lino floor to the kitchen unit and poured the yellow-tinged milk down the sink. It glugged into the drain hole and sat there, as Richard made two pieces of toast and drained a glass of orange juice. He glanced at his reflection in the kitchen window and ran his fingers through his hair, attempting to flatten down some of the wayward brown curls. Immediately, they sprang back into place. He stared at the window for a second. A shadowy, drawn face stared back at him. Countryside living did not seem as healthy as he had been led to believe in the unit. The black mould which crept across the outside of the caravan windows did not look that healthy either. He would have to stop at the Witherleigh Store and pick up some of their industrial strength bleach.

Richard grabbed his anorak and slipped his blue backpack over one shoulder. He opened the door and breathed a sigh of relief as he found no dead animals swinging on his porch. Country people might be generous but why couldn't they just leave a pot plant or a plate of cookies like normal people, he thought glumly.

Richard locked the door of the caravan and rattled the handle twice to make sure it was indeed locked. Then he squelched across the field to his car.

***

Half an hour later, he was outside the church. The autumn sun peeked at him through a clouded sky, its delicate rays of light tumbling through the grey clouds like a waterfall.

The autumnal dampness made him shiver as he approached the church. The heavy iron chain lay coiled around the tall black post, which flanked the heavy gate. Tentatively, Richard unlocked the gate. It swept open and he walked down the grey brick path, surrounded by the final resting place, of generations of villagers.

The grave markers to the right of him consisted of shining light grey crosses built upon rocks or stepped pyramids indicating rows of modern dead, while those to his left seemed much older. Their thin, crumbling headstones stood covered in green and white speckles, as nature eagerly reclaimed the stones. Richard read the names as he walked past the graves. He recognised some of the family names; the Butts, the Ashcroft's, a lone White, several Bells, and the unfortunate family of Zebadiah Strange, probably ancestors of Andrew Strange, the proprietor of the Witherleigh Store.

The modern grave markers proudly displayed their Christianity, while the older headstones possessed small, jagged crosses which appeared to have been hastily chiselled above the neatly inscribed occupiers name, along with two sets of significant dates, and a relatively loving message.

Richard chipped off some of the green mould with his caravan key and read the inscription.

'Here lies the body of Eliza Butt aged ninety-two, the Lord will judge.'

'Christ! that doesn't sound too good for poor old Eliza,' he mused.

Richard spread the thick tufts of grass which covered her dates. She had died in 1863. Below the date someone had cut a roughly made triangle of intersecting lines. The insides of the lines were stained black with a form of creeping algae, which made the triangle stand out in contrast with the greyness of the headstone.

Brown clumps of earth covered the pristine lawn between the graves as the local moles delighted in the sanctuary of the church. A lone bird sang hidden among the clouds of dark green leaves, on the spreading branches of the ancient yew, which dominated the crumbling graves.

'Well, hello there, Richard!' The vicar's voice boomed

through the stillness. Richard jumped with the shock of the sudden noise, but the vicar did not seem to notice.

'No need to go into the church today, may as well keep it clean, and anyway if we unlock it, who knows what riffraff will drift in,' the Reverend added.

'Just give the black railings their winter coat. Oh yes, and before I forget. Mrs Bell said you are most welcome to have lunch at the community centre today. Apparently, Monday is 'sausage and mash day', and very popular with the older parishioners. She wants to talk to you about a doll. Whatever that means?'

Richard blushed and shrugged his shoulders. 'That's very kind of her,' he muttered.

He thought for a moment and gestured towards the headstone. 'Have the Butts been here long?'

Reverend Anderson stared at Richard, a look of confusion crossing his face, and then he smiled. 'Ah! It's good to see you taking an interest in local history. Keep your mind off your own problems, eh? But you will have to check out the old church records I'm afraid. I was only transferred here from Ashdurton a few years ago. They needed someone to reorganise the Three Moors Mission community in North Devon. I was chosen by the Archbishop himself to do so.' Anderson beamed. His pristinely white teeth sparkled in the sunlight.

'Here's the key to the shed. It's behind the church.' Reverend Anderson produced a small key from his pocket and handed it to Richard. The smile changed to a grimace. The vicar straightened and rubbed the small of his back.

'Are you alright?' Richard queried.

'Yes, yes, I just need to go and lie down for a bit. I had parish duties to perform last night… and they took longer than I expected to complete. Some women are just never satisfied, always screaming out for more… er… spiritual counselling.'

Richard nodded. 'If you ever need any help, just let me know. I have had some small experience with these matters in London.'

Reverend Anderson's flushed and he frowned at Richard. 'I'm sure you have, young man. However, I am fully capable of catering to the needs of my parishioners.' Now, lock up when you have finished. I need to go and lie down.'

The Reverend turned and cut across the graveyard, shaking his head and muttering as he went.

Richard pinged the band around his wrist twice. He was not doing too well in his bid for allies, but then the Lord worked in mysterious ways… perhaps Mrs Bell had been sent to help him?

His stomach rumbled at the thought of sausages and mashed potatoes, swimming in a sea of thick, brown gravy.

A shadow flickered across the stained glass window towering above him.

Richard looked up to see Saint Anthony. He was in a dark tomb surrounded by three demonic manifestations. A hissing serpent towered over the saint. Next to the snake was a scorpion, its tail raised ready to strike, and lastly, a huge black bull stood behind him, its front hooves raised ready to strike the saint. The window was a warning to its congregation to remain vigilant because demonic creatures walked through the land of the living and reaped the souls of the unwary.

Unfortunately, those parishioners who actually took notice of the windows assumed their warning to be allegorical and not literal. It was a literary mistake with a heavy cost.

A small light appeared in the church. Richard watched the light move through the church. His face illuminated by shades of blues, yellows, and reds as they streamed down from the stained glass window above.

A heavy grey cloud hid the morning sun and the vibrant colours vanished.

Richard sprinted across the grass towards the first high arched window, which was nestled beneath the bell tower. The window depicted Saint Teresa surrounded by a sea of red and orange flames. Within the flames was a black outline of a man, his eyes red slits of fire.

The man began to walk towards Richard.

Richard felt his world begin to crumble and slide. He grabbed hold of the church wall and gripped it until he felt the rough bricks cut into his hands. Richard closed his eyes and prayed, murmuring the same prayer over again until the world stabilized. He sank to the ground. The springy grass felt cold and damp under his touch. Richard brought his knees to his chest and covered his face with his hands as he prayed for inner strength.

It was happening again.

He was drawn to them. It was the path of thorns God had set before him.

There was a demon trapped in the church. He could feel it. The saints depicted in the great stained glass windows – Michael, Anthony, and Teresa - had been specially chosen to stand guard over, and protect the perimeter, of the church from the demon. These three saints were the Gatekeepers of the *Vitalis*, guarding the world of the living from the world of the damned, forever locked in an eternal battle against the devil and his legions of darkness.

Their protective images had been fashioned into the very fabric of the church of St Anthony because somewhere inside the church, there was a circular seal or demon trap, and one extremely angry demon.

The trap must have failed and leaked its evil throughout Witherleigh, causing the dead to rise and souls to warp.

This was why the exorcisms were not holding, as soon as the spirits were sealed below, the demon freed them. It was an eternal circle of the damned.

A grating noise caught Richard's attention. He spun round.

A little girl stood watching him through the bars of the church fence. In her right hand, she held a Barbie doll by the remains of its long blonde hair, dragging its body along the pavement.

Richard waved to the little girl.

 The girl stared back at him. her almost black eyes devoid of any expression. Her black irises were so large that they completely covered the white of her sclera. Her black hair was scraped back behind her ears into two severe twisted plaits. She was not in the navy blue of the Witherleigh Primary School but perhaps it was a non-pupil day, or she was ill, or just a victim of general parental apathy.

Her head fell sideways onto her shoulder and she vanished. The clawing smell of sulphur permeated the dank autumn air.

'But you're a demon, that's impossible!' Richard gasped in horror, as he fell backwards against the church for support. 'How did you escape the Gatekeepers?'

He breathed heavily as the sulphur burnt his lungs and his heart raced. He had borne witness to the coming of the black-eyed creatures before, when he had worked in London. Their eyes had evolved a black liquid covering to protect them while traveling between the extreme heat of the *Abyss* to the chilly emptiness of the *Mortalis*, the afterdeath.

They were the sign of the fallen.

The demon must have broken free from the church seal and was walking the streets of Witherleigh. This was why the church was closed. Reverend Anderson must have known that the demon had escaped.

Richard swore and pinged his yellow band four times. He needed help. He could not fight a demon alone. However, his list of potential allies was not long.

Bethany thought he was mad, and the Reverend was too busy catering to the needs of his female parishioners to be of much use.

The rounded face of Mrs Bell floated into his thoughts. Mrs Bell could see ghosts, exorcise spirits, and she wanted to talk to him. Perhaps they could join forces?

He looked at his watch; it was 11.30 am. Slightly early for lunch but he knew Mrs Bell was in the centre cooking, by the delicious 'sausagy' smell which was wafting across the village square. Richard looked at the black iron railings which stood untouched by paint and a pang of guilt prickled at his conscience. He would begin painting after lunch, but first, he needed to get some supplies.

A cold wind blew in from the fields and howled up the quiet main street of Witherleigh. He zipped up his jacket and crossed the road.

Richard looked through the cluttered window of the Witherleigh Store. In the centre of the window were three grime-ridden boxed Barbies. The dolls were displayed like open coffins. Their eyes unblinking as they stared back at him. He was not a Barbie expert, but the three 'Party Time' Barbie dolls looked more like prostitutes in their thigh high boots and minidresses than party girls. It was not the image of womanhood he would want little girls looking up to; but then he was an outpatient in a mental unit.

To the right of the Barbies, were cereal packets displayed in a stepped pyramid in the shop window. He was unsure of how long they had been positioned there, but the whiteness of the packets was yellowing to that of a neglected beige.

The tins in the left corner of the window were decorated in cobwebs and an indistinguishable brown stain circled their base. It was the type of place where rats came to feast if they were feeling suicidal. Food shopping would have to be done in Ashdurton, an hour's drive through the moor, but a bottle of bleach should last for many year's Richard reasoned. He opened the shop door, and a little brass bell jingled his arrival.

Instantly, the shopkeeper appeared. A wizened old man in an ancient brown shopkeeper's coat.

'Welcome to the Witherleigh Store, I've been expectin' 'ee. You're that young curate, Richard Radcliffe,' the shopkeeper announced and thrust out his hand.

Reluctantly, Richard shook it. The shopkeeper's grip was surprisingly strong, and he had to pull his hand free from the old man's grasp.

'I'm Andrew Strange, proprietor of the Witherleigh Store. This 'ere shop has been in my family for four generations,' he said proudly. He waved towards the rows of once white shelves, stacked with cardboard boxes of seasonal fruits and vegetables, which lined each side of the narrow shop. A flopping carrot hung dejectedly over one of the muddy boxes marked 'fresh.'

The shopkeeper disappeared behind his counter and reappeared with a slatted wooden box emblazoned with a smiling hen, with the words 'Happy Chicken Company' stencilled across the top.

'May I recommend this for a carefree young bachelor like yourself? It's our weekly organic food box fresh from Arthur Butt's land up at Witherleigh Cross. 'Ee's organically certificated, you know,' Andrew said proudly feeling his potatoes.

Richard peered dubiously into the box. To his surprise, the box looked well-stocked. There was an open egg tray of a dozen brown eggs and several brown paper bags overflowing with a variety of seasonal fruit and vegetables. Richard poked a green apple. Its skin was shining and firm, unlike the wrinkled spongey affair, he had bought from the Ashdurton Express.

Richard rubbed his chin. 'How much is the food box?'

'If 'ee collects it from 'ere every Friday, I can give it to 'ee for a tenner,' the shopkeeper replied, rubbing his hands together.

Richard's eyes lit up.

In London, prices for organic food boxes were almost triple that. With the savings he could make on petrol costs on trips into Ashdurton, his meagre salary might just make it through the month. Perhaps he could pick up some fresh cartons of milk at the same time. He looked around the tiny store. Behind the shopkeeper was a row of dubious sounding dark brown bottles all bearing the image of a very happy, rotund, red-faced bishop and the name 'Bishop's Finger Scrumpy.'

Andrew Strange saw Richard looking at the bottles and his eyes lit up. 'Aye, the 'Bishops Finger,' that's a man's scrumpy. It'll put hairs on your chest.'

Richard smiled and moved quickly away. He had no desire to grow any more chest hair at present. He had a small tuft, but if any more appeared, he might have to start shampooing it or something.

A tall, white fridge stood against the far wall adjacent to the counter. It looked clean and its shelves were filled with milk, homemade cheese, and butter, all bearing the Happy Chicken logo. Richard had not realised Witherleigh had such a big food company. He helped himself to the dairy produce and placed his shopping on the countertop, along with a two-litre bottle of pine-scented industrial strength bleach, chosen from the store's extensive range of bleach, general detergent, and mould removing products.

'Sign me up for the Friday box and I'll take these too please.'

The shopkeeper's eyes twinkled with delight and he wiped his hands on his brown overcoat. 'A very wise choice, Curate. Witherleigh Cross will not disappoint.'

The shopkeeper took out a navy-blue ledger from beneath

the counter and wrote in the new order in slow, neat writing. Richard stood and watched him write, feeling slightly awkward.

The shop bell tinkled, and the heavy blue door swung open as Mrs Bell charged in.

'Mornin', Andy.' She smiled and spied Richard, 'Ah, the young Curate, you be wantin' your sausages an' mash soon. Oh, don't look at me like that - I met Reverend Anderson in the square, poor man, that back of his gives him terrible pains. He suffers so for his parishioners. Oh, anyway I must be away in case the sausages need turning. I just popped in for some extra milk, put it on the tab please Andy.' She smiled at the shopkeeper who nodded and took another hard-backed ledger from below the countertop. This one was dark green.

Mrs Bell bustled to the fridge and took out a two-pint carton of semi-skimmed milk and after waving to Richard and the shopkeeper, disappeared from the shop. The brass bell jingled as she left.

'Aye, that's a fine-looking woman. I like something meaty to hold onto at night,' Mr Strange grinned as he watched her leave the shop.

Richard looked at Mr Strange in confusion. The shopkeeper and Mrs Bell were both well past fifty and quite wrinkly. He took his change from Mr Strange and quickly vacated the premises, desperately trying to blink a series of disturbing images from his brain.

CHAPTER NINE

A delicious smell wafted through the little square. An elderly man crossed the main road and headed towards the dreary, white buildings of the community centre.

Richard followed the man.

'Afternoon, Mrs Bell,' the old man called out as he held the centre door open for Richard. 'Sommat smells grand.'

'Aye, Mr Thomas, that'll be the Witherleigh Cross organic sausages. They won the Three Moors best sausage in show last month at Ashdurton.'

The old man grinned at Richard, showing a row of yellow stained teeth. 'Aye well, I hope them's not the same ones, Mrs Bell.'

Mrs Bell stopped scrubbing at a crumb covered table and laughed. 'Why, Mr Thomas, you an' that tongue o' yours will get 'ee into all sorts of trouble.'

'Aye, that's what I'm hopin', maid,' he said winking at Mrs Bell.

Mrs Bell's naturally ruddy face went a shade redder, and she flapped the dishcloth at him. 'We'll have none of that now, come an' sit yourself down while I turn the sausages.'

'You can turn me sausages anytime,' Mr Thomas purred

seductively in his deep, gravelly voice.

Mrs Bell spotted Richard hovering awkwardly in the doorway.

'Ah… Curate, you look like you are gettin' thinner by the day, sit you down by the window an' don't you worry, I'll sort you out.'

Mrs Bell bustled from the serving area and disappeared into the kitchen.

Mr Thomas leaned backwards, tipping his chair onto two legs. 'You lucky bugger. I think 'ees on a promise there, lad.'

Richard was shocked. He had no idea the portly Mrs Bell was such a prize catch in Witherleigh. He blushed and stammered, 'Er… Mrs Bell, is a very kind, er… woman.'

The old man roared with laughter and opened the *Three Moors Star* he had taken from a vacant table and began to rustle through its well-thumbed pages. The papers front-page headline blazed 'Milk Yield Ten-Year Low Crisis;' underneath was the sad looking face of a Friesian cow.

Apparently, the cows were not doing their bit for the local economy.

'It's probably the miserable weather,' Richard mumbled.

Mrs Bell burst through the kitchen door, her face beaming as she placed a plate of steaming food, consisting of a mashed potato mountain, surrounded by a sea of thick brown gravy, into which was thrust three shiny brown pork sausages.

'There you are, my lover, that'll see you right for the day.'

Richard smiled his thanks to Mrs Bell.

Mrs Bell leant closer, her voluptuous left breast inches from his face, and whispered, 'We need to talk. There's a wickedness in the village an' I knows you can see it too.'

She patted his shoulder and disappeared back into the kitchen.

The old man raised his mug of tea and saluted Richard.

Richard looked around the centre. The lunchtime rush had begun. The elderly couple sat silently in their corner, patiently waiting for their food. The man looked up from his phone and glared across the room, muttering something to his wife about 'incomers.' Richard nodded to the man and shovelled a mouthful of gravy-drenched mashed potato and sausage into his mouth. Some of the gravy dribbled down his chin, plopping in dark splodges onto his shirt. The elderly man pulled a face and looked away. Richard smiled to himself. One of the many things he had learnt in the unit was, that if you made people uncomfortable, they would look away and leave you alone.

The centre door flung open and Farmer Butt stamped a trail of dirt across the centre floor, closely followed by his mud-drenched cow dog. He sprawled onto the table behind Richard and stared hungrily at the kitchen doors.

There was a gust of icy wind and Snowy appeared sitting at the tiny table at the back of the centre. His eyes were fixed on the window, scouring the dark green fields. His appearance, never attractive, had changed since his last hanging. Richard stared at the new appearance of Snowy and wiped his sweaty palms on his jeans as he fought the urge to vomit over Mrs Bell's sparkling table.

A thick red mark circled Snowy's neck. His faded blue eyes had elongated, and the whites of his eyes hung down onto his face, which had taken on the grey taint of death. His lips were black had shrivelled into his face as he chewed on the remains of dirt-encrusted fingernails.

A thick khaki liquid dripped slowly down his chair leg and pooled on the white-speckled lino.

Snowy twisted his head round until he faced Richard and nodded. 'Well, fancy seein' 'ee 'ere, Curate. Eat up quick as they'll be comin' for 'ee next. By the by… 'ave you seen my Martha? She went to Ashdurton to sell 'er cheese wheels an' I've not seen 'er since.'

Beads of perspiration trickled down Richard's forehead. He was not sure, but he thought Snowy was decomposing. A disgusting, clawing smell began to ooze through the centre. Richard opened the nearest window, sending a blast of damp air into the room, as he tried to finish his remaining sausages as quickly as possible.

The centre grew darker.

A grey shadow passed over his plate.

Richard looked through the window and saw a black haze had spread across the glass, obscuring his view of the square. He leant closer and inspected the window. It was covered in a series of black mould spots with spiked edges, that seemed to reach out and join with other spores, until a wave of mould grew across all the windows of the centre.

'Oh Christ! That is just not normal,' Richard whispered.

Subconsciously, his hand reached for the plain gold cross which hung around his neck.

Richard pointed at the window. He had to warn the other customers.

'Look at the mould!' he shouted. 'Something evil is coming.'

The silent couple looked up from their mobile phones. They gazed at the window for a second and shrugged at each other. Then stared into their screens once more.

The loud farmer tutted loudly, 'Grockles, 'tis only a scrapin' of Devon mould, grows everywhere in thee damp. It's nothin' to make such a gert fuss about. Bloody foreigners,' he tutted. His dog, busily munching on a juicy brown sausage, woofed in agreement.

'Them's can't see it. Them's think 'ees mad,' Snowy laughed. Several blackened teeth fell onto the bleached white plastic table.

Something metal crashed onto the kitchen floor.

A scream rang through the centre. It stopped suddenly, in mid-screech.

Farmer Butt jumped to his feet. 'Are you alright in there, Mrs Bell?' he asked, as he walked slowly towards the kitchen. The collie slunk behind him.

'Shit!' Richard murmured. He stood and tucked his chair under the table.

'Everything alright in there, Mrs Bell?' the farmer called, louder this time.

Something brushed past Richard's legs and sent electrical pulses through his body. He felt his stomach sink and chest tighten.

'After you,' he whispered to the frowning farmer.

There would be no need to rush.

Gingerly, the farmer opened the kitchen door and peeked inside Mrs Bell's domain.

The kitchen shone white; its appliances scrubbed until they

glistened. Piled neatly on the left-hand side of the sink were a toppling array of used dishes, mugs, and sundry strangely shaped utensils Richard doubted had any culinary use. On top of the stove, a huge sauccpan of yellow custard bubbled and burst, squirting yellow droplets across the stovetop, which cindered in the heat of the hobs. The oven door stood slightly ajar as the smell of slowly desiccating spotted dick filled the kitchen.

A large white table ran the length of the wall, opposite the pristine appliances. Eight empty white dessert bowls were laid on the table, complete with their accompanying spoons, all carefully wrapped in white paper napkins.

The collie pushed past Richard and dived under the table, its tail swinging against his legs, as earnest licking sounds came from beneath the table. Richard squatted down and swore.

Mrs Bell lay under the table, her back pushed up against the kitchen wall.

Her face was twisted towards him; mouth wide, frozen in a scream that would never finish. A black tarlike liquid ran from her mouth and nose. Mrs Bell's eyes stared unblinking towards Richard, her pupils fixed and dilated. Thin dark veins ran across the whites of her eyes. The rims of her eyelids had turned black, and a mass of drying blood spread across her forehead.

A dark stain covered the cream blouse clinging to Mrs Bell's bosoms. Richard stared at the cook's chest, willing it to rise and fall. Nothing happened. He bent down and examined the stain. What seemed a solid black mark at first was, on closer inspection, a series of tightly packed mould spores, which were slowly disappearing.

The farmer squatted down next to Richard, one hand holding onto the collar of his collie, as it tried to lick Mrs Bell's forehead.

'I think she be dead,' Butt said flatly.

'Er… I think so too,' Richard replied.

'Aren't you goin' to say a prayer over 'er corpse then? Send her spirit off nice an' proper like? Last rites an' all?'

Richard stared at the frowning farmer. There was fear in his face. The type of fear which could only come from experience.

'You've seen them too,' Richard whispered.

'Seen who?' said the farmer suspiciously.

'The dead.' Richard replied.

The farmer recoiled as if Richard had slapped him in the face. Butt looked around the kitchen. Satisfied, that no one was listening, he nodded.

'I ain't seen no dead but I heard 'em in the woods. Everyone knows the dead walk in Witherleigh, have been doin' so for centuries. But don't 'ee worry Home Farm is protected. Old Butler has surrounded his woods with the shiny and the cuttin'. Now send 'er off, an' best do it proper or she'll be back, an' they never come back same as when they leave.'

Richard breathed heavily trying to drag back memories of his two years of seminary college. The time had been marked by a series of new experiences. His first time away from home, his first encounter with a demon, and his first stay in a mental hospital. His second year was a blur of sedative drugs, memory gaps, and static images he could not thread together.

'You doin' it now, then, curate?' the farmer asked, his eyes never leaving the corpse

Richard cursed under his breath.

The only Latin he could remember was *Ave Maria, gratia plena, Dominus tecum* – the first line of a prayer they had learnt in religious studies – 'The Catholic Experience'. He repeated it twice. Then did the sign of the cross over her body, as he recited a few half-remembered lyrics from the *Requiem for Evita*. It was one of his father's favourite West End shows.

The farmer thumped Richard on the back.

'There, I knew 'ee weren't as useless as everyone says!' he grinned.

'Er… thanks,' said Richard crawling out from beneath the table. He put his hands behind his back and secretly pinged the rubber band twice as he prayed for forgiveness, hoping that one fake last rites ritual would not condemn his soul to the *Abyss* for eternity.

Farmer Butt rubbed the field of black stubble across his broad chin. 'Well, best ring up the police now. It'll take them a good 'our to get across the fields from Exhaven an' I can't be late for milkin'.'

He eyed the empty bowls on the table.

'It don't seem respectful to leave 'er spotted dick to burn in the oven though. We best serve it ourselves. It's what she would 'ave wanted.'

Richard took a step backwards, the sausages and mash churning in his stomach.

'Er… I suppose wasting food is wicked. Did you know Mrs Bell well?' he questioned the hungry farmer.

'Oh aye!' said Butt as he grabbed the spotted dick from the

oven and spooned out steaming wedges into the bowls. 'The custard's ruined but there should be ice cream in the freezer.' He nodded towards a little fridge freezer standing in the corner.

Richard dutifully retrieved an industrial-sized tub of vanilla ice cream bearing the Happy Chicken logo and handed it to the farmer. He chiselled pieces off with a large knife and scattered ice cream shards across the bowls.

''Ere you go serve 'em, then.' He thrust three bowls into Richard's hands. 'I've known 'er all me life. The Bells and the Butts have lived in bloody Witherleigh forever. It's our curse, we can't leave 'ere… never.'

He balanced four bowls in his hands and headed towards the doors. 'It's not that I'm not sad to see 'er pass but then 'tis the only way to escape yere. Feet first an' all, an' I do keep pigs, best bacon in the three moors.' He nodded to his dog, who wagged its tail hopefully at Richard.

Richard did not understand the relevance of pig keeping but nodded, eager to gain the farmer's trust.

'Hmm… yes. I see your point,' Richard said as the farmer disappeared through the doorway.

Richard walked slowly after him, the bowls of spotted dick shaking unsteadily in his hands. He thrust the bowls under the noses of the elderly couple and a silent woman with a plait of long brown hair, he had not noticed before, who sat knitting by the window.

He shrank back behind his table as Butt announced the tragedy to the diners.

The spotted dick stared up at him from a melted puddle of ice-cream. Richard pushed it aside and stared out of the window. He shivered as an icy breeze ruffled his serviette, which lay discarded on the table.

'Hello John,' Richard greeted the presence lounging over the chair opposite him.

Reverend Sparke grinned back at him. 'Ah, Richard! Dining at the community centre I see. Mrs Bell certainly makes a hearty meal. I would have some but this afternoon I have been invited for a delicious Sunday roast at the manor with the Ashcrofts, which is the reason I've got the best suit on.'

He stroked the shiny blue material lovingly.

'No, you're not,' Richard whispered. 'You're dead, try to remember. I need your help. Mrs Bell has been murdered.'

John looked at Richard in confusion and then nodded thoughtfully. 'Ah yes. Sorry, things get a little fuzzy when you are a tad lost and just wandering around the *Mortalis* with all the others just searching for the entrance to the *Postvitum*. It's a rather embarrassing state of affairs for a curate to be in, to be completely honest, old man.'

Richard nodded sympathetically.

'Hmm… but if Mrs Bell is indeed dead, who's that over there waving to you?' John asked.

Richard looked up. Mrs Bell smiled at him from the kitchen doorway, turned, and vanished.

'Shit!' Richard swore running a hand through his tangled hair.

'Oh, I wouldn't worry about her,' John replied. 'What I would worry about is who the devil is killing us and what have they done with the bodies?'

'The bodies?' Richard frowned.

'Well yes,' replied John. 'Where are the bodies of the

Curates being kept? Find them, and you will find your killer.'

Light beams pierced through his shimmering best suit. 'Oh bother, I'm fading.' John looked up at Richard. 'Please find my body and give me a decent Christian burial. I am so tired of just wandering.'

Richard nodded. 'I will try my best.'

John vanished.

***

The door of the centre swung open, and Reverend Anderson walked in. He scanned the room. The diners put down their spoons and averted their gaze. Farmer Butt strode solemnly across the community centre and thrust his hand towards the Reverend.

'It be a bad day for Witherleigh, Reverend,' he announced.

The rest of the diners murmured their agreement.

'She was a fine, robust woman,' the vicar declared. 'Such a tragedy, but then entering the gates of Heaven is a cause for joy not sadness.'

'Aye, Reverend, that's what we thought too,' Butt agreed.

He nodded towards Richard, in close conversation with the empty chair at his table, his pudding untouched.

'Oh dear, this seems to be all too much for our young London guest,' the Reverend said shaking his head with compassion. 'I had better see the body.'

The farmer nodded, and they walked towards the kitchen. Richard looked up and rushed after them.

'Oh, bugger me!' swore the farmer as he pulled his dog from the body. Red paw prints criss-crossed the pine scented floor and the white blaze on the front of Spud's face was matted with blood.

''Ee's always hungry, that bloody dog is,' the farmer sighed.

Reverend Anderson nodded.

The Reverend stared at Mrs Bell for a minute and shook his head. He bent down to examine the oven. Farmer Butt had left the oven door in the half-open position, just as it had been, prior to the removal of the spotted dick. The Reverend produced a set of reading glasses from inside the pocket of his tweed jacket and examined the oven door. Red liquid had splattered against the glass and trickled down the inside of the door.

'Hmm, she must of hit her head on the oven door, fallen backwards, and rolled underneath the kitchen table,' the Reverend decided, rubbing his grey stubble.

'Aye, that's my thinkin',' Farmer Butt agreed, struggling to hold onto Spud's collar as the dog lunged for the oven.

The Reverend stiffened as Richard leant over his shoulder.

'I think the demon that escaped from St Anthony's silenced her. It knew she wanted to talk to me,' Richard whispered, blinking away tears, as he fixed his gaze on the kitchen tiles.

'What did 'ee say?' Farmer Butt turned and stared at the Reverend.

'Oh dear! I thought this would happen.' The Reverend grabbed Richard by his shoulders and turned him away from the oven. 'Mrs Bell wanted to talk to you about your doll, nothing more.'

Farmer Butt snorted and burst out laughing.

'There are no demons, witches, or unclean spirits, Richard.

What do you think this is… the sixteen hundreds? The modern Anglican church does not condone such reckless scaremongering. Look to the *New Testament*, dear boy, and you will find your way,' Reverend Anderson commanded.

'You're wrong!' Richard argued, as he tried to pull away from the vicar.

Anderson held him fast, digging his fingers into Richard's narrow shoulders until he flushed with pain.

'I can see you are getting overwrought. Go back to your caravan and ask yourself why you choose to see wickedness everywhere you go,' the Reverend hissed into Richard's face.

Beads of sweat formed on Richard's forehead as he squirmed under the digging fingernails.

'But what about the black mould. It's all over her chest and I've seen it here too,' he gasped. His eyes opened fractionally wider as an idea exploded in his thoughts. 'It's the demon. It leaves trails of mould wherever it walks, it's been here before, that's why everything is bleached – the demon travels…'

The Reverend slapped him hard in the face. Richard over-balanced and fell face first onto the floor. His head inches from Mrs Bell's body. A drop of blood rolled down a cut on his lip. Richard looked up at the vicar in confusion.

'You will stop all this mould and demon nonsense, immediately. There is no mould here. Mrs Bell kept an extremely clean establishment. I warn you, do not speak ill of the dead.'

'The poor boy is getting hysterical,' Anderson stated to the farmer.

Butt nodded in agreement.

'Take him back to his caravan.'

Farmer Butt nodded to the vicar and hauled Richard to his feet. Spud growled and sniffed hungrily at his ankles as Butt manhandled Richard through the kitchen doorway.

Reverend Anderson thought for a minute, his anger subsiding as quickly as it came. He had promised Reverend Radcliffe that he would try to protect the boy. 'Oh yes! And Richard!' he called.

Farmer Butt and Richard turned.

'You need not come to work for the rest of the week, the shock of poor Mrs Bell's passing has obviously been too much for you to bear.'

The vicar cast a glance in the direction of Butt and raised his hand. 'And do not worry about your church maintenance jobs. I will do them all, along with all my other ecclesiastical duties.' He nodded at Farmer Butt, who smiled back as he pushed Richard into the dining area. The Reverend followed them at a more befitting, religious pace.

A stout policeman stood in the café taking statements from the elderly couple, who stared unhappily into their dessert bowls.

'But me an' the missus didn't see nothin',' the old man whined as he crossed his arms.

'I see,' said the policeman. 'Just don't leave the village,' he growled.

'But we never do,' the old woman commented as she scraped the last remains of custard from her bowl.

'And who's that?' said the policeman, staring at Richard suspiciously.

'Only my new helper down from London,' Reverend Anderson replied softly, as he appeared behind Richard and Farmer Butt.

'I see,' nodded the policeman. ''Im's got blood on 'is lip, did 'ee kill Mrs Bell then?'

Richard opened his mouth to protest.

'Oh, good Lord no! He fell over in the kitchen. His father is Reverend Radcliffe, head of the church commission for morality and ethics in the twenty-first century, and a rather well-known missionary. He has his own television channel, you know. His godparents just happen to be the Archbishop of London and his wife, Alison,' Anderson added.

'I see,' said the policeman. 'Fancy bloke then is 'ee?'

Anderson signalled to Farmer Butt to take Richard away.

'Well, let's just say his connections could be of great use to Witherleigh.'

Police Constable Bates nodded and flipped his notepad back open. 'I See. So, she died of natural causes then?'

'Oh no!' replied the vicar. 'Accidental death, she hit her head on the corner of the cooker door, while checking her puddings.'

'Oh aye,' said the policeman, as he wrote the information down.

'At least she died doing something she loved,' Anderson stated sadly.

The policeman nodded and placed his notebook in the breast pocket of his uniform. 'Open an' shut case then vicar. SOCO will be 'ere sometime today or tomorrow at the latest, to gather up the evidence an' the body an' all. It'll need to go to inquest, but the magistrate will do a proper job an' have the death recorded before the week is out, so there's no need to fret.'

The Reverend nodded in agreement.

Mr Ashcroft senior was an exceedingly able magistrate.

CHAPTER TEN

Butt rattled the door handle. The lock clunked and the door to Buttercup Cottage swung open.

'So much for locking my door, Farmer Butler must hold a duplicate key,' Richard muttered, as he looked around the little caravan. The duvet was piled in a heap in the middle of the bed, his unwashed underwear lay across the floor, and the sink was overflowing with dirty dishes.

At first glance, everything seemed as he had left it.

The big farmer manhandled Richard onto the little seating area by his kitchen table. He gripped Richard's shoulder and pointed a dirt-stained finger in his face, as if he were giving instructions to his cattle dog.

'Now you just stay 'ere an' keep your nose out of village matters,' he said, his brown eyes glaring at Richard. 'You'll get what's comin' to you soon enough.'

'Are you threatening me?' Richard said, trying to wriggle away from the farmer's grip.

''Tis no threat, everyone in the village knows, he'll be comin' for you soon,' he nodded at the window. 'He's called already.'

'Who has called?' Richard asked.

The farmer released his hold on Richard and strode to the

doorway, calling to his dog. Moments later Spud's black nose appeared in the doorway. The dog lay down flat against the mud as if trying to make itself invisible. A low growl rumbled through its trembling body.

'Best you don't know,' the farmer replied grimly. 'The whole village is cursed. Once you enter Witherleigh you'll never leave, but feet first. I'm sorry but there's nothin' that can be done.' Butt shook his head, called Spud to heel, and left the caravan.

Richard watched the farmer trudge wearily down the mud-drenched field, as he followed Spud, who had raced across the field, and was waiting for his master at the end of the track by the Land Rover.

Richard breathed a sigh of relief and shut the caravan door. Butt was right. The village felt cursed. Its people subdued, as if held hostage by some insidious force. However, curses could be broken, and demons trapped. Richard did not fear the creatures of the *Abyss*. Their desires were base but simple and easily discernible. It was people who scared him.

Richard stood for a moment as he looked around the caravan. Something felt wrong.

There was no sunlight.

A thin layer of black mould covered the caravan's tiny windows, filtering out the light. The air smelt acrid, a mixture of rotten eggs, wet soil, and decay. The demon had been here. It knew where he lived. He had to be prepared.

Richard took a battered cardboard box from beneath his bed and emptied its contents over the kitchen table. Then he made a cup of tea and sat down as he sorted through the heap of old books with cracked spines, notebooks, and dog-eared papers filled with scribbled diagrams. If he could work out the nature of the Witherleigh curse, then he could break it, and release the villagers. He opened an ancient book its front cover made of brown leather with the initials LFD entwinned together. The LFD or *Liber Fieri Dæmoniorum* was an encyclopaedia of demonology created by St Michah of Canterbury, detailing the demons he encountered on his pilgrimage to the Holy land in the sixteenth century. Richard flicked through the yellowed pages and sighed. St Michah alone had encountered over one hundred and sixty-six demons on his travels, anyone of which could have relocated to Witherleigh. Richard closed the book with a satisfying thud. He needed more information; he would have to go back to St Anthony's and try to gather some information from there.

Richard took another sip of tea and frowned as he tried to remember where he had put the Jaffa Cakes.

The caravan door flung open as a frozen gust of wind crashed against the caravan, rocking it from side to side. The temperature inside the caravan dropped.

Richard grabbed his mug from the shaking table as papers swirled and danced across the caravan.

A grey shadow floated past his window as it approached the door. Ice crystals spread across the caravan windows, sparkling in the afternoon sun. The doorway shook for a second. The little hessian bag, filled with what Richard had assumed to be parsley, toppled from the kitchen ledge, its contents splintering across the floor.

The dried leaves fractured into dust particles which infused the air with pungent peppery hues. The smell burnt his eyes and they streamed. Richard wiped them with the sleeve of his shirt and cautiously looked out of the caravan.

The shadow had vanished. The wind died away, and the maelstrom of papers fell to the floor.

Richard felt his breathing accelerate. He shivered and clutched his mug to his chest for warmth. His heartbeats filled the silence of the caravan. He tried to hold his breath and whispered, 'And this to will pass,' over and over again, as they had taught him in the unit.

'It was just the wind,' he muttered. 'Reverend Anderson is right. I am seeing way too many ghosts and demons. Perhaps I should start taking the pills again and this time make it a double dose.'

There was an unopened packet of emergency sleeping pills in a chipped cup, hidden at the back of the little kitchen cupboard. If he could sleep the rest of the day away, he might feel better tomorrow.

A long, slow, scratching sound cut through his thoughts. Something was being scraped across the kitchen window.

Richard glanced up at the frozen window.

A distorted, pale face stared back at him. Wavy black hair, caught in the wind, flew madly around a gaunt, grey face. A cream scarf was tied tightly around his neck, its ends trailing in the wind. The man opened his mouth and shouted something to Richard. His words were illegible; the vowels elongated, and then rushed together. Richard raised his hands to his ears and shook his head. The man cocked his head to one side, so it rested on the left shoulder of his billowing shirt. Then he straightened his head and glanced behind him, squinting into the green cow field. Slowly, the gaunt man began to carve a series of lines into the ice covering the plastic caravan window using a strange-looking, heavy-bladed knife.

Richard frowned as he tried to unravel the meaning behind the lines.

A deep rumbling sound came from somewhere beneath the field as the mud began to ripple. There was a spark and fire leapt across the field and died, leaving a smoking triangle burnt into the muddy grass.

The grey man watched the field burn, his mouth, and eyes wide with terror. The knife fell onto the mud as his long, grey fingers desperately tried to cling onto the grey plastic surround of the window.

Another gust of wind crashed against the caravan, almost knocking it onto its side. Richard fell to the floor, curling into a tight ball. Cups, assorted cooking pans, kitchen knives, and cutlery fell around him, clanking noisily against the lino.

The gaunt man screamed and banged against the window with his fists.

Richard watched in horror as the man was ripped from the caravan and tossed like a ragdoll through the air. A forest of brown tendrils rushed out from beneath the cow field and grabbed the falling man. Richard jumped up and raced from the caravan. The tendrils retracted and pulled the grey man backwards into the triangle, pinning him against the grass. The man waved his hands frantically as its body disappeared beneath the soil. Richard lunged across the mud and grabbed a flailing wrist, but his fingers slipped through the spirit. The man disappeared inside the triangle, reclaimed by the *Mortalis*.

The triangle faded into the field.

Richard rolled onto his back, gasping for breath. 'That really looked like a ghost,' he muttered. He shook his head and lay there for a moment, shivering as the damp soil soak into his back.

The afternoon sun peeked through the clouds and Richard looked across to his battered caravan. The sun's rays touched the lines the ghost had scrawled onto the plastic window. Illuminated by the sun. the lines joined together to form a sentence - 'Where are the bodies to?'

Richard frowned and ran his hand guiltily through his muddy hair. He had been so caught up with unmasking the demon, that he had totally forgotten about the disappearances. He shook his head. He had to do better.

On the ground, beneath the windows, lay a silver shiny object. Richard crawled over and grabbed it. The blade cut across his fingers. 'Oh shit!' he cursed to the cows huddled together in the furthest corner of the field. The blade was deadly, sharp, and real. He flipped the dagger over. Written along the length of the blade in decorative, cursive script were the words 'Property of Richard Dicken.'

Instantly, Richard recognised the name. Reverend Dicken was one of Bethany's missing curates, and he obviously wanted to be found.

The ground began to move.

Holding the knife in one hand, Richard tried to stand but something in the soil refused to let him.

'The *Mortalis* cannot take me. I am not dead!' Richard shouted.

Small, electrical charges pulsed through the grass around

him, filling the air with static electricity and singeing the affected grass.

'Oh crap! A hell pit… really?' Richard groaned, as the electric current expanded creating a circle of dead, black grass approximately six feet in diameter.

The earth around him began to heat and sink, creating a tunnel down into the *Abyss*.

It would be a one-way trip.

Richard felt the skin on his hands and knees blister and burn. Beads of sweat formed on his forehead and dripped into his eyes. Among the smells of cow and damp earth, Richard could just make out the faint, clawing essence of sulphide. His eyes began to itch and run but he remained trapped by an invisible force.

He felt a demonic presence lurking beneath the soil, waiting for him.

'Your pit will not hold me!' he screamed. 'I vanquished Se Irim, the sower of death, from London and I will cast you from this world too.'

'Er… are you OK, Vicar?' Bethany asked.

The circle vanished.

Richard sat up, kneeling back against his heels, as he blinked the sweat from his eyes.

'What are you doing here?' he asked.

'Well, that's a nice welcome. I just came to see if you were OK. Word around the village is that you had a complete mental breakdown and had to be escorted from the centre shouting about being touched up by ghosts or something,' Bethany replied, frowning down at him.

'And to be honest, for once, I might actually agree with the village gossip,' she added, putting her hands on her hips as she scrutinised Richard.

Richard staggered to his feet and brushed the sweat plastered hair from his face.

'Actually, I'm probably the sanest one in the village,' he smiled.

Bethany laughed. Her chestnut ponytail swished through the air, as red streaks glimmered in the brown. 'You're probably right, but there's really not that much competition. So, why are you crawling in the mud and carrying a rather cool knife then – if you're not crazy?' she countered.

'A ghost gave it to me, see for yourself,' Richard said as he passed the dagger to Bethany.

She flipped the knife over and read the inscription, her eyes gleaming. 'Where the hell did you get this? It's Richard Dicken's… that curate from Polmouth, who disappeared in November 1810.'

'I don't know if hell had anything to do with it, but he dropped it as he was carving that message onto my window,' Richard pointed to the lines scrawled onto the caravan window.

Bethany rushed over and traced the lines with her fingertips. She turned and eyed him suspiciously, 'Hmm… so can you really see ghosts then?'

'No, it's just an elaborate ruse to make everyone think I'm mad, so I can be penniless and ostracized from mainstream society for the rest of my life,' Richard laughed.

'Fair point,' Bethany nodded. 'There are whispers in the village that the dead walk. I've felt them watching me.' She shivered. 'Hopefully with you helping me, I can find the missing curates, and put the dead below ground where they belong, and stop them popping up all over the place.'

She opened the caravan door and marched inside.

'Well, don't just stand there, hurry up, we have ghosts to bust and plans to make. Christ Almighty… you live like a pig! Do you have any heating? It's freezing in here!' she shouted.

Richard hurried inside the caravan.

***

Anderson saw the red bricks of Armitage Hall outlined against the dark green moorland and eased his foot off the accelerator.

The only property for miles, it dominated the empty landscape.

The house was typically Georgian with three rows of tall, narrow, white-barred windows, which blazed gold in the failing sunlight. The entrance consisted of an overlarge white door, covered in thick ivy, which trailed across to the two adjacent windows. In spring, the ivy twittered with nesting birds but in autumn it fell silent and clung to the house for protection.

Reverend Anderson slammed his car door shut, pressed the button on his key fob and the car beeped its reply. Naturally cautious by nature, Anderson always ensured his possessions remained firmly under lock and key. He checked his appearance in the reflection of the wing mirror and strode towards the manor house. The vicar enjoyed being at the manor but felt rather sad that he had been called to attend on such a sombre occasion. The tragic passing of Mrs Bell would spoil the normally frivolous atmosphere of opulence.

Anderson pulled the ancient chain and a bell chimed from deep within the soul of the house. After at least a minute of waiting, the front door swung open. Dr Ashcroft stood in his deep pink designer chinos and white Ralph Lauren polo top, unbuttoned enough so that the Reverend could see a thick gold chain nestled amongst his greying chest hairs. The doctor thrust out a hand and the Reverend shook it, noticing the heavy gold bracelet which clunked against the two-toned Breitling Chronomat gold watch.

'It's an extremely sad day for the village,' said the Reverend.

'Indeed, it is,' replied Dr Ashcroft. 'Shall we take tea in the orangery?'

Their footsteps echoed down the hallway as they walked through the main house and into a majestic greenhouse with vaulted glass ceiling. The orangery contained an array of exotic tropical plants, many of which Reverend Anderson could not recognise.

Long-limbed banana trees had been planted in raised beds, dug into the four corners of the orangery. Their fanned leaves almost touched the glass ceiling, and cast grey shadows across the pots of ferns, citrus, and orange trees which covered the floor of the hothouse. Ancient metal radiators with grey heating coils, fixed to the supporting brick walls of the lower part of the conservatory, groaned as they churned out heat, while waterfall displays recreated rainforest-like humidity. In the summer, the orangery was extremely unpleasant, but in the chill of autumn it was most delightful.

Mrs Ashcroft was sitting next to a decorative white metal table with a silver-rimmed tea service and matching silver

117

three-tiered cake stand, filled with macarons, mini-scones, and tasting slices of gateau. Reverend Anderson beamed as he strode towards Mrs Ashcroft. 'You have my deepest sympathies for the loss of your friend,' he stated in his most sincere voice.

Mrs Ashcroft nodded and poured him a cup of Earl Grey tea. 'Thank you. It's such a tragedy,' she agreed. 'Please help yourself.' She waved an arm gracefully towards the cake stand.

Reverend Anderson smiled and helped himself to three mini-scones, bursting with thick cream with red jam oozing down their golden crusty sides, two strawberry macarons, and a bunch of grapes from a strategically placed fruit bowl.

Dr Ashcroft handed his wife a cup of tea. She delicately sipped the refreshing liquid. Her ivory skin was almost glowing in the failing afternoon sun. She leant forward and replaced her teacup gently in its saucer. The Reverend could see down her exquisitely cut, cream blouse and into the dark crevice of her white breasts which pushed against the lace of her brassiere. He felt something stirring in his trousers. Anderson put the napkin over his groin and then placed his plate of scones firmly on top of the napkin.

Dr Ashcroft left his tea untouched and leant towards the vicar, his elbows on the table, fingers interlinked as he observed the Reverend. As always, Anderson felt uncomfortable under the doctor's gaze, as if his soul had been ripped open. Dr Ashcroft smiled slightly. Anderson blushed, squirming under the doctor's gaze, hoping he had not noticed his pastry predicament.

'Is it too hot in here for you?' Mrs Ashcroft enquired. 'Get the Reverend a glass of ice water, darling. He appears a little flushed.'

'Yes, my dear.' Dr Ashcroft nodded and rose, sauntering slowly through the terracotta pots.

The Reverend had no desire for water but was pleased with Mrs Ashcroft's attentiveness. He peeked another glimpse at her chest; the raised contours of her bra made inviting shadowy shapes under the cream of her blouse.

'Do have some more cake.' She smiled, waving at the cake stand.

The Reverend helped himself to the macaron layer, taking a white, blue, and green macaron respectively, for sampling.

Dr Ashcroft slid the glass under the Reverend's nose, his cold black eyes flickering up and down the Reverend. Anderson shifted uneasily in his seat and muttered his thanks.

'We need to talk to you about your new… er… helper, is that the word? Young Richard Radcliffe,' Dr Ashcroft stated, retaking his seat.

The Reverend groaned inwardly.

'I must apologize for his behaviour and any embarrassment it has caused you and your most delightful wife,' Anderson said shaking his head sadly, flakes of coconut macaron showering his black shirt.

Mrs Ashcroft raised her hand, a silver bracelet filled with heavy charms jingled down her narrow wrist.

'We are just very worried about him.'

Dr Ashcroft nodded.

Reverend Anderson frowned for a moment.

'Yes, I am too, such a lost creature, which is why I offered him shelter and support when he was released from the psychiatric hospital. His father is a very important man. He has his own television channel, you know,' the Reverend added.

Mrs Ashcroft raised her left hand. Silenced, the vicar stared at his remaining macaron.

'Mrs Bell told us about him cutting himself in the toilets of the centre and carrying around a mutilated doll,' Mrs Ashcroft said solemnly.

'Then this morning he was seen talking to himself in an extremely agitated manner and had to be removed from the centre screaming about monsters and ghosts,' Dr Ashcroft stated.

'He needs help. Professional help, before it's too late and he does something... terminal,' Mrs Ashcroft added.

The Reverend looked horrified and placed a half-eaten chocolate macaron on his plate. The Ashcrofts were correct. Richard was unstable and if he did, even accidently kill himself, the parish, and himself in particular, would be cast in an extremely bad light. However, Reverend Radcliffe had vouched for Richard and the support he could give to the parish.

The Reverend put his hand to his forehead and sat for a moment in deep, contemplative prayer. When he looked up, he saw the Ashcrofts staring at him.

'Unfortunately, you are right, I have tried to offer him solace, counselling, and the support of the word of God, but his problems need more professional help than I can offer,' the Reverend announced.

Mrs Ashcroft took his hand and pressed it between her pale, white fingers. 'It would be for the best.'

Anderson blushed. 'I had better go to the vicarage and

phone Reverend Radcliffe, immediately.'

He thanked the Ashcrofts for the delicious cakes and rose from the table. If Richard was thinking of doing something stupid, he was not going to do it in this parish; that sort of thing would not look good on his already fairly tarnished record at the diocese central offices in Exhaven Cathedral.

Reverend Anderson almost ran from the orangery.

***

Richard entered his caravan and had to admit that Bethany was right. It looked more like a squat than a holiday caravan. The books and papers which had been spread across the little table, had been tossed around the caravan, like leaves caught in an autumn gale. He tiptoed over the cooking utensils, which littered the lino floor and sat in the booth seat of the table, underneath the scratched window.

Pain soared through his hands. He laid them on the table to examine them. In the centre of each palm, were three intersecting burn lines in the shape of a red triangle with overlong lines.

Richard recognised the markings. It was a sigil, designed to summon a demon from the *Abyss* and open a gateway into the land of the living, the *Vitare*. He picked up a leather backed book from beneath the table and flicked through its thick, yellowed pages.

Bethany thumped two mugs of steaming tea onto the table.

'Do you take sugar?' she demanded.

'Er… no thanks,' Richard replied.

'Christ! What have you done to your hands?' Bethany took

his hands in hers and examined his palms carefully. 'Well, they've definitely blistered!' she stated, as she ran a washing-up bowl full of cold water and thrust both his hands into it.

Pain seared through Richard's body as the sigil bubbled and hissed under the water.

Bethany sat down and gulped her tea. She had found his hidden stash of Jaffa Cakes and three disappeared in rapid succession.

Richard thought about telling Bethany about the demon and the battle which had raged across the earth since the beginnings of time. He could show her the The LFD or *Liber Fieri Dæmoniorum* or perhaps the slightly more modern *Triangulum,* an ancient book he had borrowed on an unofficial, permanent loan basis. from the dust covered religious vaults of the British Library.

The *Triangulum* was a detailed account of demonology from a late-medieval perspective, but he doubted Bethany could read medieval Latin shorthand or would feel the electromagnetic energy, which pulsated through the manuscript.

The tome in his possession was a seventeenth century copy of the *Triangulum*, written in slightly suspicious, faded brown ink, some of which was illegible. It described how one legion of the angelic host, the *Solise*, had fought the other legions for control of the earth. They had lost the battle. Their punishment had been swift and eternal. Their outward appearance had been altered to match their internal corruption. The *Solise* legion had been transformed into monsters and cast down from the land of God, the *Elisium*, and sentenced to wander the barren firelands of the *Abyss ad infinitum*.

Hidden lands lay between the living world and the worlds of the immortals.

A passageway or 'convergence' could occur where the walls of the worlds touched. Demons, both the powerful and the weaker summoned ones, could enter the land of the living through these convergences. Ghosts also used these passageways to cross into the *Vitare*, but being much weaker than demons, could only spend short periods of time in the living world.

The ghosts witnessed in Witherleigh were inhabitants of the *Mortalis* or afterdeath. It was an ethereal, veiled land were the spirits of the lost dead walked next to the living, as they waited to enter the *Mortalis* or afterlife and receive their eternal damnation or reward. Richard was not sure if the *Mortalis* was not some form of *pre-Abyss* torment. The spirits witnessing life and their loved ones move on without them as they stood and watched on from behind a veil.

No wonder most of the spirits he had met had been insane. It was not something he wanted Bethany to know about.

He flicked to the back of the book. Its once empty pages filled with scribbled notes and annotated diagrams depicting hideous horned demons and their sigils, the individual mark of each demon. The notes were unfinished. An ominous sign for their author.

Richard had a nasty feeling that the book cover had been made from human flesh, tanned, and dried to an almost black colour. He smelled the book. It smelt slightly singed. He closed the book, his fingers tracing along the outline of the embossed picture on its cover - a large gold cross with ornate flouted terminals, superimposed over the triangle. Tiny electric sparks flew from the cover as his fingers moved.

He decided to say nothing about the book or its cover and hid it under his pillow, while Bethany checked the rest of his kitchen cabinets.

She deserved a protected life.

Bethany sat down at the table, opening a packet of cheese and onion crisps as she read from an old school exercise book; she had taken from the depths of an overlarge, sunflower-themed bag.

'Richard Dicken disappeared on 29th November 1810. He was last seen taking tea with three parishioners at the Old Vicarage. The parishioners left around 9pm after losing all their money at cards. They saw Dicken walking back towards his lodgings at the Bishop's Nod. The following morning his bed was empty. Dicken's jacket was found hanging over the back of his chair. His hat, leather belt, and an empty money wallet lay undisturbed on his dressing table. However, his riding boots and breeches were missing,'

'Did anyone investigate his disappearance?' Richard enquired.

'No, it was assumed he had taken a ship to the colonies, as a newspaper advertising passage from Polmouth to America on the Mermaid's Joy, lay open on his writing table,' Bethany tutted.

'So, case dismissed and hidden then?' Richard asked.

'Too right… you need to keep your hands in there for another ten minutes or you'll end up in hospital,' Bethany replied firmly.

Richard shrugged and wiped his hands dry. The sigils had

faded to a slight red shadow crossing his palms. He felt no pain, just the light tingling touch of electricity which ran up and down his arms. Richard disappeared into the bathroom and reappeared moments later with both hands securely bandaged from prying eyes. He took a sip of tea. It was lukewarm. Tiny black tea flakes had formed a slight skin on the top but most of his tea was consumed this way; made and forgotten, while he pottered on, only to be rediscovered half an hour later, and then drunk out of guilt.

'It's getting dark, I need to get back. I'm on the late shift tonight,' Bethany announced, draining her cup, and charging for the door. 'I'll be back tomorrow for skeleton finding duties.'

'I think it might be best if I found them myself,' Richard said quietly. 'It could be dangerous…'

'Oh please!' Bethany cut in. 'You said it yourself, the ghosts want their bodies to be found, they will help us. I'll be in more danger tonight from the wandering hands of those stuck-up arses from the hunt. If they try to touch me, I will rip their little danglies off and feed 'em to their dogs,' she yelled as she pulled a disgusted face and slammed the caravan door shut.

Richard smiled and waved goodbye to the closed door.

He was looking forward to tomorrow. Richard stood up and viewed his destroyed caravan. It was not the bachelor pad of his dreams, but at least he could clean it. He gathered up the scribbled notes on demon catching and took the *Triangulum* from under his pillow and placed them in his backpack. Then he placed the more socially acceptable books regarding ghost hunting on the table. Finally, he put the kitchen utensils back in the kitchen nook and rearranged the herbs and spices in the correct alphabetical order. Fortunately, most of the china – two plates, assorted patterned bowls, and three mugs, had survived the assault on the caravan.

The yellow mug that informed the world 'Happy Chickens make tasty dinners,' was chipped and had a large crack running down its handle, but Richard could not remember whether the damage was recent or more of a long-term problem. He shoved it to the back of the kitchen cupboard and hoped Farmer Butler would not notice.

He washed the remaining two cups, then swore as he noticed the neatly upturned little floral jug on the draining board. No wonder the tea had tasted slightly strange.

His stomach began to churn at the thought of Farmer Butler's finest cream. He tried to swallow the rising bile, but it was no good. The tea and Jaffa Cakes reappeared all over his freshly cleaned sink.

CHAPTER ELEVEN

Richard lay in his narrow bed, his duvet wrapped around his sweat soaked body. In his nightmare, the duvet became a living entity, pulling him downwards into the earth. Richard gasped and he sat up in bed. His eyes blinked open and slowly adjusted to the dim early morning light.

Every surface inside the caravan was covered in a layer of thick black mould. The overpowering stench of dirt laced with sulphide made him choke. His chest constricted, as if a heavy force were pressing down upon him, squeezing his heart.

The bedside light switched itself on and unplugged itself. Its lead rose serpent-like over the side of the bed and swayed as it watched Richard.

The tiny floral jug flew across the caravan. Richard ducked and the jug shattered across the duvet. The electric lead struck. It wrapped itself around his neck and tightened. Richard choked and clawed at his throat.

A black simian-like shadow crossed the caravan with preternatural speed. It leapt on to the end of the little bed and watched Richard struggle with interest. Small amber eyes glowed in the darkness of its shadow.

'Why fight, Richard? Accept the inevitable. You were born

to die, it will just be a bit sooner than you had hoped,' the shadow whispered softly.

Richard tried to speak but the pressure on his neck was too great.

'You need to pass now,' the shadow smiled, holding out a shapeless black hand. 'I am going to release you from the torment of this world.'

The caravan grew quiet. Richard felt as if he was withdrawing from the world as he floated upwards, away from his body. He tried to scramble back inside his body but the force pulling his spirit upwards was too strong. Richard closed his eyes and prayed, as he waited for his spirit to land.

Richard found himself standing in front of two colossal wooden gates, set into an ancient grey stone wall, which stretched away into the distance. Swirling grey mists lapped around the bottom of the wall.

Richard knocked loudly and a smaller door set within the great door opened.

His grandfather appeared in his Sunday ceremonial robes and stared down at Richard.

'Oh crap!' Richard groaned. His grandfather, a tyrannical zealot, had passed over twenty years ago, drowned in a boating accident on Wimbleball Lake while holidaying in Somerset and everyone had been rather relieved.

'Well, grandson. I am not surprised to see you ascend so early. You are weak and foolish like your mother. I told your father he should have chosen more wisely.'

'Er, hello Grandfather,' Richard said, wondering if he had entered some *pre-Abyss* torment.

'You cannot enter here,' Bishop Radcliffe announced. 'Begone and do something useful with your life.'

The Bishop shook his head, and the door was firmly closed.

Richard flew at the door, banging his fists against the heavy wood, but it was too late. The ground fell away. Richard felt himself fall through the swirling mist. 'I've had enough. Do not abandon me!' he screamed, as he desperately tried to hold onto the giant door. However, no one was listening.

***

'Er… I'll just put yer jug down on the step for 'ee. Daisy-Bell's not doin' so grand today, so it's only half as thick as when she's workin' proper,' Farmer Butler shouted through the caravan door. 'I'll not come in an' disturb 'ee. You seem a mite preoccupied. Come, dog.'

Richard felt himself fall back inside his body. He felt a surge of electricity run through his body and took a deep, rasping breath as his life force returned to the *Vitare*.

Richard found himself lying on his bed and cursed. He was back in Witherleigh.

The insidious black mould had vanished. The dancing ambers of the early morning light glistened through the caravan windows. Richard sat up in bed and frowned. He felt no demonic presence; just a twisted duvet, sticking to his sweating body.

'Thank you,' he croaked, to the retreating footsteps.

Richard rolled from his bed and opened the caravan door. The chill of the night was still hanging on the morning air. Grass sparkled with haw frost. The wind howled as it ran in from the surrounding moorland. The caravan swayed gently and a lone hessian sack hanging from the porch, hit Richard in the face.

He sneezed as a cloud of parsley particles wafted into the air, only to be taken away by the wind. In the distance, the topmost branches of the woodland trees waved and bent. The protective wire of shining objects, which encircled the woods, chimed together in anti-demonic harmony.

A scythe of crows wheeled through the air, black specks against the lightening blue sky, as they cawed out a warning. Something in the woods was moving.

It made the trees shake and the birds take flight. Richard squinted through the trees but saw nothing. The interior of the woodland was lost among the thick, slightly blurry undergrowth.

Farmer Butler knew what walked in Witherleigh. The whole village knew. What he did not understand was if everyone knew the dead were walking, why didn't the villagers ask for help?

Because they're hiding something.

The curates had been disappearing for centuries. This was a secret that had run through the generations. Richard thought of the ill-assorted customers at the community centre – the nameless elderly couple, Arthur Butt and Spud with his marginally organic vegetables, the obnoxious Jacko, his wife, and their benefits fraud, and poor Mrs Bell who was murdered because she had wanted to talk to him. They did not seem like people supernaturally blessed with good fortune, health, or money.

Just what type of demonic pact had they entered into? And

why had it silenced their families for generations?

Guilt. The word popped into Richard's head as he ran a hand through his wild hair. They were all involved in the murder of the curates.

'Just what the hell are you doing now?' Bethany stood, hands on her hips, as her ponytail blew in the wind.

'Er, just thinking,' Richard replied blushing as he realised that he was standing in the cow field wearing only a rumpled pair of boxers and vest.

Bethany sighed dramatically.

'You really can't look after yourself at all, can you? Get some clothes on for God's sake. You will catch pneumonia or something like that.' She viewed his scrawny body. 'Yes, I thought you wouldn't be able to feed yourself properly either. So, I brought you this from the Nod.'

She thrust a tinfoil covered plate under his nose. The smell of bacon and sausage wafted around the caravan. Richard threw on a relatively clean pair of jeans and a jumper, and sat down at the tiny table, ready to devour the full English breakfast.

'Shall I make a cup of tea then?' Bethany asked.

Richard lowered a forkful of sausage and shook his head. 'No thanks, black coffee please.'

Bethany rolled her eyes and stomped across to the kettle. 'So, ghostbuster – where do we begin?'

Richard pushed the empty plate away from him and stared at her intently. 'Are you sure you want to do this? Mrs Bell is dead. The curates are dead, and their ghosts are walking. Witherleigh is not a safe place. You could get hurt.'

Bethany banged a mug of coffee down on the table in front of Richard. 'My father's bones are buried somewhere here. I'm not going anywhere until he is found and given a Christian burial. You ready or what?'

Richard sighed, zipped up his anorak, and slid his backpack over his shoulders.

'Right, let's go find some ghosts then.' He smiled as they headed for her four-wheel drive, a mud-spattered, boxlike green and white Land Rover.

The Land Rover looked like it had been bought from a scrap merchant. Both front and back bumpers were crumpled. A long rusting tear ran along the length of the passenger side, which appeared to have been repaired with some sort of grey plaster. While the headlights seemed to be attached to the car with brown duct tape.

Richard jumped into the passenger seat and quickly fastened his seatbelt, as Bethany revved the engine and tore up the bumpy farm lane.

***

Twenty minutes later, Bethany's car drove into Witherleigh. Richard let go of the door handle and breathed a sigh of relief.

The village was quiet and sombre. The church of St Anthony dominated the background. A sombre grey outline against the sky. The Witherleigh Store stood to the right of the church, its clean white paintwork at odds with the dust-covered window display. Next to the shop, was a row of four tall, terraced cottages, their walls white-washed and scrubbed clean of all traces of natural Devon dirt. Two inverted triangular willow hanging baskets hung next to the front door of each house. Each one filled with white winter pansies. The only irregular thing about the cottages were their ill-aligned small, Elizabethan white-barred windows, which peered out from beneath the overhanging thatch.

'Well, that didn't take her long, did it,' Bethany growled and pointed towards the community centre.

Mrs Ashcroft stood outside the centre.

She wore a black mourning dress, and a finely knitted shawl which she hugged to her slender figure for warmth, as she supervised the removal of the community centre sign. Propped against the wall of the centre was a gleaming new yellow shop sign, declaring the 'Happy Chicken Café' in vivid red letters. Inside the café, the windows were being polished by a series of severe looking women.

'It's the Happy Chicken mafia,' Bethany hissed.

Richard frowned. 'You don't approve? I thought farming cooperatives were the only way forward against the supermarket monopolies?'

Bethany shook her head. 'They're all as bad as one another. You try to sell your produce in the village without a Happy Chicken logo. No one will touch your stuff. In the Nod, if we want to bring in delicacies like feta cheese, the boss has to smuggle it back from Ashdurton in his sports bag – double the cheesiness, if you know what I mean,' Bethany winked.

Richard laughed, then he made a mental note never to order a Greek salad at the Nod.

'Anyway, let's get down to business,' Bethany stated as she flicked through a hardbacked notebook emblazoned with sunflowers. 'The first detailed case regarding the missing curates was Richard Dicken. He disappeared while lodging at the Bishop's Nod. So, we may as well start there and see if you can pick up any vibrations or freaky ghost stuff. Just keep the weirdness to the minimum. I need this job. OK?' Bethany stared intently at Richard.

Richard nodded solemnly.

'No weird, freaky ghost stuff. I promise,' Richard said as he crossed his fingers.

Bethany took Richard round the back of the Nod and down the crumbling stone steps, which led directly into the almost subterranean kitchen. A wave of airless heat hit him like a furnace. Richard quickly stripped off his anorak and jumper to reveal a crumpled, rather grey shirt. He shoved his winter layers into his backpack as he felt Bethany watching him.

'I guess you've never heard of an iron then?' she commented as she marched into the kitchen.

An array of black cast iron pans hung from an iron frame which protruded from the low, yellowed ceiling. Richard noticed dried herb bunches had been tied to the iron frame. It was not a good sign. His fingers automatically went to his wrist. He groaned as he realised his rubber band was missing. It must have snapped while he slept. A feeling of panic fluttered in the pit of his stomach.

Richard pinned a smile to his face and followed Bethany.

A thin Chinese man with white hair tied into a long ponytail, which dangled down the back of his chef's whites, stood behind a long kitchen table, breaking up plucked yellow chickens into various sized metal bowls of different chicken parts. Richard swallowed a wave of nausea as the chef decapitated a scrawny looking chicken.

The head was thrown into a bowl on the opposite side of the table. Its juice splattered across the table, as he fished out another jaundiced chicken. The chef looked up and stared at the intruders, cleaver in one hand, limp chicken in the other. Richard nodded to the chef. The chef growled something which sounded Cantonese, spoken in a such a way that it did not seem to be a welcome greeting, but Richard could not be sure. He nodded to the chef and quickly followed Bethany from the kitchen. The sound of the hatchet followed them into the corridor.

'Don't mind Chef Sheng,' Bethany stated. 'He's a bit sensitive today. A customer complained that his beef Wellington was chewy.'

A white door to the left of the kitchen was marked 'Staff Only'. Bethany turned and put her finger to her lips as she held the door open and signalled for Richard to go through, then quietly closed the door.

'If the boss sees you in here, tell him you got lost,' Bethany whispered as she bounded up the claustrophobic, wooden staircase to the guestroom landing.

The landing was a complete contrast to the old servants' stairs with deep, red, heavy pile carpets. An ornate, frilled lamp jutted out between each of the four guestroom doors.

A series of dark oil paintings ran along the inside wall, depicting memories of the Devon countryside from long ago: a white manor house surrounded by trees, a long-legged chestnut horse and its equally equine-faced rider, and a family of rosy-cheeked farm labourers forking dried hay onto an overflowing haycart, while a grey carthorse grazed.

The final painting was of a demure lady, her grey hair scraped into a severe bun, as she sat at a mahogany writing desk, reading a letter. Her black eyes lifted momentarily from the letter and stared out at Richard from the painting. There was something familiar about the lady's haunting gaze.

'Christ, that's an Ashcroft!' Richard exclaimed.

'Shh!' Bethany hissed as she came up behind Richard. She squinted into the painting.

'That's Lady Youlden, of Armitage Hall. Could be some distant ancestor of Dr Ashcroft, I guess. Most families have been here for generations, so there's a good chance everyone is kind of related.'

'Hmm… not too related, I hope?' Richard raised an eyebrow.

Bethany laughed and punched Richard hard on the shoulder.

'I didn't realise girls were so violent!' Richard winced, rubbing his shoulder.

Bethany looked as if she was going to hit him again.

Quickly, Richard turned his attention back to the painting. The words of the letter were illegible, paintbrush marks. However, in the right-hand corner, hidden among the black lines, was a mark he had seen before, a sigil in the form of an extended triangle.

Richard felt his chest turn cold.

'We need to hurry up before we get caught,' Bethany hissed and grabbed his arm, dragging him down the remainder of the landing, stopping in front of an arched doorway marked

'Private'. Bethany rattled the handle a few times and the door begrudgingly creaked open.

'This heads up to the attic, to the room where Richard Dicken was staying,' she whispered.

Richard nodded and followed her up the creaking stairs. A small dust-covered window cast a thin ray of light onto the staircase. Richard glanced through the glass. From this height he could see the woods crowding around the manse. The land cut in two by a narrow brown path. Neither looked inviting.

A dark grey shape appeared at the beginning of the path. Richard rubbed his eyes and squinted through the murky window.

Snowy stared back up at him and waved. His face repaired but emptied of emotion. If this was a warning sign Richard could not decipher it. However, something stirred in the pit of his stomach. Perspiration began to trickle down his forehead as warnings of impending doom pinged in his brain.

Bethany stomped up to the top of the stairs and disappeared. Richard followed her, bending his head as he found himself in a tiny wooden hallway.

The attic was divided into halves with two guest rooms on either side, lit by a large circular window, cut high into the wall of the attic, where the eaves of the roof fell away diagonally.

Bethany stopped outside a small wooden doorway marked 'Juniper Room'. Its white paint faded to cream. A rough keyhole had been chiselled to the right of a small black doorknob. Bethany twisted the doorknob and pushed hard on the door. The door shuddered but would not move.

'Christ!' Bethany exclaimed. 'The doors are not meant to be

locked. There aren't any keys.'

She pulled again. The door creaked and groaned but would not budge.

'Let me have a try,' Richard suggested.

Bethany looked him up and down. Richard could tell by her slightly amused expression that she doubted he would ever move the stuck door.

He reached out but before he had even touched the doorknob, the door creaked open.

'I loosened it for you!' Bethany stated and pushed Richard through the doorway.

The attic room had been abandoned since the curate's disappearance. The air smelt stale. A cloud of dust rose caught by the sudden draft. Dusty spiderwebs hung by the tiny, circular attic window, waved in the sudden breeze, and then fell limply against the glass. White sheets covered the furniture, which bulged out from the covers forming strange shapes.

'Pull the sheets off slowly. We don't want to disturb anything,' Richard whispered as he gently removed the dust cover from the curate's wash basin stand, which stood opposite a shrouded, wooden bed.

Bethany rolled her eyes and threw back the sheets covering the bed and an avalanche of dust rolled towards Richard, mushrooming into a cloud of white, stifling dust. Underneath the window, the white sheet covering the curate's writing desk fluttered and slid onto the floorboards.

A pile of papers stacked neatly on the writing desk rustled slightly and then shot upwards, plastering the ceiling in quivering cream papers.

Leather boots squeaked as footsteps marched along the passageway, stopping outside the door. Someone knocked loudly, and a key rattled in the lock.

The door flickered and swung open.

'What the hell is happening?' Bethany whispered as she backed slowly into the wall.

***

The little wooden bed remade itself with starched white linen pillows and sheets covered by a thick, navy blanket.

The blanket bulged and moved.

Three men appeared in the doorway. The two scruffily dressed men ran into the room towards the bed, while a gentleman wearing cream breeches, a white waistcoat with short skirts, and a black coat with curving back fronts stood with his arms crossed and watched. A narrow smile on his thin lips.

The navy blanket was tossed to one side, as a young man dressed in a white nightshirt sat up in bed, startled by the sudden intrusion, and dived towards his bedside table.

The man in the ripped, brown greatcoat lunged forward, grabbed the young man by his shoulders, and pinned him down against the bed. While the huge man in a brown shabby coat and three-cornered hat kicked the table into the wall. The table shattered onto the floorboards and a heavy-bladed knife clattered against the floor. The young man struggled and kicked out at his attackers. The huge man in the brown coat, grabbed hold of the thrashing feet, and held them firmly against the bed.

'Get off me! You will all be damned to hell!' screamed the young man.

'Remove the good curate and make sure you spill no blood today.' The gentleman walked into the room and gagged the curate using the wrinkled, white neck scarf which had been hanging over the back of the chair. He took two lengths of thick red cord from his coat pocket and bound the curate's hands and feet together. The gentleman then signalled to the others who unceremoniously wrapped the struggling man in the navy blanket.

The men grabbed either end of the blanket and carried the swaying roll from the room.

The gentleman surveyed the mess in the room and tutted. He strode to the writing desk and laid an open broadsheet across it, one of the small print columns had been circled in black ink.

'Butler!' he yelled into the empty hallway.

A ragged, young boy rushed into the room and stood before him.

'You will tidy this room,' the gentleman commanded, and threw a large brown coin on the floor, in front of the boy. He walked over to the chair, where the curate had carefully folded his clothes, before retiring to bed.

'And burn these rags!' he ordered, waving a hand across the curate's clothes, as he walked from the room without a backward glance.

Butler glared after the man. He felt the warm wool of the coat between his fingers and his eyes narrowed as he listened to the creak of the footsteps descending the wooden staircase.

He made a rude gesture to the man's back and quickly stuffed the coat, riding boots, and breeches into the bedsheet, which he tied into a ball and hid in the hallway. Then he knelt as he began to pick the pieces of table from the wooden floor.

Time shifted. The boy disappeared. The room remade itself and died.

***

'Oh Christ, what just happened? Was that real? I mean not real, but like ghost stuff. Is that what happened to my father?' Bethany rambled as she unpeeled herself from the wall, furiously blinking tears back from her red-rimmed eyes.

'I think we have just witnessed a *resonare*, an echo of Richard Dicken's abduction. They were not ghosts. Just a memory of violence, which has scarred the room, which we somehow triggered… Spill no blood… that doesn't sound very good, does it?' Richard muttered, half to himself, as he ran his hand through his hair.

'Oh, are you alright?' he frowned, his breath coming in white clouds.

'I'm fine, It's just an allergy.' Bethany sniffed as she wiped her nose on the sleeve of her Puffa coat. 'It's really dusty in here.'

She wrapped her arms around her waist.

A discordant yell split the empty silence of the attic. Its words cut into pieces of sound, which were flung around the room, some whispered, some shouted so loudly the window rattled as the sounds flew by.

The delicate, square-backed chair pushed neatly underneath

the oak writing desk, flew across the room. Richard ducked as it hit the wall, inches from his head, and scattered across the floor, while an icy wind howled around the room. Its power increasing with each circuit of the attic.

'Something's trying to break through!' Richard shouted. His voice almost lost in the howling of the wind and the discordant sounds.

Bethany crawled into a corner and tucked her legs tightly to her chest. The papers, once more neatly arranged on the desk, were grabbed by the wind, and tossed around the room. One caught Richard's face, scratching a red diagonal mark across his cheek. A drop of blood seeped from the wound and fell too slowly onto the floor. The blood formed a perfect circle on the wooden floorboards and disappeared.

The white china wash bowl hovered momentarily above the washstand and shot upwards towards the ceiling. Then it dropped to the floor, spraying jagged china shards across the room.

Bethany screamed in pain as one shard ripped through her jeans and lodged itself in her shin. She started to crawl towards the door.

'Don't move!' yelled Richard.

A painting of a vase of overlarge flowers, flew diagonally across the room, and bounced off the windowpane, and fell face down on the debris-ridden floor.

The noise stopped.

The windborne papers fluttered gently over the floor.

Richard pushed his hair from his eyes and quickly scurried across in Bethany, who gingerly pulled the shard from her leg.

'What was that?' she whispered her face grey and covered in sweat.

'Someone trying to make contact, I assume,' Richard said quietly.

'Well, let's not stick around here then. Help me up. I want to get out of this room. Now.' Bethany decided.

Richard nodded and pulled her to her feet. She winced and put her arm across his shoulders.

'You're have to help me out of here. Now put your arm around my waist,' she commanded.

Richard nodded and slid his arm around her waist. His face turned scarlet. 'It's just her waist. Don't blow it or say something stupid,' his inner voice whispered.

'I thought your waist would be smaller and less squishy,' Richard observed.

Bethany looked at him for a second before she punched him hard in the stomach.

'But I like it squishy.' Richard gasped as he clutched his stomach.

'Just open the bloody door,' Bethany growled.

CHAPTER TWELVE

Richard twisted the door handle. It refused to turn. He felt his heart sink to his stomach. The black iron handle froze white, burning his fingers as a veil of sparkling ice crystals grew across the door and spread onto the walls, as the temperature in the attic began to drop.

'Something doesn't want us to leave here,' Richard stated. His breath froze, hanging in the frigid air.

Bethany shivered and zipped up her red Puffa jacket. She grabbed the door handle and pressed her shoulder against the door and pushed, as she tried to force the door open.

The door would not move.

'Well, don't just stand there. Do something ghostboy!' Bethany nodded towards Richard, her eyes demanding instant action.

'Hmm....' Richard said, as he reached out and touched the spreading ice crystals. 'This inn must be the site of a convergence, a gateway between the worlds. The walls of the *Mortalis* and the *Vitare* are very thin around Witherleigh, which is why the dead can walk. These cold spots occur when a ghost or something is passing through a convergence from the *Mortalis* into our world.'

'Er… OK,' said Bethany nodding intently. 'Is it dangerous though?'

Richard shook his head.

Bethany smiled with relief.

'Cold spots aren't at all dangerous. It's what comes through them… that is,' he said grimly.

'Huh!' Bethany replied. 'Don't these ghosts realise we are trying to help them? Talk about the ungrateful dead!' she muttered.

There was a crash. Richard and Bethany spun round. A picture of farm workers armed with pitchforks, throwing hay onto a wagon, lay shattered on the floor. Richard sneezed as the grassy smell of fresh hay, wafted through the attic, and a light sprinkling of hay fell from the attic ceiling, covering the floorboards.

'Don't touch the painting,' he warned Bethany. 'It will drag you into the convergence.'

'Don't worry. I'm not going to touch any of this weird shit!' Bethany growled as hay stalks fell around her. She grabbed the door handle and rattled it up and down.

The door would not move.

'We're trapped,' she whispered, as she stared back into the room. A small leather notebook flew across the room towards her. The book thumped against the door and burst open, its pages flying across the room.

A set of icy footprints came towards them.

'Watch out!' she screamed. It was too late.

An unseen entity dragged Richard across the attic room and threw him against the wall. Richard fell heavily onto the little bed, which cracked under his weight.

Bethany slumped to the floor by the door.

The freezing air inside the attic became denser, pressing Richard into the bed. He tried to struggle free, but his arms and legs would not move. An icy wind howled past the bed, pulling at the sheets, scattering the pottery shards around the room like missiles. Richard felt his chest tighten. His breaths became shallow gasps of air.

Something cold touched his cheek.

A grey, wild face appeared above his, its black hair caught by the surging wind. The rest of the body of the curate materialised; this time wearing a torn, yellowed nightshirt. The figure sat on Richard's chest. One grey skeletal hand covered his mouth and nose. The ghost opened his mouth and shouted something into Richard's face.

The dissonant sounds cleared for an instant.

'Save my soul!' the curate screamed.

'Are you Richard Dicken?' Richard whispered, as he struggled to breathe.

The ghost paused for a second, stared at Richard, and slowly nodded. The ghost of the curate began to speak. Consonants jumbled over each other as the sounds mixed together. Richard thought he heard the words 'Witherleigh' and '*Daemonium*'.

'Speak clearly. Your words are becoming too jumbled as they pass through the convergence,' Richard shouted at the curate, desperately trying to communicate to the ghost through the boundaries of the corporeal realm.

However, Richard could the feel energy in the attic room change. The convergence was closing. The curate was being pulled back. Dicken glanced over his shoulder; his black eyes widened in terror. He opened his mouth to speak but the sound was stolen. A black shadow fell across his body. The curate jumped up and tried to run to the wall, but the shadow reached out and grabbed his foot, dragging him down into the floorboards. Richard watched in horror as Dicken disappeared. Their eyes met for an instant. Richard felt the pain of centuries flow through his body.

The pressing force moved from Richard's body and he lay on the bed panting. His whole body shook. The ice crystals vanished as the temperature in the room rose.

Richard breathed a sigh of relief.

The room began to turn, slowly at first, and then faster and faster, until all he saw was a circular flash of yellowed ceiling. Richard grabbed the bedframe with both hands as the bed rose towards the ceiling. He closed his eyes and tensed his body, as he waited for the impact.

The bed hung suspended for a moment. Then plummeted downwards. It hit the floor, its wooden frame creaking as it almost collapsed under the force of the impact. The mattress sagged as the legs of the bed buckled inwards. Richard lay there for a second not daring to move as the bed creaked and groaned beneath him.

'I'm still alive,' he whispered.

The shaft of sunlight, which sliced the attic room in two darkened, as a swathe of black mould moved across the round attic window and blocked out the sun.

Slowly, the window opened.

Richard tried to sink into the bedding, holding his breath

and trying not to cough, as an acrid smell filled the attic room. From the corner of his eye, he saw a dark shape land on the windowsill.

'May the Lord protect me,' Richard prayed. Slowly, he turned towards the noise.

A large raven strutted through the open window. The bird spread its blue-black wings as it flew onto the wooden posts at the bottom of the bed.

The bird sat silently observing Richard.

Richard propped himself up onto his elbows and peered at the raven. Beads of cold sweat appeared on his forehead and trickled down his back, sticking the dead man's sheets to his shirt.

'Name yourself, demon,' he said in a voice braver than he felt.

The raven's long black beak opened into a grin and it cawed loudly.

'Name yourself!' Richard shouted.

The raven stretched its wings. Several feathers fell slowly onto the detritus covering the wooden floor. The raven cawed again.

'You are the fallen of the *Solise*, cast out from the *Elisium*. Your disguise does not fool me,' Richard said, pulling a necklace from beneath his grey shirt. On the end of the necklace hung a golden cross.

'Be gone, demon,' he commanded.

The raven cawed and dived at Richard. Its talons ripped across his chest. Tracks of blood appeared on his shirt. Richard grabbed the bird by the throat and pulled its claws out of his chest. The raven twisted free, and flapped squawking towards the ceiling.

Richard sat up and shouted to Bethany, 'Quick, get out of here. Now!'

Bethany staggered to her feet and lurched against the door as her bad leg collapsed under her. The door wobbled. Black branchlike tendrils unwound from the wooden panels of the door and snaked towards Bethany. They wrapped around her, dragging her towards the door. Her large brown eyes searched for Richard.

'Help me!' she screamed.

'Hold on!' Richard shouted.

Gingerly, he swung his legs to the floor, testing them. They felt wobbly but still worked. He ran towards Bethany and desperately grabbed at her hand, as the rest of her body was sucked inside the door.

A loud rustling came from somewhere above his head. Richard looked up and saw a snapping black beak inches from his face. He dropped Bethany's hand as he tried to cover his face with both hands, but he was too late. The raven plunged its sharp claws deep into his left eye.

Richard screamed as pain exploded inside his head. He fell to the floor, holding his face, the blood from his empty eye socket oozing through his fingers, making red paths down his torn sleeves.

The raven held the bloody eye in its beak and flew cawing with laughter through the tiny, attic window. The shrivelled string of the remaining optic nerve swung through the air as it flew.

The window wobbled and closed itself.

The black mould disappeared, and sunlight poured into the attic room.

'Richard!' Bethany screamed; the outline of her mouth pressed against the inside of the door.

Richard twisted around, so that he was lying on his front. Only Bethany's hand remained free, sticking out from the wooden door, her fingers opening and closing, as she searched for his hand. Richard dragged himself towards the door, as he followed the sound of her voice. He reached out to try to grab hold of her hand but missed. Her hand was pulled backwards into the wood.

'No!' Richard screamed and collapsed face first onto the wooden floor.

***

It was the screaming that first alerted the diners to the problem.

Reverend Anderson was taking morning tea with Miss Norman, his parishioner from an isolated hamlet, in the middle of Witherleigh Moor. The moor made its own weather. In the course of a single day, the sun could shine so hard the tracks criss-crossing the moor cracked and the grass withered to brown. While in the afternoon, grey clouds could gather and drench the arid tracks, recreating ancient stream beds, which poured in channels through the grass, isolating the little hamlet from the rest of his congregation.

Consequently, Reverend Anderson made sure that whenever the outlying villagers managed to overcome the weather and struggle their way into Witherleigh, he took time out from his busy schedule to cater to their spiritual well-being.

Miss Cecelia Norman pulled her long brown hair to the side of her head and stroked it. The chestnut colours glinted in the mid-morning sunlight. Her hand was almost stroking her right breast, which threatened to burst from the restraints of her bulging, green silk shirt. She held a crustless cucumber sandwich in her right hand, which waved in the air, as she spoke animatedly about her latest painting, a Dadaist interpretation of the Church of St Anthony being attacked by red splodges of demons. The blue birds hovering above the jumbled mass of brown tombstones were apparently angels. It was a wonderful modernist interpretation of the age-old battle between good and evil, reimagined for the modern, more discerning art lovers of North Devon. As a churchman, it was his duty to encourage his parishioners' creativity as a celebration of God's wonderful creation.

When Cecelia bent forward to nibble on her sandwich, he could see the bouncy pinkness of both her breasts.

A high-pitched scream made the cucumber sandwich drop to the floor.

Chef Sheng raced from the kitchen; the doors slammed against the wall. His chef whites covered in brown stains. 'Is another diner sick?' he demanded to a horrified waitress.

The waitress shook her head. 'It came from upstairs. I think it might be the attic. Thems ghosts in the attic.' She crossed her chest and hid behind a customer.

'Ah, that's good,' the chef replied. 'I will go and throw out the brie. It has too much green mould.'

The chef bowed and disappeared back to the subterranean depths of the kitchen.

151

The chatter resumed.

The Reverend was about to order a replacement sandwich, when a second bloodcurdling scream silenced the dining area.

Dr Ashcroft drained his teacup, stood up, and announced, 'I will go and investigate. All this talk of ghosts and hauntings just upsets people. It's probably just some young farmers having a bit of good-natured fun.'

He marched from the room. The sound of his leather boots stamping up the staircase, echoed in the silence. Reverend Anderson sighed and cast one last lingering look at Miss Norman, who was staring up at the ceiling, her hazel eyes wide with terror.

The Reverend leant forward and squeezed her delicate hand in his. 'Do not worry, my dear child, I will get to the bottom of this.'

He stood up and slowly followed the footsteps of Dr Ashcroft, who had disappeared around the corner of the dark oak guest staircase. The Reverend further reduced his speed. A series of stern-faced men and women stared down at him from tarnished gilt frames. Personally, he could never see the point in painting ugly people, but then most people did not share his understanding of the spiritual purity of beauty.

The old stairs creaked under his footsteps and he looked around uneasily and whispered, *'Peace I leave with you; my peace I give you. I do not give to you as the world gives. Do not let your hearts be troubled and do not be afraid. John 14:27.'*

Anderson turned a second corner and followed the stairs into the attic. He ducked as he walked through the attic doorway, just in time to hear Dr Ashcroft exclaim,

'What the hell is going on in here? What in God's name have you done, young man?'

The Reverend felt his heart sink as he entered the Juniper Room. He saw a figure rolling on the floor, clutching his face, and moaning like an animal in pain. To the left of the doorway, sat the attractive but always angry barmaid Bethany, huddled in a ball clutching her knees tightly. There was blood on her legs, hands, and smears of blood across her face. A clump of brown hair hung over her face, hiding her eyes.

'What did he do?' Dr Ashcroft demanded as he stood in front of Bethany.

'I'm sure he did nothing,' Anderson cut in, sweating profusely, and wishing he had called Reverend Radcliffe.

'Help me,' Richard groaned. 'I have been blinded!'

The Reverend leant over Richard and peered through the hands covering his face. There was no blood. His face was dirty but undamaged.

'Hold the boy down,' he called to Dr Ashcroft. He grabbed Richards' wrists and pulled them away from his eyes. Two wild blue eyes stared back at him.

'I can't see… the demon has taken my eye!' Richard screamed, blinking in the sunlight.

'Oh Christ!' Reverend Anderson muttered. 'He's gone completely insane.'

'Quick! Tie his hands and feet together,' Ashcroft ordered, producing two pieces of thick red cord from his coat pocket. 'He is a danger to himself and others.'

Ashcroft nodded towards Bethany.

Anderson caught Richard's flailing arms. He stretched them

across the floor and kneeled across both the outstretched arms as he bound Richard's wrists together. Richard kicked out, his battered white trainers flying across the room. Ashcroft turned Richard onto his front and stood over him. Anderson rearranged his tie, smoothed down his silver-streaked blond hair, and turned his attention towards Bethany.

'Now then Bethany, what happened here? Were you and Richard up here for some sort of secret sexual liaison which turned violent? Do you like it a bit rough then?' He looked down at Bethany.

Bethany glared up at the vicar, shaking his hand from her shoulder. 'We weren't doing anything like that!' she hissed.

'So, what exactly were you two doing up here then?' Dr Ashcroft demanded.

Bethany swallowed and stared at the dirt-covered floor. 'I just heard something moving around up here and went to investigate the noise. I found him like that. I was going downstairs to get help, but I tripped over and banged my knee.'

Bethany motioned towards her ripped and bloodied trousers.

'Thank you for being so candid with us, Bethany.' The Reverend smiled with relief.

He turned towards Dr Ashcroft. 'There you are. Richard just had a seizure up here. No harm done but obviously he is very sick. I will phone his father immediately to arrange transport back to the mental hospital.'

Dr Ashcroft nodded. 'That's lucky for you, then, isn't it? It wouldn't look good if people thought you had invited a dangerous lunatic down here to play with their children, would it, Reverend? After all, I hear you are still under diocese investigation, aren't you? It would be awful if the Archbishop received another complaint.'

Anderson felt his heart stop for an instant and then beat on.

'The people here trust me and know I would never do anything to harm them. I will open the church's doors to those in need. I am a man of Christ. What about you?'

Anderson left the question hanging in the hostile air.

He stood up and pulled Bethany to her feet. 'You will be fine, go downstairs and clean yourself up, there's a good girl. Your mascara has run.'

Bethany nodded and staggered through the doorway.

'And what shall we do about you?' The Reverend stared down at Richard, who was struggling to break free from the cord ties.

'You have to let me go!' Richard shouted. 'Someone has summoned a demon to Witherleigh. I need to cast the monster back into the *Abyss* before it's too late.'

Dr Ashcroft shook his head, 'Paranoid delusions. The ramblings of a disordered mind, I'm afraid.'

'His affliction seems to be religious in nature; perhaps I can take him back to the manse. Just until his father arrives,' Anderson suggested, as he helped Richard from the floor, so he was sitting with his back against the wall.

'I'm afraid I can't allow that,' the doctor stated and took a leather case from his jacket pocket. He opened the case, pulled out a syringe, and a small glass bottle. Ashcroft stabbed the lid with a long needle and proceeded to draw off some of the clear liquid.

There was a loud cough from somewhere outside the Juniper Room.

'Enter!' Ashcroft commanded, glancing through the open doorway.

Four heavily built estate workers marched into the diminutive Juniper Room.

'Escort the cleric back to the manse,' Ashcroft ordered. He gripped the vicar's face. 'If you want to remain here, you will do exactly as I say.'

The nearest two workers seized the Reverend and frogmarched him from the room.

'Leave him alone!' Richard shouted, as he struggled to free his hands.

'This will calm you down.' Ashcroft laughed as he stabbed him in the right thigh with the needle.

Instantly, Richard flopped against the floor.

'Haldol. It never fails. Right men, if anyone asks, we are taking him to the surgery.'

The two men dragged Richard to his feet and half-carried him down both flights of stairs and through the Bishop's Nod.

CHAPTER THIRTEEN

Richard winced as a sharp pain pounded through his head. A series of yellow and orange dots danced in front of his eyes. He blinked them away as his eyes adjusted to the gloom. His body felt heavy; every muscle ached and screamed for more sleep.

The bed felt hard against his back, which seemed strange, because the mattress in the old caravan was so soft, he often woke half-submerged inside it. Strands of wayward hair itched against his face. He tried to brush them aside, but his hands would not respond.

Richard lifted his head from the bed and cursed.

His hands and feet were spread-eagled, cuffed, and chained to each corner of the narrow metal bed. His old trainers had vanished, and he had a big hole in his right sock. A pale big toe stared at him through the semi-darkness of the room.

The toe wobbled out of focus and Richard felt his world disintegrate.

He was back at the Nightingale Unit.

Richard pushed his head into the thin pillow, the sound of his heartbeat pounding in his ears, as he listened for Dr Berghaus' quiet, measured footsteps echoing along the corridor. The last time he was sectioned, he had lost six months of his life to the treatment. Blurred pictures of nurses staring over him and Dr Berghaus' thin smile surfaced through his empty memories.

This time, I might not escape.

The thought shocked Richard into action. He tugged on the leather restraints, straining against them. Chains rattled against the bedframe. He collapsed back onto the bed. If they knew he was awake, the nurses might come back, and send him into another drug-induced haze.

Richard lay back against the pillow and stared up at the white ceiling tiles.

Something was not quite right.

The white tiles had been replaced by a red brick ceiling. The walls were brick too. Black cracks ran through the topmost bricks which were decorated with tattered spider webs; their strings covered in old dust. The familiar choking smell of artificial pine had been replaced by an earthy smell of damp, laced with apple.

Slowly, realisation dawned.

He was not in the caravan or back at the unit. In fact, he had no idea where he was. Richard stared at the crack in the ceiling and tried to focus his drug-scattered thoughts. Fractured images floated through his mind.

He remembered Dr Ashcroft, with two grim-faced looking men, dragging him down the stairs of the Nod.

The raven flying through the closed attic window, his dripping eyeball held triumphantly in its claw. The raven had turned its head backwards in mid-flight and winked at him. Its amber eyes glowing through the shadows as it flew back into the *Mortalis*.

'Oh crap!' Richard groaned. *'Be sober-minded; be watchful. Your adversary the devil prowls around like a roaring lion, seeking someone to devour, 1 Peter 5:8.'*

He had been tricked by the demon. The consequences for his foolishness would be severe. The village was now witness to him screaming about his plucked eye and his obvious descent into madness. The images of the horrified faces of the diners made his cheeks burn.

Other thoughts took shape in the blackness.

He remembered the leather restraints being put around his wrists and ankles. Dr Ashcroft bending over him, as he muttered under his breath. It had sounded like 'too soon.' Then the memories disappeared.

A tingle of electric warning pulses ran up and down his spine. Richard did not want to be trapped down here when the doctor was ready.

He tried to wriggle his right hand free, but it was strapped down too tightly. Richard breathed deeply for a minute, gathering his strength, and then pulled hard against the cuffs, desperately trying to force the restraints to widen just an inch. The bed groaned, the chains rattled, but the restraints held fast.

Richard flopped back against the bed, panting heavily.

'Hello there, old man. What are you doing down here?' A familiar Home Counties voice boomed jovially behind him.

'John. John Sparke, is that you?' Richard shouted.

'As I live and breathe,' John replied. 'So, what are you doing all chained up down here, then? You haven't joined the cricket club, have you? Their initiations can be pretty wild. I remember the time that Jonty Peterson was tied naked to…'

'John!' Richard interjected. 'Please come here, now.'

'Well, really,' John said reproachfully. A cold breeze blew across Richard's face. The curate appeared next to the hospital bed.

'Christ, what has happened to you?' Richard gasped.

The normally well, if eccentrically dressed curate, had decayed rapidly since their last meeting. The shiny blue suit was ripped, the suit legs torn and ragged. His patent leather shoes were missing, revealing holey black socks, which like the rest of him, were caked in dried, brown mud. The curate's blond sculptured hair was plastered onto his once rosy face, which had sagged and greyed. His faded blue eyes were ringed with large black circles.

John looked confused and following Richard's gaze, stared down at his clothes.

'Oh damn! The best suit is ruined! What the hell am I going to wear to lunch now?' he frowned.

Richard groaned.

'You've got to try to concentrate, John. You are not going to lunch at Armitage Hall. You are dead, and you died rather a long time ago,' Richard said firmly, his chains rattling against the metal bed as he spoke.

The curate looked reproachfully at Richard. 'Well, there's no need to shout, old man. I maybe dead but I'm not deaf. Besides, it's awfully hard to keep track of time and memories when you are dead. Death is quite a complicated business really. It's such a shame I can't write a sermon about the difficulties of being deceased. Guaranteed it would have filled the church. Perhaps I should go and visit Rev…'

'I'm sorry,' Richard cut in, 'but please, is there any way you can get me out of these?' he raised a manacled hand.

John rubbed his chin and stared at the chains.

'I don't think so, I'm really rather dead,' John stated apologetically.

'But can you just give it a try?' Richard smiled encouragingly.

John reached out a grey hand, the sleeve of his jacket and shirt hanging loose from the elbow. Richard noted what looked like the grey outlines of bites and jagged cuts, covered the lower part of his arm.

Richard felt a slight breeze against his face as the curate leant over and tried to undo the cuff around his right wrist. The grey bony fingers fell through the restraint.

'Damn!' John exclaimed. 'I'm so sorry, I can't. I really am a terrible ghost.'

'Don't be too hard on yourself, at least you tried. I'm sure being a ghost is a lot harder than most people realise,' Richard replied.

John looked extremely crestfallen for a moment and then smiled. 'Don't move, I will be back!'

He disappeared in a gust of wind.

The breeze blew Richard's hair from his eyes. A shower of dust fell from the cobwebs, freed by the gust of wind. Richard lay back against the bed and thought for a moment. Perhaps Sparke had gone to get Bethany? She had seen the ghost in the attic. Therefore, she should be able to see John too. In fact, too many people in Witherleigh saw ghosts. Something evil had been lurking in the village for centuries. Its taint had touched the villagers' souls through the generations and corrupted them.

A breath of icy wind swished through the room. John reappeared.

'It's going to be fine now, old man. I have found someone who can move objects. Just don't mention the dead thing. He gets rather touchy.'

Richard nodded eagerly, the chains clinking against the bed, as he looked for Snowy.

A discordant scream ran around the room, followed by an echo of heavy boots, which approached the back of the bed.

'Oh crap! It must be Dicken…' Richard muttered, as he tried to twist around.

A strong wind howled and blew through the basement, ripping the cobwebs from the wall. Richard felt his bed begin to shake.

The little bed was lifted from the floor, hovered for a moment, and then thrown against the brick wall. The bed rebounded and tipped to one side, leaning diagonally against the wall, its four castor wheels spinning in different directions.

Richard hung from the bed, his weight pulling against the chains as the cuffs dug into his wrists and ankles. He gasped for breath as the pressure of the unseen force sucked the air from the brick room. The walls began to wobble. Powdered cement trickled down from the loosened brickwork and was blown across the grey stone floor.

An amorphous face appeared, hovering inches from his.

'Richard Dicken, is that you? I command you to make yourself known to me,' Richard shouted above the wind, summoning the spirit to him.

The head disappeared.

'No, don't go!' Richard screamed. 'Whoever you are... *Veni ad me!* Come to me!'

The howling wind retreated, dragging John along with it, through the open doorway. The door slammed shut. The only sound left in the room was the creaking of the bed wheels as they continued to turn.

Richard coughed as the pressure eased from his chest. An oppressive emptiness filled the room.

'Damn it! I really need to learn how to control spirits a bit better,' Richard muttered crossly to himself.

Richard looked longingly at his rucksack, propped up against the wall opposite him, hoping the knowledge contained in the *Triangulum* would magically appear in his brain.

A wavy shadow moved across a rectangle of light cast by the skylight. Richard raised his head trying to peer through the narrow window. The doctor's surgery was situated at the end of the little row of Victorian terrace houses which led from the market square. Even though it stood slightly apart from the terrace, people walked up and down the road. Perhaps one would hear him and help.

'Help me, please! I'm trapped down here!' he screamed.

The shadow disappeared.

'No wait!' Richard shouted and tried to pull his hands from the wrist restraints. He winced as the cuffs cut into the skin around his wrists. Even if they heard me, who would come to the aid of a madman? Richard thought, as he desperately tried to blink tears of frustration from his eyes.

The bed jolted forward, spun away from the wall, and

flipped onto its side.

Three of the bed wheels stopped spinning, while the top wheel nearest his head, changed direction and began to spin counterclockwise. He felt a stabbing pain in his chest as his heart struggled to beat.

Positional asphyxiation was not the most honourable way to die but was slightly better than auto-erotic asphyxiation. Richard closed his eyes and prayed for death to come quickly.

A cold breeze blew against his face.

John Sparke reappeared inches from him, his face reanimated, and his clothes repaired to his pre-death appearance.

'John, you're back, thank goodness! Go outside and tell someone, anyone, that I'm trapped down here!' Richard gasped.

John looked puzzled and stroked his chin pondering the request. 'I'm terribly sorry but I don't see how I can do that, Richard.'

Richard stared at the ghost.

'Look, just go onto the street and grab someone. I am sure that most of the villagers can see ghosts, even though they pretend not to.'

'Hmm…' John said shaking his head, 'I would and you're right they do but there's no one here.'

'Well, go and look in the Happy Chicken café or whatever it's called now… just do something!' Richard panted as his heart beat through his ribs.

'I can't go back to the café. I'm sort of located on you, old man, I'm afraid,' John smiled apologetically.

Richard frowned.

'So where is everyone? And where the hell am I?' Richard said, desperately trying to squint through the skylight.

An echo of footsteps ran across the room.

'Oh! dear me! This doesn't look good at all!' John said frowning over Richard's shoulder as he quickly vanished back into the *Mortalis*.

'Oh crap!' Richard groaned as he realised, he had no choice but to summon the new spirit.

'Et tu iubes, veni ad me, I command you to come to me!' he yelled, crossing his fingers, and hoping for a friendly spirit.

The running footsteps hesitated.

A gust of wind pinned Richard back onto the bed and flipped the bed back onto its four wheels. Instantly, Richard felt the pressure release from his chest and lay on his back panting.

'I'm sorry if I upset you Snowy, I know you loved Martha but please help me,' Richard pleaded to the silence.

A grey figure began to walk towards him from the shadows. The figure clicked his fingers and the bed stood to attention on its back legs. Richard found himself standing vertically, but still strapped to the bed. Another gust of wind blew, and he watched in fascination as the shadowy figure crossed into the living realm.

'And a good morning to you, sir, but who is this Snowy? Some wench, I wager?' the ghost replied grinning at Richard.

'And who the hell are you?' Richard asked the scruffily dressed man in front of him. 'Oh crap, I'm sorry! Where are my manners. Are you another curate?'

'Well, sir,' the man flashed Richard a lopsided grin and

bowed, 'I like to think of meself as a man of God, I help redistribute the wealth so the poor, meaning meself, don't starve to death.'

Richard glanced up at the apparition in front of him.

The ghost was of a rather muddy but affable young man. His brown hair was shoulder length and unkempt, half-tied back with a black ribbon. He wore a roughly cut leather jerkin which hung open to reveal a large cream overshirt, its ties left undone and barely concealing a taut, muscular chest covered in a sprinkling of brown hair. His cream breeches ended at his knees, just above a pair of ancient riding boots which showed a patch of bare skin, where his stockings should have been.

Around his neck was a thick, red mark.

'Thank you for coming to me. I need your help. Please release me. I'm trapped down here,' Richard said, frowning at the ghost, his eyes lingering on the mark which circled the ghost's neck.

'An' why should I?' the ghost enquired, putting both hands on his hips.

'Look!' said Richard. 'Dr Ashcroft will be coming to get me soon or else leave me down here to rot. Either way I don't trust him, and if I don't stop him, people here will keep dying.'

The ruffian's large hazel eyes narrowed with disgust. 'Ashcroft, you say. That devil made me swing.'

A white frosted veil lifted from the figure as it materialised fully in front of Richard and started to undo his ankle restraints. The ghost smelt unwashed and earthy but otherwise looked robust and red-cheeked, even in death. With the last cuff undone, Richard collapsed forward onto the floor.

'Thank you… um… sir,' Richard muttered as he sat on the cold stones and rubbed the circulation back into his numbed wrists and ankles.

The ghost put out a hand and helped Richard to his feet. Richard stood up and looked down at the ghost, who was smaller than he had expected.

'You are a long'un, grown up on the fine food from a rich cleric table, I 'spect?' the ghost teased. 'Oh, where are me manners afore gentry? The names Turner, Nathaniel Turner, highwayman an' all around na'ar do well, at your service.' He gave a half-bow.

'Er…Hi! I'm Richard Radcliffe, I am… hmm… well now, probably unemployed.' He smiled and bowed in return.

A door slammed shut from somewhere above them and muffled greetings were exchanged.

'You might be wantin' to take your leave now,' Turner suggested, his hazel eyes flicking upwards towards the voices.

Richard nodded and hobbled towards the thick oak door. He crossed his fingers and pushed. The door creaked open. His captors had obviously felt no need to lock it, considering his predicament. They walked through a low, sloping red-bricked corridor which opened out into a large room with a low, vaulted ceiling. The walls of the room were lined with huge dark oak vats, encircled with metal stays, which towered above them as they walked past.

The smell of apple was intoxicating.

'Does Witherleigh have a cider mill?' Richard asked.

'Aye, it does an' plenty 'o spirits from the Frenchies come along this way too.' Nathaniel grinned as he touched the side of his nose with a grubby looking finger.

A white sign had been nailed into each vat naming them respectively as 'Organic', 'Extra Strong', 'The Finger', and 'Tourist'. At the bottom of the vat marked 'The Finger' was a triangle with one overlong line, carved deeply into the oaken cask. Richard touched the vat. The wood felt warm. Its apple aroma tinged with a slightly bitter flavour.

He removed his hand and hurried past the vat.

At the far end of the vat room was another larger corridor, ending with a stone staircase leading upwards to the main floor. The corridor acted as a channel, funnelling the voices down to the subterranean level. Richard was about to follow the sound of the voices, when Turner signalled to him and disappeared between the last vat and the red brick wall.

'One way for the excisemen an' one way for the honest countryfolk.' Turner winked and pressed a brick in the wall. A small door hidden in the wall swung open to reveal a narrow, dusty staircase.

The lower end of the staircase was sloped downwards and was wide enough to roll a barrel, while the upper staircase consisted of narrow, steep steps which twisted around following the outer contours of the building. The outer side of the staircase was red brick and cold to touch, while the right-hand side was wooden panelled. Richard shivered. He felt as if he were walking inside his own coffin.

'How do you know so much about all this?' Richard asked.

Turner motioned him to come closer. Richard leant forward, and Turner whispered in his ear, 'A little ghost told me!' He roared with laughter and galloped up the stairs.

Richard shook his head and smiled as he followed the highwayman. Half-way up the stairs, Turner pushed him against the wall, a dirt-stained finger to his lips.

'That's him! The bastard, that hanged me,' Turner whispered. He motioned to the wall. 'Look through the peephole an' you can see the devil himself.'

Richard saw a rusted iron slide fixed to the wall and drew it back to reveal two holes. He bit his lip as he stared through the peepholes.

Dr Ashcroft was sitting behind an enormous mahogany writing desk, sipping a cup of tea from a gold-ringed china teacup. A half-eaten almond brioche sat unwanted on a matching side plate. His arms were crossed as he stared at the gathering of people in front of him, all dressed in various shades of brown and green. Two large men stood behind him, their arms also crossed, wearing identical green sweatshirts with a picture of a very happy chicken drinking a pint of cider on their right breasts. Underneath Richard could just make out the words 'Witherleigh Scrumpy Makers Est. 1770'.

An old man shuffled forward, twisting a green flat cap in his hand, ''Ere's the thing, Dr Ashcroft, sir. We can't afford a rent rise this year. Me an' me wife can barely afford to pay the rent as it is. The crops are rottin' in the fields. We won't get half for them as what we got last year.'

'Aye, but I'm just surprised you got any time for ploughing, Jacko. You lookin' after that disabled, invisible son of yours, an' as your wife's on disability now too an' you bein' their sole carer an' all.'

Jacko glared at the tall, weather-beaten farmer, standing

at the back of the group. 'Well, here's the thing, Arthur, I've seen yon orchard. At least my apples don't look like withered old prunes but then the ones in yon veg boxes are all red an' plump. How can that be so?'

'An' what do you mean by that?' Arthur growled.

'You can stuff your fancy organic label up your arse, as it ain't worth shit. That's what it means, Arthur.'

Arthur flew at the old farmer but was held back by the rest of the villagers. Dr Ashcroft smiled and shook his head.

'So much fuss over an organic vegetable box. You people can never see the big picture, can you?' Dr Ashcroft took another sip of tea.

Someone coughed and hesitantly stepped forward. Richard recognised him. It was Andrew Strange, proprietor of the Witherleigh Store.

'It's not just the farms that are in trouble, sir. There's barely enough local produce to stock my shelves,' Strange spoke, as he twisted his cap in his hands.

'I see,' said Dr Ashcroft, replacing his teacup in its saucer. 'And what do you want me to do about your poor business skills?'

The office door opened. Mrs Ashcroft sailed silently into the room. She placed a delicate pale hand on her husband's shoulder and whispered softly in his ear.

Dr Ashcroft nodded.

'Very well, we will postpone the rent increase till after the harvest. We must all pray for a bountiful one.'

He stood up, carefully pushed his chair under the table, and taking his wife's arm, they walked from the office. Their tenants lowered their gaze as the couple walked past.

The two workers ushered the people from the room.

Richard was about to turn away from the peephole when a black shadow passed the study window. He moved round and peered through the eyehole, just in time to see a breath of blackness blow across the office window and vanish.

'Christ! What's wrong with these people?' he muttered.

'Oh! They're just desperate. Landlords are all the same, selfish brigands. See your family starve to death in the gutter rather than go without their rent. The devil take them all.'

Richard frowned at Nathaniel.

'I'm sorry about your family, I truly am, but at this precise moment I'm slightly more concerned with the fact that a demon is watching us through the window.'

'What the devil! What do you think this is? the 1600s? Ain't no demons nor witches, are you mad?' Turner stared at him suspiciously.

'Yes,' Richard replied. 'And I have the certificate to prove it. Are you sure you didn't see the demon trail?'

Turner shook his head. 'The only demon I saw was still very much alive.'

'I'm sorry to disappoint you but that's not your demon. However, Dr Ashcroft is probably a direct descendant of the judge that saw you hanged, though. Families never seem to leave Witherleigh.'

The memory of a tall man looking around Richard Dicken's attic room in disgust and watching as the curate was carried off to his death, flickered across his thoughts.

'There is something rotten at the very root of this village, but all I really know is that about four centuries ago Ashcroft's ancestor kidnapped and almost certainly was involved in the murder of Richard Dicken, while his descendent had me strapped to a hospital bed and left in the cellar of a cider mill. It's weird but not exactly a watertight case for denouncing the Ashcroft family as having made a *Daemonium Foedus*, an everlasting contract with a demon centuries ago, is it? If I went to the Archbishop with this, he would throw me out of his office without so much as a cucumber sandwich,' Richard said, rubbing the day-old stubble on his chin.

'Don't forget Judge Ashcroft murdered me too,' Turner growled.

'Murdered you or sentenced you to death?' Richard asked.

''Tis the same, he got me hanged then left my body to rot in the gibbet at the crossroads. He didn't need to do that,' Turner said sadly, his gaze drifting past Richard.

'I'm sorry,' Richard replied. 'So, you didn't get a Christian funeral either?'

Turner shook his head and vanished.

Richard called after the ghost, but it was too late.

'Well, I will just add that to my list of things to do – give Nathaniel Turner's bones a Christian burial and let him pass on. While trying to locate the bodies of the missing curates, defeat a demon, and try not to look completely insane,' Richard muttered to himself.

Hopefully, a convicted highwayman would be allowed into the *Elisium*. Richard was not quite sure of Turner's suitability. Fortunately, that was not his responsibility.

Richard followed the narrow pathway back down past the

vat room and below. A string of small, electric light bulbs was strung along the low ceiling and cast a dim yellow light across the darkness of the passageway. He noted the absence of cobwebs and dust. The passage was obviously well used, but he doubted it was for smuggling tobacco or scrumpy.

Richard walked along the tunnel. Its cold rocky floor prodded painfully into his socked feet. The passageway ended in a heavy wooden door. He pushed hard and it swung open. A shaft of mottled light filtered into the passage bringing with it the smell of stale air and old dust.

'Oh Christ!' Richard groaned. 'It's a bloody crypt. That's all I need…'

A row of four grey marble carvings of people lay on tombs in front of him. The two males were dressed in ornate looking doublets with high collars, that fanned out around their necks, and voluminous, striped hose which encircled their thighs. The women's faces were framed by elaborate headdresses. They both wore long, heavy dresses. Fine marble hands clutched small books to their ample bosoms, which peered out over the straight line of their bodices.

The remainder of the dead lay on narrow ledges in alcoves chiselled into the stone of the crypt. Richard touched a marble foot. A slight electric pulse hummed through the statue.

The dead did not sleep well here.

One of the alcove tombs seemed familiar. He walked over. A recumbent effigy showed a carved figure of a tall man dressed in a frock coat with large buttons running down the length of its front seams. The coat lay open to reveal a waistcoat, breeches, and long riding boots. Richard felt the hairs on the back of his neck prickle. Warning signs flashed through his brain as a voice inside his head whispered, 'Do not look into the eyes of the dead for they will steal your soul.'

However, he could not help himself. There was something too familiar about the angular outline of the features.

Richard leant into the alcove and stared into the carved face. Half-hidden beneath a curly stone wig were the carved, pointed features of Dr Ashcroft.

He read the inscription chiselled above the alcove.

William Ashcroft
Born 1770
Died 1830
Memento Mori

'Remember you too will die' – it was not the cheery inscription he had expected. Richard took a step backwards.

The carved figure flickered.

Its eyes opened and turned slowly towards him.

Richard felt his knees give way as panic surged through his body, sending electric pulses through his limbs. He raced through the tomb, towards two heavy looking wooden doors recessed into the archway of the crypt. The doors were reinforced with thick bands of rusting orange iron. A ring-shaped iron handle hung on either door.

'Shit! Handles on the inside of crypts are never a good sign,' he muttered.

Richard looked over his shoulder and scanned the remaining tombs for movement. He rattled the iron rings and thumped his fists against the door screaming, 'Let me out!' After a minute, Richard paused, and listened through gasping breaths for signs of help.

In the distance, he heard a lorry rumbling through the village, possibly a milk lorry? However, he really had no idea when milk was collected. Or perhaps it was stuffed with Happy Chicken produce? If there were any crops left to harvest. The farmers had seemed adamant that the crops were failing.

A slight rustling was vaguely audible, over the murmuring autumn winds. Richard listened hopefully and banged against the door again.

'Hello out there! I've been locked in here, please help me!' he shouted.

Richard waited for a few seconds. There was no answering echo. He banged again and rattled the door ring. Then paused.

'Oh Christ,' he murmured, as he realised the rustling was coming from within the crypt.

He turned, half-expecting to see the marble figure of the past Ashcroft standing behind him, hands poised inches from his neck. There was nothing. No trapped ghosts had risen, wandering through the tomb in confusion. No statues had woken from their eternal beds and the ancient Ashcroft effigy continued to stare up at the ceiling.

The crypt was deadly still.

Richard banged his head against the wall.

'Keep it together,' he whispered and slumped down against the cold, stone steps.

The rustling sounded again. It was coming from one of the alcove tombs to the left of him. He tentatively approached a recumbent effigy. The carving was small, only half-filling the alcove. The image of a young girl lay in front of him, her eyes closed as if asleep. Coils of braided hair fell past her shoulders and onto the deep pointed collar of her dress. The collar reached to her narrow waist, which was accentuated by a full skirt, flattened by the stone mason, which stopped just below her knees, to reveal a pair of buttoned boots.

An angelic chubby face peered up at him from the semi-darkness. A tiny ball gripped firmly in her hands.

He glanced at the tomb's inscription.

Henrietta Armitage born June 1870
departed this life April 1878
Nobilis Sacrificium

''In noble sacrifice' of what?' Richard frowned.

He touched the stone shoulder of the little girl and said a prayer for a life cut too short. There was no electric energy emanating from her tomb. It was cold and empty; her spirit had passed. Richard breathed a sigh of relief.

'Well, at least you are free now, rest in peace,' he whispered.

Something brushed against his ankle.

The small ball fell from the girl's tomb and rolled across the stone-flagged floor. The ball rolled to the centre of the crypt and stopped.

A stifling silence covered the crypt. Richard held his breath and waited.

Small, electric charges exploded, barely inches above the stone floor, and filled the air with static electricity. Richard stood frozen to the spot as a glowing yellow current arced across the crypt floor, turning the grey stones black. The air inside the crypt began to heat.

Richard screamed in pain, as the demon sigil etched into his palms, burned bright red.

Among the smell of burning dust and electrified air, Richard could just make out the faint clawing touch of hydrogen sulphide. His eyes began to itch, and tears streamed down his face, but he remained still, holding his breath, as he sensed an insidious presence searching for him from beneath the stones.

A black shape rippled through the stone floor.

The floor began to bubble and then imploded, to reveal a gaping black pit directly beneath the crypt. Green-tinted clouds of sulphide rose and poured over the sides of the hole, its smell choking him, squeezing the breath from his body.

Richard felt the floor collapse under his feet. He clawed at the sides of the pit, his fingertips burning as they touched the steaming stones. Something grabbed hold of his legs, dragging him downwards, as his nails gouged deep lines in the melted floor.

'Help me!' Richard screamed, as he fell into the darkness.

CHAPTER FOURTEEN

'Oh, dear me,' Anderson's worried face peered over him. 'Well, you gave us quite a scare, young man,' the Reverend said, his quiet voice betraying his relief.

'I'm sorry,' Richard whispered, his throat burning. 'What happened? Where am I?' He tried to sit up, but the Reverend put his hand on his shoulder.

'You're in the guest bedroom at the vicarage. You must have had a funny turn or something. I found you collapsed on the steps leading down to one of the old graveyard vaults.'

'Do not look mad.' A voice warned inside his brain.

'Thank you,' Richard muttered. 'I think I must have slipped and fell.'

'Hmm…' The vicar rubbed his chin thoughtfully. 'And just what were you doing in the graveyard, Richard?'

His keen grey eyes fixed on Richard's face.

Richard smiled weakly. 'I was just checking their condition; grave upkeep is part of my job.'

The Reverend nodded. 'Very true, the dead should be honoured and respected. So, no more apparitions or demons?'

Richard shook his head. 'It's fine, they've all gone now. I've started taking my pills again,' he said as he crossed his fingers which were hidden beneath the pristine white duvet, sprinkled in tiny pink embroidered roses.

Reverend Anderson almost beamed. 'Excellent news. Your father is on a very hectic tour of America, bringing Christianity to the colonies, but as soon as his schedule permits, he will make arrangements to have you put safely back in the Nightingale Unit.'

'So, he's not sending me back straightaway?' Richard raised one eyebrow.

'Oh no, well you must understand, Richard. Your father is very important to the church. If the media got hold of the fact that his son was in a mental institute, it just would not send out the right message at all.'

'Of course not,' Richard nodded wearily.

He spied a glass of water on the bedside table and gulped the refreshing water down, wayward drips ran down his face.

Reverend Anderson's piercing grey eyes lingered momentarily on Richard's hands, which were covered in thick bandages.

'Be careful Richard. A couple of years in seminary college does not equip you for fighting the monsters that walk among us. Sometimes its best left to those with the right sort of training,' Anderson whispered.

Richard looked up at the vicar and frowned.

Reverend Anderson put on one of his Sunday after-service smiles.

'When you are feeling better, I will run you back to the caravan. I have important church duties to attend to in Temperley tonight. Now get some rest. Mrs White is preparing one of her delicious sausage casseroles… with extra-cheesy dumplings,' he added and turned to leave.

'Thank you,' Richard said, frowning as he peered under the bedsheets. He was wearing a pair of itchy, red-checked pyjamas. 'Er… where are my clothes?'

'Mrs White has very kindly washed them. They were covered in black soot and tar. You really must try to take more care with your appearance.' Reverend Anderson nodded and left the room.

Richard paled. He did not know which was worse, the Reverend or Mrs White undressing him, but neither was an image he wanted to keep in his head.

He poured himself another glass of water and fell fast asleep.

***

In his dreams someone kept calling his name.

The voice was faint but persistent.

'Bethany…' Richard whispered as his subconscious fixed on her pixie-like features and the swish of her ponytail. Perhaps it was time he tried to get a girlfriend. He was not that bad looking, and his father had money. According to the glossy magazines scattered about the unit, that was what most girls were looking for.

The figure grabbed him by the shoulders and shook him. 'Wake up Richard. He is coming!' it whispered.

Richard sat bolt upright. The image of Bethany shattered. John Sparke sat cross-legged on his bed, watching him intently.

'Is that you, Bethany?' Richard whispered.

''Fraid not, old man. It's only me,' John Sparke replied.

Richard rubbed his eyes as they adjusted to the semi-darkness. 'Oh Christ! What time is it? The Reverend is meant to be driving me home!'

'I think you have slightly bigger worries at the moment!' John nodded towards the pink floral wallpaper that covered the guest bedroom. Richard squinted through the darkness.

The room was empty.

No sinister looking shapes moved through the dusk. The manse was silent. Even Mrs White had stopped singing hymns as she cleaned the invisible dust, in the squeaky falsetto of a natural contralto.

'Er… thanks for the warning, John, but I don't think anyone's there,' he whispered and fell backwards into the deliciously soft mattress, hoping for another dream of Bethany.

An icy breeze blew across his face.

Richard groaned and opened one eye. 'Seriously John, everything's fine, no one is here. You're just a bit confused. Now please let me sleep.'

John gave Richard a reproachful look and whispered in his ear. 'He's watching you. If I were you, I would turn the lights on.'

'Oh Christ!' Richard swore and lunged for the rose-inspired pink and cream light. He flicked the switch. The room filled with shades of pink, as he propped himself up on his elbows.

'Oh shit!' he whispered.

Rips of stained floral wallpaper were peeling away from the walls. The curtain pole hung on straining supports and lunged diagonally towards the floor. The heavy pink curtains were missing. The bedroom windows had been flung wide open, pinned against the outer wall of the manse, as the cold early evening air entered the room. Every drawer in the pine chest was open, its linen left dangling from the drawers. One of the doors of the tall pine wardrobe had fallen inwards, held up by a twisted hinge. Richard stared at the gilt-edged oval mirror directly opposite his bed and watched as black cracks ran across the glass, splintering his reflection.

A swathe of thick black mould crossed the room. The pink roses on his duvet turned dark green. Instantly, its warmth evaporated, and it felt cold and damp against his skin. The smell of decay and wet soil permeated the little room, as the freshly cut pink and cream arrangement of roses in the vase on the vanity table, turned brown and shrivelled. Their petals crumpled to dust as they fell onto the carpet.

Richard's hands felt as if they were on fire. Two amber triangles burned through the bandages. He ripped them off and emptied the jug of water, left on the bedside table, over them. The water hissed as the searing pain abated slightly. Richard leapt from the bed and searched for his clothes. He was not going to fight a demon in borrowed, red-checked pyjamas.

The floorboards in the centre of the room bubbled and dissolved as a black hole appeared in front of the little bed. The clawing odour of hydrogen sulphide oozed across the room. Richard covered his face with the bleached white guest towel, positioned carefully at the end of the bed.

'*Ostende te daemonium*, show yourself demon!' Richard demanded, hoping the demon would not be able to enter the vicarage.

A large brown and white owl appeared at the window, its wings banging against the window frame. Richard rushed forwards trying to shoo the frightened bird away. The owl managed to perch on the windowsill. Its talons digging into the white wood. The majestic wings folded neatly together. The bird twisted its head towards Richard, its round amber eyes glinting with amusement.

'I see your dress sense hasn't improved since our last little meeting. You will never get a girlfriend dressed like that,' the owl sneered, its unblinking eyes staring through Richard.

'What do you want?' Richard asked, knowing full well the dangers of discourse with a demon.

'I want many things, dear boy, what do you want? That's the more interesting question.' The owl blinked slowly at Richard.

'Why are you in the village? How did you escape the church?' Richard demanded.

'Obviously, I am here because I was asked to come. Such a very long time ago. I stayed because village life is just so delightful. I have everything I need here. You, on the other hand, I'm afraid are not wanted here... but then you are not wanted anywhere. An only child. Your parents were so proud when you were born. It is such a great pity you grew up to be such a disappointment. In fact, it would have been better if you had never been born. That's what your father says.'

The words hit Richard like a punch. He felt his heart contract as tears pricked his eyes.

'Get a grip!' he muttered to himself.

Words of a demon were like poison. Their victims' biggest

fears ripped from their subconscious and whispered back at them, to destroy their world.

'Probably,' Richard answered forcing a smile onto his face, 'but I called you and you are bound to answer me. Who summoned you here?'

The owl stretched. Its grey-brown wings covered the length of the window and its sharp talons dug deeply into the windowsill, splintering the white wood.

'About five hundred years ago, an old crone summoned me to this hamlet to perform a small favour. They wanted better crop yields, more gold coin from the harvests. I just showed them the way to improve it. That's all,' the owl replied as its head fell to one side.

'How did you escape from the demon trap inside the church?' Richard demanded, filtering through the information.

'I didn't escape. I just left you pathetic imbecile.' The owl jumped off the window ledge and spread its wings as it hovered just below the ceiling.

'You lie. You were sealed in there. I saw the protecting angels. How did you break the seals?' Richard asked.

'If the circle is incomplete it is not a circle,' the demon sneered and dived towards Richard. Its powerful brown beak and razor-sharp talons aimed directly at him.

Richard ran to the door and rattled the door handle. It would not move.

'Not again!' he groaned.

He took a deep breath, banged against the door with both fists and yelled, 'Reverend Anderson, get me out of here now!'

Richard felt the owl's talons pierce his skin and screamed

in pain as they raked down his back. His legs threatened to collapse under him. He turned around to face the demon, his arms covering his face. The owl flew into the centre of the room. Richard's blood dripped from its talons and splashed slowly onto the floor. The sound of its wings beat through the room.

'You bore me. Accept your death with just an ounce of decorum,' the owl said as it launched at Richard.

Richard covered his eyes with his hands and screamed, 'Reverend Anderson, please get me out of here!'

Talons pierced through his pyjama top.

Richard screamed as he felt the owl carve a circle around his heart and then rip down into his skin. His heart shuddered under the strain, pounding through his chest. Richard looked down. Blood spread across his pyjama top and ran onto the cream carpet.

'Get off me!' he screamed as he tried to punch the bird from his chest.

The owl cackled and dug its talons deeper into Richard's skin.

Richard felt the world retreating as his vision narrowed. He stumbled against the bed as he became light-headed. Bells rung noisily in his ears as blood rushed to his brain. Richard clutched at the bed for support, but his legs gave way and he slumped onto the floor.

The bird hooted in triumph and relaxed its grip.

Richard lunged forwards onto his front, trying to crush the owl between his body and the floor.

The owl growled and released its grip. It flew backwards, its back almost touching the ceiling as it watched Richard try to staunch his wound with a fluffy, pink guest towel. Richard crawled back towards the bed. He yanked a trailing white wire and the floral bedside lamp smashed onto the carpet. Richard grabbed the lamp by its stand, flicked the switch, and watched as electricity pulsed through its jagged remains.

He propped himself up against the bed and waited.

The demon-owl swooped.

Richard reacted too late and the sharp talons raked across his face. He screamed as the owl hooted, gloating in its victory, and bent over Richard, its sharp beak inches from his left eye. The owl lunged forward. Richard smashed the jagged remains of the lamp against the bird's back.

The lamp rebounded off the feathers and rolled noisily across the floor. The owl lunged again. Richard covered his face with his arms and screamed, 'No!'

An old phrase he had once read in the *Triangulum* floated into his thoughts. '*Abiit potest daemonium*! Be gone demon, go back to the shadows!' He screamed as the beak pecked through his arm.

The owl stopped for a second, its face an inch from his and tutted, 'We aren't in the Dark Ages now, you know. Your father was right, you really are too young and inexperienced. He should never have sent you here. Reverend Anderson would have been better off on his own.'

The owl lunged, beak open, towards Richard's left eye.

'No!' Richard cried as he realised in horror the events of the attic had been an echo of his future blinding. He desperately tried to punch the demon-owl from his face.

The bedroom door swung open.

Mrs White screamed.

It was such a high-pitched scream, both Richard and the demon turned towards the door.

The owl launched itself from Richard's chest and dived headfirst into Mrs White, who was propelled backwards through the doorway. Richard heard her body thump heavily against the corridor wall. The owl landed, folded its wings into its red-stained, cream body, and followed Mrs White out of the room.

Richard pushed himself away from the side of the bed and tumbled heavily onto the carpet, dragging himself across the floor towards Mrs White.

A thin trail of blood followed him.

'Run, oh God... run,' he whispered weakly.

Richard collapsed halfway across the carpet and lay there panting as he blinked the blood from his eyes. 'Mrs White, speak to me, are you alright?' he whispered as he tried not to attract the attention of the demon.

Mrs White walked back into the room.

Her light blue eyes fixed straight ahead of her., her naturally pale complexion, ashen white with shock. Richard raised his head and smiled with relief. There were no blood stains marring her crisp pink dressing gown. She was shocked but otherwise unharmed.

He held out a shaking arm. 'Everything will be alright... just help me up.'

Mrs White walked past him.

Richard frowned and called out again, but the words stopped on his lips.

187

The back of Mrs White's dressing gown was shredded. Her pale skin hung in strips. Blood-soaked pieces of her white nightie stuck to her back. She collapsed to her knees and fell forwards, her chest crunching against the remains of the lamp. Her remaining blood pooled around her body.

'Oh God, no!' Richard groaned.

The owl sauntered back into the bedroom, a strip of bloodied flesh hanging from its beak. It threw its head backwards and guzzled the meat.

He surveyed the body. 'For a skinny bitch, she certainly had a lot of blood.'

'Why did you do that?' Richard whispered, a tear rolling down his cheek, making a white track through the red.

'Well, I am a little hungry... but to be brutally honest, mainly for the sport.' The owl winked at Richard, jumped onto the windowsill, and flew out into the darkening sky.

'Why don't you just finish me off then?' Richard called out after the demon.

'No need, dear boy... no need.' The owl's reply came back to him, carried on the night air.

Richard grabbed a pillow, pressed it to his chest, and frowned after the demon. He looked across at Mrs White's body. It was glowing faintly in the fading light of the early autumn evening.

'I know your game demon,' Richard said grimly.

An unnatural, violent death at a vicarage would create an angry, unstable spirit. He looked at the broken body of Mrs White. She had not been particularly pleasant in life. In death she could become a murderous fiend.

Richard crawled towards the body and turned her over onto her back. Her faded light blue eyes were fixed and open in the shock of her unexpected death. Her body was tense, and he could feel a slight electrical current pulsing through her corpse. He put his hand on her forehead. It was hot to touch.

The demon had cursed her soul. Her spirit was returning to its body.

Mrs White's body flipped onto its back. It arched upwards; her limbs taut as her body contracted into a bridge shape. Her head twisted beneath her body and her empty face stared at him. Her white hair, loosened from its bun, dragged along the floor as she scurried towards him.

'*Cara Deo, obsecro vos. Hoc regnum accipe animam ire tui.* Dear God, let her pass on. I really do not want to meet her ghost,' he yelled, curling up into a tight ball, his back against the bed.

Mrs White jumped, landing next to him. Her upside-down face inches from his as she sniffed his face.

Tentatively, Richard touched her forehead and made the sign of the cross.

'*Transire in lucem,* cross into the light,' he commanded as he raised his arms above his head and shouted, '*Spirituum venit ad lucem,* come into the light and find eternal rest.'

Mrs White howled, her eyes rolled into her head, her back arched higher, so only her fingertips and toes touched the floor. Slowly, she rose into the air, hovering just above Richard. The blood dripped from the ends of her white hair onto Richard's face.

A bolt of white light shot through the open bedroom window and caught Mrs White's body in its beam. A shadow of her ghostly image crossed the ruined bedroom wall, as Mrs White was pulled into the trail of light.

Her spirit had been gathered. She was passing into the *Mortalis*.

Richard breathed a sigh of relief and closed his eyes in a prayer of thanks.

'Fear me and my armies!' Mrs White screamed, her eyes blazing amber as her fingers gouged marks into the window frame. She thrust her hand into her chest and pulled out a rib and hurled it with demonic strength at Richard. He ducked as the rib flew across the room, slicing his cheekbone as it embedded itself into the remains of the flowery wallpaper.

She laughed hysterically as the receding light dragged her backwards through the window.

Silence descended.

Richard collapsed exhausted on the floor next to her empty body and closed his eyes.

CHAPTER FIFTEEN

Richard woke with a start. Rays of light cast from an apathetic moon, illuminated the black clouds, and covered the night sky in tones of darkest blue. The guest bedroom, however, was pitch black. Richard saw a faint light pulse through the darkness as a message flashed across his iPhone. He fished the phone from the floor and examined it. Its screen was covered in a spider web of cracks. Out of habit, he checked the message.

Apparently, his alma mater was having an old boy black tie social event. A former English cricket star was going to entertain the Old Exhavians with an evening of amusing anecdotes from his cricketing career. From what Richard had read in the papers, it was surprising that the cricketer, Aubyn Hamilton-Hill, a former Exhavian himself, could remember enough about the last two decades to actually give an hour-long talk.

Two tickets would only cost £90 and include a glass of wine.

Richard deleted the message and switched onto torch mode. He shone the feeble beam of light around the ruined bedroom.

The first thing he noticed was that the room had been transformed to its former appearance and then destroyed once again.

The wallpaper filled with tiny pink roses was still a vision of bright pinkness. However, the roses were covered in red droplets, which had been sprayed in drifts across the room. The duvet lay rumpled, abandoned on the floor, while the white under sheet was polka-dotted red.

Richard rolled onto his front and assessed the window.

It was concealed by two velour pink curtains that draped onto the carpet. There was no sign of movement from the curtains and the bedroom felt warm and dry. The demon must have repaired the damaged window. However, the mirror remained cracked and shards of glass had fallen onto the carpet, leaving behind black spaces where his reflection should have been.

It was not a good omen.

Gingerly, he moved the torch beam to where Mrs White had fallen.

'Oh Christ!' Richard groaned. The body was gone.

The remains of the lamp lay scattered where she had fallen. A pool of blood had soaked into the cream carpet next to him, and a smeared blood trail led from the carpet, to the red-splattered duvet. He dragged himself over to the duvet, pulled back a corner, and stared in horror at its contents.

Mrs White's exsanguinated face peered out from the duvet cocoon; her light blue eyes dulled to grey. Her mouth open. Her final words stolen by the demon. Richard carefully rewrapped Mrs White.

He sat propped up against the side of the bed.

Things did not look good for him. A convicted mental patient, about to be readmitted on the grounds of a remission into the madness of delusions and paranoia, found in the company of a dead body. He was not a police expert, but he had watched a few episodes of *CSI* at the unit. He had always thought this programme to be slightly inappropriate and rather dangerous, to broadcast in a forensic psychiatric unit - a way of teaching the criminally insane how to cover their tracks better.

Even he would suspect himself.

Mrs White was lying by the bed he had used, wrapped in his bed linen, with the remains of a lamp covered in his fingerprints sticking out of her chest. He scanned the room. The demon had left no trace of its presence.

This was the second middle-aged woman who had died while in contact with him, anymore, and he would be classed as a serial killer.

He looked at his phone. It was a little after one. The Reverend would not be back until around ten in the morning if Bethany's information was correct.

He had nine hours.

Richard stood up and prised the pyjama top from his chest wound. The wound was dry and had formed a red-tinged crust, he was healing.

He was not destined to die today.

Richard peeled off the pyjamas, stripped the sheet and mattress protector from the bed, and rolled them into a ball. He dragged the heavy ball of bedding down the stairs and went off in search of a washing machine.

The front door opened, quietly.

Richard ran back to the staircase. He dragged the duvet ball behind the navy, velour hallway curtains and looked around for somewhere to hide. Under the panelled stairway was a black doorknob. Richard ran over. He pulled the knob and a tiny diagonal door set inside the staircase opened. Quickly, he squeezed into the broom cupboard, wedging himself between the vacuum cleaner and a cardboard cut-out of Father Christmas.

Quietly, he shut the door.

Muffled footsteps crept down the hallway and stopped at the bottom of the stairwell.

'Thee keep watch for our Violet. She would have had 'er sleeping tablets by now. I've seed her after taking 'er pills an' she be dead to the world. Trust me. And thee follow me, it's time that grockle went home. He's upsetting everyone with his raucous an' wild ways. We'll bundle him up an' drop him in Exhaven market. Them's a peculiar lot in Exhaven, he should fit in fine over there,' a gruff voice filtered through the wooden panels.

'Right you are, Willis boy. 'Ee's bin nothin' but trouble since 'ee arrived. What with poor Mrs Bell dyin' an' all, 'ees brought bad luck, 'ee 'as,' a fading voice answered, as it disappeared up the stairs.

'Aye an' the man from the organics said he won't certify my crops, says he found nitrates in the potatoes. Nitrates, the bastard. It's just a bit of run-off from last time the leat flooded, that's all. Charlie's right though, the new vicar's brought nothin' but bad luck to this village. Spud don't like 'im neither. 'Tis time for 'im to go back home,' said a gravelly voice.

Richard instantly recognised the deep growl of Arthur Butt.

Spud started whimpering. 'Heel Spud. See 'ee don't want

to go anywhere near 'im an' dogs 'ave a nose for wrong'uns.'

'Aye, that they do,' Willis Boy replied.

Heavy footsteps trampled up the stairs, their sounds magnified in the cramped space of the broom cupboard, which groaned and shook with each step. Richard silently retreated to the back of the cupboard and waited for the explosion of noise.

'What the bloody hell has been going on 'ere then!' Willis Boy yelled. 'There's blood everywhere, it looks like old Blightie's slaughter room.'

Booted feet ran across the landing and stopped.

'Mrs White is not in 'er bedroom!' a worried voice called out.

'No, she ain't, you stupid turnip. He's gone an' wrapped 'er up in yon duvet,' Willis replied.

''Ee's gone an' killed 'er. 'Ee probably wanted 'is wicked way with 'er an' she rejected 'im. Then 'ee killed 'er. Londoners are like that. I seed it on the telly,' Arthur Butt snarled in disgust.

'Away with 'ee Spud. Don't lick that,' he added hurriedly.

'Aye, that will be 'bout right. Bloody Londoners comin' down 'ere an' trying to steal our women,' Willis Boy tutted.

'Aye, bloody Londoners,' Charlie agreed. 'An' Mrs White being a properly righteous woman would 'ave rejected 'is amorous ways.'

'Aye,' chorused Willis Boy and Arthur. 'She rejected ours.'

'She was a fine woman an' deserves a proper Christian send off,' Willis Boy announced.

The others agreed with a chorus of grunts. 'We need to call the police.'

'Oh aye,' replied Arthur slowly. 'But the fancy man is gone

an' we is 'ere. How do we explain that, then boys?'

A cloud of silence descended.

Richard tiptoed through several bulging cardboard boxes and circumnavigated the Father Christmas. Cautiously, he pressed open the broom cupboard door, tiptoed to the side of the stairs, and peered through the dark oak railings. One of the men stood with his hands on his hips, legs splayed, as he surveyed the guest bedroom. The others were hidden from sight, safely secured in the guest bedroom.

Richard tiptoed towards the front door. The grandfather clock struck two. Richard bolted behind it.

''Ere that almost frightened the life out of me!' Charlie exclaimed.

Footsteps crossed the landing towards the stairs. Richard held his breath.

'Well, the young vicar ain't 'ere,' Arthur announced. 'So perhaps he's gone.'

'Aye, but we can't be 'ere neither. We don't want the police poking their noses into our affairs. I've got my position to look after. Been a postman here for near twenty years an' not so much as one complaint,' Willis Boy said.

'Aye, but what about these?' Arthur replied.

Richard peered around the side of the grandfather clock.

'Oh Christ! that won't do at all!' Willis Boy exclaimed in horror. 'Them's our footprints in the blood.'

'Bloody hell!' Charlie swore. 'I can't go to prison for murder, me Ma would kill me!'

'Aye,' Willis Boy muttered. 'Arthur, you're used to washing down carcasses. Strip her, change her, an' put her back in her room nice an' respectful like. Charlie… you an' me will strip this room an' load it all in the post van round back. We'll dump it all in Exmoor marsh.'

'Oh aye, an' remember to take off yon boots too. Them's all got to go,' Arthur stated, looking at Charlie's blood-splattered trainers.

'But that's not fair!' Charlie moaned. 'These are Reeboks, I only 'ad they last month for me birthday. Them's almost brand new.'

'Aye, 'tis a great shame,' Willis Boy commiserated, taking off his black wellies, to reveal a pair of thick grey socks, 'Bloody Londoners,' he swore.

'Aye,' the others chorused, as they stood in their socks, 'Bloody Londoners.'

***

Richard had heard enough.

He tiptoed through the front door and disappeared naked into the night.

The autumnal night air blew against his skin. Richard shivered as he stood behind an azalea bush, planted just underneath the front room window. From this position, he could see the shadowy forms of the three villagers as they scurried across the upstairs landing. The glow from the first-floor windows cast a shallow light across the innermost flower beds, lengthening the shadows of the sleeping ornamental cherry trees.

There was a bang and a stream of cursing flooded through the window, as something heavy bumped down the staircase.

Richard left the safety of the azalea, tiptoed through the front garden, and followed the path around to the back of the manse.

The back garden consisted of a large expanse of lawn which melted into the surrounding woods. To the left of the garden hidden discreetly by a dwarf apple tree was an umbrella washing line. Its metal and plastic arms shining through the darkness like an alien antenna. Richard crept along the shadows of the herb garden, dived out, and grabbed the grey shapes which were hanging limply from the line.

'God! I hope these are mine,' he prayed, hoping that his luck had changed, and he was not sitting in a rosemary bush with an armful of Mrs White's underwear.

He smiled with relief as he recognised his own rather tatty but now spotless clothes. Spotless but still damp. At least he would not have to walk up Fore Street naked.

Richard breathed a sigh of relief.

More swearing filtered through the darkness as doors were slammed shut and the post van drove off, its wheels spinning as it accelerated away. Richard skirted around to the front of the house, following the retreating yellow lights of the van.

The dark trees seemed to lean forward and rustle their dying leaves, whispering to each other as he walked past. He scanned the darkness for glowing amber eyes, but the woods seemed devoid of animal life. He walked quicker. Bad things held back by the light, were unleashed at night, and he had no wish to meet them here. An owl hooted from the inner wood. Richard ran down the path, his feet skidding in the mud.

Eventually, he reached the manse gates and turned right

heading towards the central square, where his car had been parked. His keys were lost but the central locking system had broken months ago. Luckily, he had a spare car key on the Saint Dymphna key fob holding his parents' house keys. The fob had lain forgotten and hidden in the back of the glove compartment, under a pile of screwed up paper balls, a packet of jellybeans, and his old college tie.

In the distance, he saw the rectangular grey shape of a lone car, parked by the village green. He hurried across the road.

The door of the Witherleigh Stores jingled open. Andrew Strange marched out in a tweed jacket and flat cap. His face, in marked contrast to their earlier meeting, was grim.

Richard dropped down and flattened himself against the road as the shopkeeper walked past and headed towards the Bishops Nod.

Strange knocked on the door of the inn three times. The door opened slightly, a shaft of light falling onto Strange's face. The door widened and the shopkeeper walked inside.

Richard saw the hunched figure of Mr Thomas, the dour innkeeper, move across the bar, a grey shadow caught in the inn's lights. Richard jumped up and ran to the Nod, watching through one of the latticed windows on the far side of the inn, as Thomas opened a door labelled, 'Cellar Keep Out'.

'Arthur will 'ave to catch us up later,' Thomas announced as he flicked the light switch, and a string of white lights illuminated the cellar stairs. The innkeeper disappeared. Strange, the two cider press workers, and Jacko and his wife, all hurried after him.

'Oh dear, you do look a bit rough, old man,' a clipped

Home Counties voice chirped in his ear.

Richard jumped and tumbled backwards, tripping over a flowerpot, and landing bottom first on the pavement. The flowerpot tottered for a second and then collapsed onto its side, spewing its contents diagonally across the empty pavement.

'You're not wearing any shoes. Did you know that?' John asked, his pale face glowing slightly in the darkness.

'Yes, they seem to have disappeared,' Richard replied glumly. 'I think they're still at the manse. I'm afraid there's been a murder at the vicarage. Mrs White is dead. God rest her soul.'

'Damn,' John said shaking his head. 'Another woman dead. Did you kill her?'

'No! I did not!' exclaimed Richard, 'but I was there when it happened.'

'Oh…' John said frowning. 'Two middle-aged women dying on you, just doesn't look that good.'

'I know,' Richard replied. 'I'm really not lucky with women.'

'Hmm...' John rubbed his chin thoughtfully. 'Perhaps it's your clothes. You need to get yourself one of these.' He smiled as he stroked the shiny blue fabric.

'Nothing like a quality suit to impress the little ladies.'

Richard sighed but said nothing.

A small shadow scurried along the road and headed around the back of the Nod. Richard recognised the swish of the ponytail, half-hidden under a black bobble hat, and blushed.

'I think I will just check round the back,' he whispered to John who stood leaning against a car, his arms folded, and a huge grin on his lips.

'Whatever you say, old man,' John grinned as he walked

leisurely along the pavement.

Richard tutted at the smirking ghost and followed Bethany. He ducked beneath the windows of the Nod and skirted around to the back alleyway, which ran next to the inn.

Crates of vegetables had been stacked against the wall of the pub, all stamped with the Happy Chicken logo, over which someone had stamped the words, 'Home Farm potatoes.' Richard peered into one of the crates. It smelt of soil and damp. Gingerly, he picked out a dark looking potato. It felt wrinkled and soft, almost squishy beneath his fingers.

No wonder the villagers were worried.

The potato crop had failed. They had rotted in the fields and were inedible. He scanned the wooden crates and found one marked 'Witherleigh Cross carrots.' Richard prised a carrot out through the hand hole of the box. He held it upwards towards the shaft of light from the inn and watched as the carrot flopped over to one side.

'What the hell are you doing?' hissed Bethany, a pair of night vision binoculars swinging around her neck. 'I thought they had sent you back to that expensive mental place in London?'

Richard hid the flopping carrot behind his back.

'And just who said that?' he asked.

'Dr Ashcroft told Mrs Ashcroft and she told Mrs Foxworthy, the new cook at the café, who then told the rest of the village,' Bethany stated.

'Well, Dr Ashcroft lied,' Richard said. 'He left me to rot in the cider mill. He's tied in with all these disappearances. His family has been for hundreds of years.'

'Hmm…' Bethany stroked her long ponytail, staring at Richard. 'Well, he obviously lied about you going up to London, but I don't know if he's a criminal mastermind. Last year he saved old Butler's prize cow, Muriel. She went into labour and her calf got stuck. The vet was caught up on the moors in the snow. So, Butler called the doctor instead. Why would a serial killer go out in the snow and bother to save a calf? It doesn't make sense.'

Richard shrugged his shoulders. 'Perhaps he's fond of animals?'

Bethany hmphed.

'All I know is the Ashcrofts are neck deep in the disappearances. I know it. I think you do too, only you won't admit it.'

Bethany glared at Richard.

'Ok, but can you blame me for being a bit cautious? The Ashcroft's are respected members of the Witherleigh community, while you… er… You don't exactly look that sane, do you?'

Richard tried to pat down his wayward curls and unrolled his trouser legs.

'I just didn't want to get my jeans dirty, that's all. I lost my trainers when the doctor drugged me.'

Bethany hmphed again.

'I don't think she believes you,' John said, as he stood behind Bethany, shaking his head sadly.

'If you're not going to be useful, you may as well leave me alone,' Richard said to the ghost, watching as John put his hand through Bethany's ponytail.

'Sorry,' Bethany replied, a hurt look on her face. 'I… I almost believe you.'

The door of the Nod jingled opened.

Richard and Bethany peered around the corner and watched as the group trooped out from the pub.

'If we shovel anymore shit on the crops, they'll start tastin' of it,' Arthur Butt muttered.

'Aye,' Thomas replied. 'An' I can't be seen buying nitrates again, them bloody DEFRA are everywhere. The co-op can't lose our organics label; prices will drop like a stone.'

'Aye,' said Strange looking up at the sky. The darkness had been replaced by a blaze of navy blue. A faint glow of pinkish light hovered just above the horizon.

'Sun's almost up. You'll have to wait to tomorrow, then spread 'The Finger'. That scrumpy's so strong it'll make your carrots stand to attention.'

'Aye,' said Butler. 'But we'll be needin' a new batch soon. We'll 'ave to tell the master. He'll not be happy. Two offerings in one covenstead, tis a lot of bother.'

'That it is,' Strange nodded, and the group splintered.

Bethany grabbed Richard by the shoulders and yanked him backwards into the alley.

'Do you know what that means?' she demanded.

Richard ran his hand through his hair and frowned.

'They're spreading cider on the crops. That's got to be a healthy alternative to nitrates, completely organic,' Richard replied.

Bethany tutted and shook her head. 'If it's completely legal then why do it at night and just exactly what is going to be offered? I don't like the sound of this. Do you think Dad found out something to do with the crops and that's what got him killed?'

She turned away and rubbed her eyes.

Richard shifted his feet awkwardly and stared at the pavement for a full minute. Say something supportive, his brain whispered.

'From what I know about covensteads, and I did attend the seminary, it'll just be a couple of sheep heads they bought from a local butcher and a lot of heavy drinking,' Richard half-smiled.

He patted Bethany's shoulder. 'And your father was just one in a long line of missing curates. Why kill all the other curates too? A hundred years ago everything was organic?'

Bethany shrugged her shoulders.

Richard quickly removed his hand.

'Look… I don't know, alright! I'm kinda new to all this ghost shit. I'll do some digging today – go to the cider mill guest room, see if any of the missing curates were somehow connected to the cider mill.' Bethany turned and pointed at Richard. 'You go back to the caravan and grab your ghost stuff then go to Stillbone Chapel. You should be safe up there. It's on the edges of the three moors, no one goes there anymore. Just drive towards Exmoor and stop at Queen Cross. It's signposted but you'll have to walk down to it, which is why no one goes there. My office is in the back. The door's unlocked. I'll meet you there, after my shift.' She rummaged inside her black backpack.

'Oh yes, and here's a little present I've been waiting to give you,' Bethany grinned, as she hurled a plastic bag at Richard's chest, and stalked from the alleyway.

Richard went scarlet.

He clutched the Happy Chicken bag to his chest and muttered his thanks, annoyed that he had not even thought of giving Bethany a gift. He would have to do better, but then he had no idea what Bethany would want. Perhaps he could drop by the Witherleigh Store tomorrow and pick up a bottle of expensive shower gel and some soap. Bethany smelt like she washed a lot.

CHAPTER SIXTEEN

The pedals felt strange under Richard's feet. Shiny green wellies were not the best attire to drive in, but it was either that or his Sunday best shoes. He was loath to wear those, in case they were ruined by the red mud, and he was left with either wellies or flip-flops to wear for church on Sunday.

Besides, he wanted Bethany to know how much he appreciated her gift.

Richard squinted through the blanket of pale, grey mist which rolled across the fields and mixed with the grey haze of early morning. Everything felt muted by the mist. Birdsongs were hushed as the countryside sat in an eerie silence. Occasionally, the dark grey shadows of treetops penetrated through the whiteness. Richard slowed down as he desperately tried to distinguish the road from the undergrowth.

Deep, mud-filled gullies clung to the sides of the lane, waiting for the unwary motorist. If their car wheels wandered into one of those, their only option would be to call the breakdown truck. Then have the indignity of being manhandled out by the local garage pickup truck, which would cost more than a week's wages. Richard could not afford the money or the long hours waiting for a breakdown truck to locate him in the moorland wilderness.

A gap appeared in the mist; part of the lane became visible.

A blanket of amber leaves had fallen across the narrow road, which appeared almost straight, as it passed by the empty fields. Richard eased his foot down gently on the accelerator.

The car skidded on a layer of thick mud, which had been washed down from the fields, and left hidden beneath the leaf-fall. The hastily thrown together luggage on the backseat of his car clunked together. Richard stamped his boot down on the brake pedal. The car spun across the lane, narrowly missing a collection of dismayed looking beech trees.

The car stopped spinning. Its front pointing backwards towards the village. Richard breathed a sigh of relief and said a prayer of thanks. The remaining orange beech leaves fell cloud-like on top of his car.

A tall, white shape loomed out from the swirling leaves.

Richard froze. His fingers whitened as they gripped the steering wheel. Several minutes passed. The shape remained motionless. Cautiously, Richard reached inside his jean pocket. His fingers searching for his mobile. It was still in one piece. He touched the screen. The phone blinked and the torchlight app beamed into the surrounding gloom.

A tall, white signpost loomed out of the trees. Its base wrapped in twisted, green ivy leaves. Its letters half-hidden from view. The early morning breeze ruffled the leaves, and he could just make out in black letters the words – Queens Cross.

The left arm of the signpost pointed back towards Witherleigh, while the right announced that Stillbone Chapel was five miles away and pointed towards a tiny lane which crossed through the ancient woodlands.

The branches of the woodland trees reached over and intertwined, forming a wooden lattice canopy, blocking out the faint rays of the rising sun.

Two wheel-sized tracks ran along the lane, separated in the middle by a mound of dirt, topped with scrub grass. After about ten feet, the lane fell away to the right, as it circumnavigated an ancient oak.

Richard reversed the car and edged his way down the lane, the sides of his car scraping against the hedgerows. He prayed that he did not meet an early morning tractor coming in the opposite direction, or they might have been stuck facing each other for hours, while he tried to reverse back through the winding lane.

Half an hour later, the lane opened slightly to reveal a barren space, cut into the hedgerows. The clearing was big enough for one small cart. He pulled into the tiny space and saw a wooden signpost which announced, 'Public Footpath - Stillbone Chapel 1-mile.' Its right arm pointed towards a narrow mud path in the grass. Below the sign someone had attached another, more homely-looking sign, using twisted wire loops. Written on this sign with dripped white paint was the warning, 'Treespassers will be persecuted and then shot.'

Richard smiled; being shot was the least of his worries.

He opened the back seat door of his car and groaned. The hastily filled cardboard box containing his charts, notes, and demonology texts had fallen onto its side and spilled its demonic-looking paraphernalia contents across the back of his ancient car. It was not the most appropriate reading matter for the son of a vicar; he grinned as he placed the research materials back in the box and closed the lid.

Demonology would have to wait till later. Bethany was not ready to face the realities of demon fighting in the twenty-first century. Richard swung his bulging rucksack over his back, as he followed the sign to Stillbone.

Ten minutes later his back throbbed painfully, the backpack seemed to have grown heavier with each step. He stopped for a minute and wiped the sweat from his forehead.

He was not as fit as he had hoped.

The path twisted upward. Richard panted as he hurried through the trees. The mist lifted and the birds woke. Their songs pierced the silent emptiness. Several took flight, alarmed as he stumbled against a hawthorn tree, its slender twigs cracked, snapping under his weight. Its brown-grey bark, knotted and fissured with age, felt rough under his touch. A thorn raked across the back of his hand. A drop of blood appeared and rolled unnoticed onto the tree. A cascade of small-lobed leaves fluttered onto the mud path.

In the distance, almost hidden by the trees, Richard saw a tiny grey stone building, lying within a steep grass valley, carved into the woodlands.

His skin prickled as he felt hidden eyes boring into his back. There was something in the silent woods watching him. It had smelled his blood and was hungry.

'Hold it together,' he whispered to himself. Paranoia was just a manifestation of fear. It was not real, and it would not impress Bethany. He followed a little stone pathway towards the church entrance, the cracks between the stones, alive with curling dandelion leaves and tall grasses.

Stillbone Chapel was a miniature version of the Church of St Anthony, surrounded by a gathering of ancient trees which dwarfed the little chapel.

The chapel's grey brick walls were speckled with white. Its vivid stain glass windows were cut squarely into the church's body and decorated with diagonal lead work.

No armed angels protected this church.

Richard scurried down the path and through the overgrown lawn surrounding the little chapel. On either side of the path were tall gravestones, bent with age, and covered in shades of rusted orange and bright green moss. Each grave had been dug so that its occupant faced towards the path. It was almost as if their spirits could rise from their graves and follow the path into the safety of the church. He shivered as a cold wind blew across the graveyard. Even the dead needed protecting in this valley.

Something wicked had happened here.

He should not have come here.

He was drawn to places of evil. He always had been. It was his curse. Richard sighed. He dropped his backpack onto the grass and opened the half-stable door of the porch leading to a stout oak door, which protected the entrance of the church. The heavy door groaned as it swung open. Richard flicked a light switch by the door. The gloomy interior of the chapel was bathed in white light.

Miraculously, the building had electricity.

The walls of the tiny chapel towered above Richard. Once they had been whitewashed, but over the centuries the white had faded to a yellowing cream. Its miniature nave consisted of four rows of paired hard wooden pews, which faced the five steps, leading up to a wooden altar. The altar table was covered in a clean white linen cloth, protected by a single wooden rail.

There were no plaques for the dearly departed or cut flowers to bring joy or life to this chapel. Its smell reminded Richard of a second-hand bookshop, musty with a tinge of sadness, for treasures long discarded. The church was an echo of Christianity from long ago. Richard could feel the ancient paths of worshippers echo through the chapel. He was stepping into the footsteps of those who had passed.

Quietly, Richard slid through the door to the right, which led from the nave, hoping his presence would not disturb anything resting in the chapel.

Richard stared at the room in confusion as he found himself in what appeared to be a 'Doomsday Prepper' survivalist camp. He felt an overpowering urge to ping his elastic band but had to make do with pinching the skin of his wrist instead.

Bethany's secret office was seven feet wide but ran along the entire length of the church. Opposite him was an empty desk and a fold-up chair, their presence dominated by a huge pinboard covered with tattered, curling newspaper clippings, photographs, and black and white line drawings. Red wool lines ran between the pictures like a spider's web. In the centre of the board, was a picture of him, ripped from the parish magazine declaring his appointment as the new North Devon church networks Children's and Youth Leader. Over his face, scratched in dying biro, someone had drawn a triangle with elongated lines. He shivered as a cold sensation crawled up his spine.

Richard looked around Bethany's secret headquarters. At the far end of the room, was a camp bed, stove, and tins of food stacked up against the wall.

A sudden wave of tiredness hit him, and he collapsed into the sagging bed.

***

Richard woke with the gentle touch of sunlight warming his face. He checked his watch and groaned. It was eleven-thirty. He had slept the morning away. Gingerly, he swung his legs from the camp bed, the movement sent shoots of pain through his spine, and he twisted around trying to unlock his body.

The low midday sun cast shortened, crisscrossed shadows across the wooden floor. Richard walked the two feet to the camp stove and helped himself to a cup of tea, poured some *'Heinz baked beans with pork sausages in a rich tomato sauce'* into a mess tin, and watched as it bubbled on the stove.

Fortified with his delicious brunch, complete with some *Rich Tea* biscuits, he had found tucked away in an old cake tin, Richard went back to examine the board. The answer to the murders had to be located somewhere within Bethany's cobweb.

Little natural light reached the near end of the room and the details of the map were darkened. He flicked a light switch. Instantly. the room began to buzz with electricity and glowed white.

Richard froze.

He had not turned the chapel lights off before he had

accidentally dozed off.

Someone had visited the church while he had slept. Perhaps it had been Bethany? He shook his head. He was in doubt Bethany would have woken him up and given him a few stern words about sleeping on the job.

Richard could hear no sirens or shouts from angry villagers. Therefore, whoever had visited him had kept his location secret. Perhaps to come back and kill him later?

He dismissed the thought.

Anyone who wanted him dead could have just turned the gas stove on while he slept. Fatal accidents were the best way to cover up awkward deaths. He had learnt that from his time in London.

It must have been Bethany.

Richard drained his mug and stared at the pin-board. The faces of the missing clergy stared back.

He recognised several of the faces. A ripped newspaper article showed a smiling John Sparke, standing next to the Ashcrofts, in front of Armitage Hall. A locket pinned to the board held a miniature portrait of Richard Dicken, his black hair neatly tied back with a black bow, painted sometime prior to his abduction from the Nod by an older Ashcroft and his men.

Some faces he did not recognise.

On a page carefully cut from a book was the circular picture of a rosy-cheeked young man with doleful brown eyes and white powdered hair, dressed in a black coat with silver-coloured buttons, opened to reveal a grey waistcoat. Richard bent forward to decipher Bethany's spider-writing – 'Charles

Blackmore, painted while a student at Jesus College, Oxford.' Richard swallowed as he recognised the cluster of medieval spires piercing the background of the painting. Blackmore had been the second curate to go missing from St Anthony's. He had taken his dog, Percy, for its early morning walk through Elfsworthy Wood.

Neither had been seen again.

A stern face stared out of the board at him, intelligent eyes piercing through the woodcut print. His face surrounded by a high white, ruffled collar. Underneath the picture, Bethany had scribbled, – 'Reverend Zacheus Versey, disappeared 1620, buried in a plague pit, w. of Witherleigh'. Beside this information was a big red question mark.

One red wool strand, ran from each of the faces of the missing curates, to his photograph in the centre of the board.

Richard traced the remaining strands with his finger. They flew across the board to pictures of Armitage Hall, the Happy Chicken monopoly, and a strangely pristine spreadsheet of monthly church offerings.

He checked the dates and nodded in admiration, as he found Bethany's pattern.

The meagre church offerings rose considerably around the time of each vanishing, only to reduce slowly over the following years.

These were offerings to ease guilty consciences, but his father's God could not be bought.

Richard scanned the faces of the more modern photographs and frowned. Everyone had a logical reason given for their absence, under which Bethany had written in angry capital

214

letters, 'NO POLICE REPORTS.'

None of the modern curates had been reported as missing.

Richard checked the note pinned beneath Sparke's photograph. The reason for his disappearance was that he had run off to France with a blonde shop girl from Temperley. Apparently, he had even sent his stepfather a postcard from Vézelay.

Richard touched the photo of Sparke and shook his head. This was a wall of men whose lives were lost and forgotten. He closed his eyes, clasped his hands together, and prayed that the lost curates would find peace.

There was a scratching sound.

'Oh Christ!' Richard murmured and stared at the board.

The lost faces began to bulge from beneath their frames.

Richard took a step backwards as the tormented faces of the lost, tried to push their way through the paper boundaries. The pictures stretched to their limit and some began to tear open. Richard could see the contours of the curates skulls, eye sockets, and their open mouths pressed up against their captured images.

The monochrome photograph of a fresh-faced, young man in military uniform, with a bright white dog collar, ripped in two. A light grey negative of the young man in the photograph, thrust his hands through his picture, and tried to strangle Richard.

Richard pulled away from the grey hands and tumbled backwards, falling heavily against the polished, wooden floor.

The remaining trapped faces silently screamed from behind their photographs, twisting their faces from side to side, as they tried to escape their paper prison.

The army Padre reached inside his boot, pulled out a thin bladed knife, and slashed through his portrait.

The silver knife glinted in the light of the naked bulb. The Padre dropped the knife, which clattered against the floor. The blade dissolved into a puddle of silver, which ran between the cracks of the wooden floorboards, and disappeared.

The grey image of the Padre slid onto the chapel floor. His eyes were completely black, and his head twitched from side to side, as he crawled with preternatural speed towards the prostrate figure of Richard.

'Find… my… bones,' the Padre hissed, as he loomed over Richard. The Padre's hands circled Richard's neck and squeezed. 'You must help me before it is too late. I can feel my soul darken.'

Richard grabbed at the hands, trying to tear them from his neck, but his fingers fell through the tightening hands.

'Let me live and I will help you,' Richard promised as the pressure on his neck increased. He felt his vision fade to black. His hands dropped from his neck as he thudded unconscious against the floor.

***

Richard shivered in the cold as the room faded in and out of view. A sharp pain drilled through the centre of his forehead. Tentatively, he touched his neck and winced as his fingers examined the bruises around his throat. He sat up and the room spun in circles. Eventually, the room stabilized, and Richard staggered to his feet.

Every face in Bethany's collection was blurred. The colour drained from each picture. Drips of black ink had run down the board and pooled on the wooden floor. Sprawled across every inch of the board in handwriting ranging from the finest copperplate to the worst doctors' scrawl were the words, 'Find our bones'.

A sudden breeze rushed through the chapel and the stable door slammed shut. Richard ran into the nave and swore.

The chapel walls had altered. They were now covered with fading brown spots and wrapped in huge, pale spiderwebs. A thick grey dust carpeted the floor. Several of the pews lay broken and a set of footprints recorded in the dust, walked from the pin-board to the chapel doors.

Something, which had been sharing the chapel with him, had been released.

Richard shivered. 'Perhaps it was a protective spirit,' he whispered to himself, but even he did not believe it.

He stood up and doubled over in pain, clutching his stomach. A faint outline appeared on his T-shirt. He lifted the shirt and stumbled backwards in shock. A series of strange, symbols made of circles and lines had been scratched across his stomach. They looked more like runes than letters. Either way he could not decipher the marks.

Richard ripped a piece of the under sheeting from the camp bed and wrapped it several times around his waist as a makeshift bandage. Then painfully pulled his sweatshirt over his shirt to hide the lumpy appearance and whispered, 'I promise that I will find your bones.'

217

CHAPTER SEVENTEEN

Richard scribbled a note to Bethany, warning her not to enter the chapel, and pinned it on the oak door. He threw his rucksack over his back and stood listening to the sounds of the valley. A howling wind ran through the encroaching woodland, knocking the empty tree branches together. The wind carried a faint voice. Something was calling to him from beyond the great elm, whose spreading branches dominated the eastern corner of the chapel grounds.

A dead branch thudded onto the grass. Alarmed, a rook cawed and flew away, hidden in the cloudy sky. Richard walked over to the elm. Behind the tree was a stone wall, its topmost stones covered with waving grasses, and spreading ivy leaves that fluttered in the wind. The wall nearest the chapel had partially collapsed, its stones spilling onto a narrow, muddy pathway.

The voice called again.

Richard followed the meandering path into the woodlands. He held his hands above his head, for fear of being ensnared by the waist high growth of stinging nettles. Above the nettles, the whitebeams were turning golden. They brushed against him. Their clusters of tiny red berries danced up and down on their emptying branches as he passed.

Richard walked onwards, following the contours of the valley. He did not know where he was going; but if there was something in the woods, he was certain that it would find him. Gingerly, he touched his stomach and winced. Some ghosts had been trapped in Witherleigh for far too long. They needed to pass into the *Mortalis* before they accidentally killed him, with their pleas for aid.

After an hour of walking, the path opened out onto one of the one-car Devon lanes which terrified its city-dwelling visitors. The road was dwarfed by hedgerows which leant over and scratched their initials on the unwelcome visitors' cars. Beyond the hedges were patchworks of fields coloured in earthen shades.

A cow mooing in the distance told Richard he was nearing civilisation once more. He continued to walk down the lane. It was splattered in wet, red mud. He circumnavigated the more pronounced piles of mud; in case they were not comprised solely of mud.

The lane led to a three-way crossroads.

The towering white signpost was situated on a green mound of grass. The signpost's left arm stated 'Witherleigh 3 miles' to the left, while its right declared, 'Quarterley-in-the-moor 11 miles'. Another, off-centre arm stated 'Stillbone Chapel – unfit for cars.'

Richard had never heard of Quarterley-in-the-moor. However, he imagined it comprised of a small cluster of derelict, rainswept, moorland farms. It was not a place he would go out of his way to visit. The name 'Raymes Cross' ran up the trunk of the crossroads.

The name was vaguely familiar. Richard closed his eyes as he tried to remember, where he had heard it before.

'Of course,' he smiled.

It had been mentioned in the leather-backed book of old Devon folklore, Reverend Anderson had insisted on letting him borrow at their first meeting in the manse. Mrs White had not been pleased, that one of the manse's library treasures, had been removed. However, the Reverend had thrust the volume in his hand stating, 'Read this Richard, and use the knowledge well.' He had thought it most odd at the time but then the Reverend was odd most of the time.

Richard's smile faded as he remembered Raymes was old Devonian for a body or skeleton.

He placed his backpack on the grass and waited.

The wind started in the trees.

Their branches shook, and leaves chimed together and fell onto the lane, surrounding Richard in a swirling golden cloud. While the grass around the bottom of the mound sparkled white, covered in a sudden frost, as the convergence opened.

A spirit was coming.

Richard shivered in the cold and prayed for strength. He unzipped his backpack and removed a crumpled Tesco's carrier bag.

The signpost blurred as it slipped from focus.

Richard wiped the sweat from his eyes. The signpost reappeared.

'Good day to you!' Nathaniel Turner sat leaning against the white post and grinned up at Richard.

'Damn!' Richard's face fell.

'Well, that's a fine greeting. I must say!' Nathaniel replied.

Richard blushed.

'I'm so sorry, I was just expecting a different ghost.'

'Aye,' replied Nathaniel. 'You be wanting one of those fancier types of clerical ghosts. All of they as mad as a hatter.'

Richard nodded. 'They sent me a message.'

He lifted his T-shirt and showed Nathaniel his stomach.

'Judas!' Nathaniel leant forward and squinted at the black symbols.

'Do you know what it says?' Richard asked. 'The message was jumbled in the crossing.'

'It looks to me like writing.' Nathaniel said as he shrugged his shoulders.

'But can you read it?' Richard asked.

'Probably not.' Nathaniel said, shaking his head.

'Well, can you at least try?' Richard sighed.

'I can… but I couldn't read my letters that well when I was alive, an' being dead don't help you see things too clearly,' he shrugged. He reached out to touch Richard's stomach.

Richard shivered uncomfortably as icy hands traced the symbols across the stomach.

'You can't read, can you?' Richard said pulling away from the ghost.

'Not a mark,' Nathaniel replied and grinned at Richard.

He nodded to the bag.

'So, you here to bury my bones all Christianlike and send me upstairs?'

Richard nodded. He could not be sure which way a

convicted highwayman would travel after his earthly liberation, so he thought it best to remain silent.

'I'm down there.' Nathaniel pointed to a grassy triangle of scrubland, separated from the field which Richard had just walked down, by a browning hedgerow.

'They hanged me, then left my body to rot in an iron gibbet over there for a month. Until one of the landowners complained the smell was turning his milk bad.' Nathaniel glared over to where the lone cow sung. 'Then they cut me down an' buried my bones without so much as a prayer. It was that magistrate, Judge Ashcroft, an' his men, that did for my soul.' Nathaniel began to twist his fingers around his shirt tails.

Richard shook his head. 'I promise I will pray over your bones.'

Richard took a folding spade from the plastic bag and walked over to the spot Nathanial had pointed to. He began to dig. The spade barely dented the topmost layer of grass. The ground was as hard as iron. Richard sighed. He fervently hoped the bones had not been buried too deeply.

The countryside flickered.

Its colours bled away until the landscape turned to grey.

***

A tall, wooden pillar with a lighter horizontal crossbeam appeared from the greyness and loomed over Richard. A man-sized black cage dropped from a wooden crossbeam. Nathaniel screamed and clawed at the soil, as an unseen force picked him up, and sucked him back inside the gibbet.

Nathaniel's clothes weathered to black rags which flapped

around his grey limbs. His dark brown hair became plastered to the flesh which was dripping from his face. A hungry buzzard swooped down and plucked an eye from the decaying skull. The bird stared at Richard for a minute, its eyes glowing amber through the greyscale, and flew off into Elfsworthy Woods.

Richard was left in the cold, grey world of the dead.

The sounds of the cattle and wild bird song were dulled. The only sound Richard could hear was the beating of his own heart which throbbed too loudly in his ears. Richard looked at Nathaniel's body sagging in the metal confines of the gibbet. He felt a dull ache grow in his chest.

No one deserved to die like that.

The gibbet creaked as it began to rock slowly from side to side. Electromagnetic pulses, flashes of brightness in the gloom, emitted tiny electric sparks which popped and crackled around Richard.

The sound of fleeing feet ran past him. He turned and squinted into the greyness, trying to locate where they had come from.

A blurred shadow moved in the distance, running down the road from Witherleigh. It flickered in and out of Richard's sight.

Richard frowned as he recognised the Jesus College gown which flapped behind the figure, and an ominous feeling fluttered in his chest. A group of grey villagers seemed to be chasing him. The tallest villager leapt feline-like onto the back of the fleeing man.

Both fell struggling to the floor. The man's square cloth hat fell, lost among the hedgerows. Two thick set villagers grabbed the writhing man by the shoulders and dragged him to his knees.

'Good morrow to thee, Reverend Versey, sir, you seem in such a hurry to leave our godly hamlet.' A hooded figure shuffled forward from the gang of villagers.

An icy wind blew. Richard shivered and zipped up his jacket.

The hood loosened to reveal an elderly woman. Her skin wound tightly around her skull; her cheeks pinched with hunger. She was dressed in brown rags, her long grey hair falling in rattails around her stooped shoulders.

'There is nothing godly in this hamlet, witch!' the vicar replied. 'I will report thee to the witchfinder and thee will be tried for witchcraft and sentenced to hang for thy crimes.'

'But I am a healing woman. A white witch. I use my potions to heal and help the infirm,' the old woman retorted.

'Lies! The devil take thee, she-witch. I have seen thee serve offerings to summon the devil from the depths of hell.'

'And that will be thy's undoing,' she hissed.

The witch covered her head with the hood of her threadbare cloak. She leant forward and touched Versey's face. 'Thy will make a goodly offering.'

'Begone, she-devil,' Versey cried as he tried to twist away from her touch.

The witch laughed. 'Bring him alive and unbloodied,' she ordered the villagers. The two burly villagers grabbed Versey by each arm. The rest of the grey villagers retreated to the safety of a spreading oak tree. Some of the women clutched their thick woollen shawls to their long dresses, as they whispered fearfully to each other and shook their heads.

The Reverend jerked his shoulder forward.

The larger villager, wearing a torn brown coat, lost their grip on his shoulder, and tumbled forward onto the muddy track.

Versey turned and punched his remaining captor in the face. There was a sickening crack as cartilage splintered and blood streamed from his nose. The villager crumpled onto the track.

Freed from his captors, the Reverend ran towards Raymes Cross.

A single musket shot rang out through the countryside.

The vicar dropped to his knees, a thin trail of blood spilling from his mouth. Versey crawled towards Richard, his lips moving silently in prayer. His eyes widened momentarily, and he fell forward into the dirt. His fingers traced the sign of the cross into the mud and then relaxed.

'You slack-brained fool!' the witch screamed. She slapped the watchman's face. 'You will die by your own musket. I have seen it.'

The watchman looked at the witch in horror and turned and fled back towards the village.

***

'That fool will die before the day is out.' The witch stated.

The villagers stopped whispering and lowered their gazes, hoping not to be caught in the witch's curse.

'No blood can be spilt. He is a spoilt offering. Captain Ashcrofte, leave no trace behind.'

'Yes, goodwife Whyte.' Captain Ashcrofte bowed and barked at his men. 'Pick up the corpse. We will retire to the hall and there you will all feel the lash for your stupidity.'

The witch laughed at the men's unease. She picked up

the tattered lengths of her skirts and skipped back towards Witherleigh.

***

The scene flickered as the greyscale was replaced with the technicolour hues of autumn. Birdsongs tweeted from the hedgerows and the air smelt of damp earth. Richard scanned the trees. The gibbet was gone, replaced by sprawling green shrubs and a golden leaf fall.

Turner had disappeared. Dragged back into the lonely wanderings of those souls lost in the *Mortalis*, those whose journey into the afterlife had not been blessed. Richard knelt in front of the crossroads and said a prayer for the Reverend's soul.

A car beeped and skidded to a halt behind him.

Richard turned and groaned as he recognised the shining BMW. Startled, a flock of rooks flew from their perches and circled the sky in a cacophony of caws and flapping wings.

An electric window slid downwards.

'Hello Richard!' Anderson shouted in a pitch slightly higher than usual.

'What on earth are you doing out in the middle of nowhere with a spade… Burying bodies or digging for treasure?' The vicar laughed heartily at his own joke.

Richard blushed and quickly put the shovel back in its bag. In the corner of his eye, he saw a decaying tree stump, its sides decorated in golden brown, saucer-like fungi and grinned. 'I'm foraging for mushrooms.' Richard nodded towards the tree.

The Reverend smiled. 'Ah, I see… All part of God's good bounty.'

He stared at Richard for a second. 'I have some bad news, I'm afraid. I'm just driving back from Raymes Farm. I have been giving spiritual council to Primrose, Mrs White's sister. Poor Violet passed peacefully in the night. Dr Ashcroft thinks it was probably a heart attack, as that was what took her mother before her. Jump in!' the vicar said, opening the passenger side door for Richard.

'That's awful!' said Richard, climbing into the seat and hugging his backpack as he tried to avoid the Reverend's gaze.

'She was a dedicated church woman, quite plain, but well-endowed. I will have to eat at the Nod until the diocese sends me a new housekeeper.' The vicar glanced at Richard in the mirror. 'Where shall I drop you, young man?' he enquired.

'Stillbone Chapel, please, my car's there,' Richard replied to the Reverend's raised eyebrow.

'Hmm… I'm glad to see you turning to God in your time of mental crisis, but that is not a place you should be visiting,' the Reverend replied. 'If you wish I can open St Anthony's up for you to pray in. You will have to have a shave and shower first, of course.'

'Er, thank you,' Richard replied not wanting to go anywhere near St Anthony's and its demon.

'Oh yes, I still haven't had time to ring your father yet, do you think you can cope? The church could do with your father's donations for a little while longer. The roof is in such a terrible state.'

Richard nodded, 'That's fine. I'm feeling a lot better now, thank you.'

'Excellent.' The Reverend beamed and accelerated

down the lane.

***

Three minutes later, the Reverend dropped Richard in the little clearing, next to his parked car, with the advice to go and visit Dr Ashcroft at the earliest opportunity. The doctor seemed extremely concerned about his wayward mental patient's whereabouts and safety.

Richard nodded and smiled at the vicar, which seemed to please Anderson. The vicar waved at Richard through the open window of his BMW, as he sped off down the lane.

Richard waved back. He had no intention of going anywhere near the good doctor.

Richard was about to get into his battered old car when he noticed a note had been shoved under one of his windscreen wipers. It was a small piece of cream paper, folded precisely down the middle and could only be from one person. He grinned as he extracted the note, imagining Bethany's hands caressing the paper. He opened it, read the note, and flushed.

'Meet me at St Anthony's 10 pm. It was the last sighting of Versey. This time don't screw it up. B. X'

Flashbacks of lights moving around the church filtered through his brain.

The armed angels standing guard in the stained windows around the church's perimeter had failed to contain the demon. However, St Anthony's had been the demon's cage for over four hundred years. Over time, the demon had begun to loosen its seals and walk freely through the village, but it would return to the church as soon as it felt her presence.

Bethany would be walking into the demon's lair. He had to arrive early and warn her. Richard looked at his watch. It was five. He had plenty of time to prepare. Richard felt his stomach flutter. She had signed the message with a 'X'. It was an uppercase kiss.

She must like him.

Richard jogged back to the little chapel and placed the hemp bags liberated from his caravan in the church porch. He was not too sure about the religious protocols for placing demon-repelling gris-gris bags in a church, but they had stopped the evil spirits from entering his caravan and hoped they would do so again. Next, he poured some water from Bethany's stores into the oval washing-up bowl, stripped, and washed himself with a dishcloth which smelt faintly lemony. He shaved and splashed on some expensive looking aftershave, a present from his mother last Christmas. A decision he instantly regretted as he felt the first layer of his skin explode.

***

Half an hour later, Richard was parked in a mud-covered layby cut out from a browning, stubble-filled field, just outside Witherleigh.

The overflowing hedgerows hid most of the layby from all but passing traffic. From what Richard knew of Witherleigh, there would be little traffic on a Friday evening. Most people would be either safely locked into their farmhouses or drinking at the Nod.

Richard opened his car boot and took some phials of holy water and the *Triangulum* from his box and put them in his backpack. Next, he pressed a panel in the plastic mouldings located in the left side of his boot. The panel sprung open to reveal a wooden stake, a blowpipe complete with a selection of brightly coloured feathered darts, and a silver switch-blade knife, which he slipped into the back pocket of his jeans.

He zipped up his grey hoody and heaved the bulging backpack onto his shoulders. Then disappeared down the darkening road towards a splattering of yellow lights, shining dimly amid the greyness of the village.

A rustle of feathers swished past his head. Richard ducked down behind a shaking fern and squinted up into the sky. An owl silhouetted against the moonlit clouds circled above him, searching the fields and woods for its dinner. No amber eyes pierced the grey.

Richard breathed a sigh of relief and walked briskly towards the deserted village square.

The square was ringed by four streetlights, their pale light barely stretching to the end of the pavement in front of them. The Ashcrofts' Range Rover sat next to a ragged selection of ancient cars, straddling two parking spaces.

The pub door opened, a raft of loud voices and male laughter cut through the silent air. Richard stayed in the shadows and watched as two giggling young men wearing baggy, checked shirts, which hung over their jeans, fell into the street, and wobbled unsteadily towards their car.

Richard shook his head. He pitied anything they met on the lanes back to their farm.

The door to the Nod closed, and the world went silent. He ducked beneath the flower-lined windows and walked briskly past the pub.

St Anthony's Church stood illuminated in the darkness by its cross, back lit with a white light, which glowed like a beacon of Christianity in the sky. The strength of a thousand years of worship emanated from its ancient walls.

Richard smiled as he felt its silent power.

The pavement in front of him, brightened as electric sparks exploded around him. A slight breath of ice-tinged wind blew against his face.

Richard swallowed and stood still, hoping to blend into the night, as a hunched, thickset man appeared.

The man's pale blue eyes shone unnaturally in the light of the cross, as he wandered down the street grumbling to himself. 'Where's me wife, Martha? Selling 'er cheeses all dolled up like a bloody whore. Wait 'til the bus comes in. I'll teach 'er to make a cuckold of I.'

Richard watched as Snowy turned towards the market square bus stop and stood glaring at the old Temperley road. He crept quietly towards the church, hoping not to attract the attention of Snowy's unpredictable ghost.

Footsteps ran towards him through the darkness.

Richard spun round as the diminutive figure of a young girl appeared behind him, holding the weather-beaten Barbie doll by the straggling remains of its once platinum-blonde hair.

Richard crouched down and smiled. 'Hello little girl, I recognise that doll, it's very… er… special. Are you lost?'

The girl looked up.

Richard leapt backwards. His back pressed tightly against the coldness of the church railings.

'Christ almighty! What happened to you?' he exclaimed. His heart pounding inside his chest.

The girl's appearance had been frozen at her time of death.

Her face was covered in deep, black scratches. Two black hollows stared up at him. Her eyes had been ripped from their sockets. She held her Barbie out to Richard. The sleeves of her pink pinafore dress rose to reveal a series of parallel cuts crossing her pale grey arms.

'Did the Ashcrofts do this to you?' he whispered.

The girl moved her head to one side, so her ear touched her shoulder, and stared at Richard.

She dropped the doll on the pavement. The corners of her mouth drooped, and her body began to shake as a gurgling sound welled-up from her chest.

Richard looked at the little doll.

Its features ran together to make an expressionless, amorphous, plastic blob. It was revolting but harmless. He picked it up and handed it back to the crying child.

The doll exploded in flames. Its plastic melting into his flesh.

Richard screamed and tried to shake the liquifying doll from his hand.

The girl threw her head backwards and laughed. Her high-pitched squeal deepened into a guttural growl.

Richard tore the doll from his hand with his free hand. The melted skin ripped, sending waves of pain through his body.

He collapsed forwards onto his knees in front of the girl, his hands falling against the pavement. Instantly, the pavement moved, and black bubbles began to form and burst on its surface.

The girl's eye sockets glowed amber in the darkness.

'Well, you are just one disappointment after another, aren't you?' said the voice of the demon. 'Have the decency to die quickly and leave us alone!'

The girl leapt forwards. Her hands grabbed each side of Richard's face as her thumbs pressed into his eyes. Richard's felt as if his eyes were going to burst from their sockets and tears of pain streamed down his face. The melted pavement collapsed, sinking slowly back into the earth. Richard's hands fell through the concrete, which instantly tightened around his wrists. The girl's thumbs pressed harder into his eyes.

In the distance, Richard heard a car slow down and park. The car door slammed shut.

'Oh God,' he moaned.

Bethany had arrived.

Richard tried to pull his hands from the pavement. The concrete tightened, as the strength was sucked from his body. He fell against the pavement. An unseen force lurking in the earth beneath him, began to pull his body downwards towards the *Abyss*. The little girl flew backwards and watched vacantly as Richard lay motionless on the path.

Bethany's footsteps rang through the air as she marched towards the church. Richard tried to raise his head from the melted pavement, but his body would not respond. He heard the heavy church gates clink open. His mind screamed a warning to Bethany.

The gate closed, and her footsteps faded away.

A wave of frost sparkled across the pavement.

'Hmm, I think you ought to get up, old man.' John appeared,

sitting cross-legged on the pavement in front of him.

'If you don't save yourself, you will die and so will she,' John whispered into his ear, as he nodded towards the church.

Richard nodded and focussed on his fingers. They flexed beneath the viscous concrete. Instantly, he was hit by an intense wave of pain.

'How dare you meddle in my affairs, Curate,' the girl screamed.

A storm of tiny electric orbs circled around the girl, casting an unnatural bright shadow against the pavement.

'Get up and run to the church,' John shouted, desperately trying to pull Richard to his feet. His hands fell through Richard's arms, his touch sent a shiver down Richard's back. It was as if something was walking over his grave.

Richard looked towards the church.

The saints glowed at him through the darkness. A strange tingling surged through his body and he felt the grip of the melting concrete loosen. Richard gritted his teeth and dragged his body slowly from the clasping concrete.

Instantly, the concrete hardened, and the pavement repaired itself.

His old vicar's frail voice broke through his thoughts. *'Be strong and courageous; do not be frightened or dismayed, for the Lord your God is with you wherever you go, Joshua 1:9.'*

'Yes, I hear you,' Richard whispered and staggered to his feet, one hand holding the iron railing for support, as he dragged his way towards the black church gates.

The metal felt hot under his touch.

'You will never make it,' the girl hissed.

Richard clung tightly to the fence and stared at the girl. 'Show me your real face, you coward.'

The girl roared. She flew towards Richard, her nails elongating to bony claws.

John leapt to his feet and flew at the girl.

Confused, the girl paused in mid-flight, her legs dangling in mid-air. John fell through the girl and tumbled to the pavement.

The girl laughed.

'Well, that is just embarrassing… little curate.' She jumped on top of him.

She landed, her pale legs astride John's chest, pinning his arms to the side of his body.

'You have no body, but I am not really interested in the flesh. I just want your spirit.'

The girl took a curved dagger from her pink wellington boot and cut a neat line across her left arm.

John turned his face towards Richard and mouthed the word 'Go.'

Richard nodded and pinched his wrist. There was nothing he could do to save John's soul. Silently, he dragged himself along the black railings.

Cursed black blood seeped from the cut; with her right hand she squeezed the droplets over the blade. She smiled and carved a triangle with elongated lines running across John's forehead.

'*Meus es tu*, you are mine,' the demon whispered in his ear. She stood up and grinned. Slowly, her head turned towards Richard. 'Well, aren't you going to say farewell to your friend? You have just damned his soul to an eternity of torture.'

Richard hesitated and turned as John's ghostly body rose inches from the pavement, hovered for a second, and then shattered, showering the pavement in soul shards. The shards melted as the fragments of his soul dripped downwards into the *Abyss*.

An icy wind made Richard shiver as he reached the main gate. He felt John's ghost disappear from the living world. Richard slammed the barred iron church gates shut. The girl flew at the gates. They flickered in greyscale and recoiled as the demon girl tried to push through. Then realigned themselves.

Overhead a dark cloud moved aside, and a beam of moonlight shone onto the church steeple. Slowly, the light moved up the spire reaching for the cross, which stood at the apex of the steeple. The moonlight hit the cross and instantly an explosion of light flashed around the church, Richard fell backwards, tumbling onto the grass verge.

The demon-girl was flung from the church gates and hurled through the darkness, landing on her hands and feet in the market square.

'Well, well, demon,' Richard said scrabbling to his feet as he looked the creature up and down, 'So, you can't break through the church's barrier without being invited, that's not really very impressive is it? You will have to try much harder to kill me. I hold the *Triangulum* – the book of the damned. I will destroy you and your hold on this village. I give you my word,' Richard promised.

'You might destroy this vessel, but I have more forms than you can comprehend, you ignorant little child. How many people will die as a result of your obsession? I see you have caused two deaths in Witherleigh in less than a fortnight. I only claim a few souls a century. So, who is truly the evil one?' the girl argued as her head rested against her shoulder. A pair of dark grey handprints encircled her neck.

'Talk to yourself, demon. I will not listen to your lies.' Richard turned his back on the demon and hobbled towards the church.

CHAPTER EIGHTEEN

The entrance to St Anthony's Church was barred by a skeleton frame door, which consisted of a framework of heavy black vertical metal bars, with a shiny silver handle incongruously fixed to the bar furthest to the right. Richard grasped the handle. It felt cold but not freezing. It had not come into contact with the electrical energy of the dead or the damned. Richard breathed a sigh of relief and opened the door.

The interior of the church was illuminated slightly, by the light cast from the soft floodlights, which beamed upwards onto the church building every night. The lights had the effect of highlighting certain areas, while other parts of the church remained hidden in the shadows.

The metallic threads of the gold altar cloth glinted under the floodlights. On top of the altar, was a simple wooden cross which overlooked the nave. Directly above the altar was the magnificent, eighteenth-century triple-stained glass window, which dominated the end of the nave. The triptych portrayed an image of Jesus dressed in a ruby robe, his head haloed in gold, standing over a cowering winged demon. His right hand raised as he banished the demon from the living world. Its bold colours shone brightly through the darkness and were reflected downwards dancing on the grey flagstone floor.

Ever since the earliest of times, when the Lord Creator divided the day into times of light and dark, the creatures of the darkness had fought to seize control of the light and rule the living world. It was an eternal battle. Only the faces of the combatants had changed. Richard knelt in front of the altar and prayed for assistance. No one important, just an angel from a minor host would do.

The church stood in sombre silence.

Two plain, white candles flickered and danced at either end of the altar. The hairs on the back of Richard's neck rose.

There was a rustling sound behind him. He spun around.

'Wow! You're as jumpy as a cat!' Bethany laughed as she waved a thin torch beam across Richard's face. 'Oh, what the hell happened to you? You look like you've just been crawling around in the dirt... again.'

Richard shifted his feet awkwardly. 'I tripped over on the pavement outside.'

'Hmm...' said Bethany. Her tone suggesting the matter would be more fully explored at a later date.

Quickly, Richard changed the subject. 'So, how did you find out about Versey? I thought his details were lost?'

'Well, that was true. He disappeared in the time of the great 1610 plague. I couldn't find another reference to him in the parish archives. However, any missing curate is definitely suspicious.' She eyed Richard defiantly.

'Definitely,' he nodded enthusiastically.

'And today Dr and Mrs Ashcroft came into the Nod for afternoon tea. They normally have the cream tea afternoon

239

special, with a double helping of scones for Dr Ashcroft and the new season's jam for Mrs Ashcroft. Unfortunately, along with every other crop this year, the bloody blackberry harvest failed. The blackberries are all overlarge, mushy, and tasteless. Chef Sheng can't make his jam and old man Strange had no Happy Chicken jam products in his store, so we had to buy a jar of the generic stuff from the store in Temperley and smuggle it in. Well, Mrs Ashcroft took one bite and spat it out in her napkin. Then she was screaming and saying how she would never set foot in the Nod again and almost had to be restrained by her husband. All over a pot of jam! It was just really embarrassing. Fortunately, me and the chef searched the kitchen larder and found some homemade blackberry jam hidden behind the flour jars.'

Bethany grinned.

'It smelled slightly dodgy – acidic with a touch of dirt. The chef scraped a layer of green mould off the top, mixed in some of the generic jam, so it tasted a bit less acidic and gave it back to her. Then she gobbled it all up. Stupid stuck-up bitch!'

'Versey?' Richard interjected, not really wanting to hear about incidences concerning either jam or scones.

'Well, once 'Jamgate' was over, I served them a complimentary pot of camomile tea and I overheard the doctor saying…'

She lowered her voice. 'He said that when he was rummaging through an old chest, that he'd found in the old servant's quarters, above the empty stable block, which Mrs Ashcroft wants to turn into a meditation room…'

Richard sighed.

Bethany glared at him. 'As I was saying, in the old chest were several documents dating from the early 1600s. One of them was a report from the vicar to The Most Reverend Gervase Babington, the archbishop of Exhaven, stating his curate had gone missing from his rooms at St Anthony's and…'

'Did you see the document?' Richard interrupted.

Bethany frowned at him.

'Don't be silly, of course not! He wouldn't have taken the letters with him to afternoon tea, would he? Ashcroft just said Versey had disappeared from the church… this church… and asked for a third scone. So, is his ghost here or what?'

'Not at the moment, but I saw him earlier today. Versey certainly wasn't anywhere near St Anthony's. He was being murdered on the old road crossing the moors up by Raymes Cross,' Richard replied.

'What?' said Bethany. 'But I know Ashcroft said it was St Anthony's, do you think he read the papers wrong, then?'

Richard shook his head and waited.

Bethany's brown eyes widened; a frown ran across her forehead. 'Shit! He lied to me. He must have realised we were working together, and that we would come to the church to try to communicate with Versey. But why the hell would he want us here…' She left the sentence hanging in the air. Her fingers whitened as she gripped the torch.

'It's a trap, isn't it? We need to get outta here now,' Bethany whispered as she turned to leave.

A tingling sensation, almost like an electrical charge ran through Richard's body.

'There's something here,' Richard whispered. He scanned

the church, his blue eyes sweeping across the illuminated areas as he searched the shadows.

The church felt quiet, but there was a faint iridescent glow in the darkness. Richard walked towards the altar. He pulled back the faded, T-shaped embroidered runner which ran up the centre of the nave, separating the two sides of the church.

'Got you,' he smiled as he knelt and beckoned Bethany to come over.

A large triangle with elongated lines had been carved into the hidden flagstone. A deep circle encompassed the points of the triangle.

'It's a demon trap,' he whispered.

Richard leant in closer to check the inside of the circle. No names had been branded into the stone. He touched the trap. There was no residue, demonic heat. The demon trap was empty.

He pointed at the carving as Bethany peered over his shoulder.

'Bloody hell!' Richard murmured. 'We just can't catch a break in this place. This demon trap was not sealed properly, the trap doesn't contain the demon's name. It wouldn't have held the demon for long.' He ran his hand through his hair. It stood on end.

'So, you're actually telling me that demons are real, and one was trapped in that stone?' Bethany whispered pointing to the demon trap.

'Of course.' Richard nodded gloomily. 'When they were cast out of heaven, the *Elisium*, and fell through earth into the *Abyss*, some clung on to this world with their teeth or dug their talons deep into the rocks. You can still see the marks they left on the land – the faults, the valleys, and the volcanoes, etcetera. To get the power they desired, the demons who stayed behind, promised weak-minded people anything they desired; material possessions, longevity, or skills they did not possess. However, bargains with demons never end well. They extract a heavy price for their promised aid. The one in Witherleigh must have been summoned over five hundred years ago. He has been receiving his payment ever since and he doesn't want to leave.'

'What payment?' Bethany asked, looking down at Richard, her hands on her hips. 'The villagers here are all broke. Most are on the social and anyway, how come no one has ever seen it? A vicious looking, winged creature like that one,' she pointed at the stained glass window, 'would get noticed even in Witherleigh.'

'Some people have seen him,' Richard replied grimly.

The barred door clunked against its stopper. The church was flooded in yellow electric candlelight as determined footsteps marched across the entrance hall, heading for the nave.

'But if he has sought solace in God, we should not disturb his prayers,' Reverend Anderson's voice echoed through the church.

'He is a danger to himself, you, and your flock. He needs complete rest and his medication,' Dr Ashcroft replied.

Bethany pushed Richard flat against the floor.

'You need to hide,' she hissed.

'But what about you?' Richard whispered.

'Oh, I'll be fine,' she said, with a smile tinged with sadness. 'I'm just a barmaid, no one even notices me.'

Richard nodded uncomfortably. 'Er… shall we meet up at your place as it's a lot closer. There's no point going back to the caravan and…'

'Just be quick about it, I go to bed at twelve,' Bethany interjected.

Richard went scarlet and nodded. 'OK. It's a date. I mean… er… not that sort of date, not a date at all really. More like a friendly meeting of er… friends or even colleagues.'

Richard's inner voice screamed at him to just keep quiet.

Richard half-smiled and reached out to touch Bethany on the shoulder but quickly withdrew his hand. He did not want to seem too forward.

Bethany looked down at Richard and shook her head. She opened her mouth to say something but then changed her mind.

The voices became louder.

'Stop talking nonsense and move it!' Bethany pushed Richard towards the altar, and he dived underneath the golden altar cloth.

'Well, well, it's Bethany the bossy barmaid.' Dr Ashcroft's voice echoed through the church as he strode up the nave. 'We are looking for your little friend. You know, the mad one who plays with dolls.' He paused for a moment. 'You do know that he suffers from paranoid schizophrenia, don't you? He thinks everyone is out to get him and even thinks that he sees ghosts.'

'But most people in Witherleigh have seen strange sights. I saw a ghost at the Nod,' Bethany said defiantly.

Dr Ashcroft shook his head sadly and turned to Reverend Anderson.

'You see, Godfrey? As I was explaining to you earlier, hysteria spreads like the plague. One person makes ludicrous statements, and the rest of the herd follows. We need to get him back safely into psychiatric care before he causes further damage.'

'But I have a responsibility to care for him. I promised his father,' Reverend Anderson pleaded.

'You have a responsibility to me and that's all that matters, vicar. I'm sure the diocese would be most interested in your nocturnal ministries,' Ashcroft growled.

The barred door opened again and moments later Police Constable Bates sauntered up the nave.

'Evenin' all. Everything alright 'ere then Doctor, Reverend,' PC Bates said, taking out his notepad.

Dr Ashcroft said nothing. He looked at his watch and back up at the policeman, who shuffled his feet uneasily.

'I came as soon as I could. There's been an incident in Temperley. Farmer White's cows broke through their 'edge an' walked through the Buttercup Estate mooin' at the top of thems voices. The townies thought they were goin' to be trampled to death. Bloody townies!' the wide policeman exclaimed, shaking his head.

'Oh, pardon my French, vicar, 'tis from havin' to associate with all them villains,' Bates explained.

Reverend Anderson nodded but said nothing.

'Ms Bond has broken into the church,' Dr Ashcroft snapped. 'Arrest her, then find that lunatic boyfriend of hers.'

His mobile rang. He waved one hand in the air to silence the group. After a series of heartfelt 'yeses,' he sighed and

245

announced, 'I have to go to Corner Cottage. Old Mrs Turner is having her palpitations again. A GP's work is never done.'

'Make sure you get that boy.' He glared at Bates, who stood scratching his left side whiskers with his pencil.

Bates nodded. 'Right you are then, Doctor!'

Ashcroft marched importantly from the church.

PC Bates took Bethany by the elbow and nodded at the vicar. 'Let's be out of 'ere, Bethany girl.'

'Are you arresting me, Bert?' Bethany frowned, pulling her arm from his grasp.

The policeman winked. 'Not if I can help it. Temperley station is closed for the night an' I ain't drivin' all the way to Exhaven an' then spendin' all night doin' paperwork. Just stay away from Dr Ashcroft. You don't want to make 'im mad.'

He escorted Bethany from the church.

Reverend Anderson shook his head and approached the transept. Richard crawled from the back of the altar. He heard the swish of cloth as the vicar walked past the altar and round to the lectern.

Glass chinked against wood.

Richard peered around the table. His eyes opened wide with surprise as he saw the Reverend sitting, his back propped against the lectern, drinking communion wine from the bottle, as he flicked through the pages of a black-fronted magazine entitled, '*Extreme Penance*, deluxe edition'.

After what seemed hours, Reverend Anderson stretched. The bottle of wine tipped over and red liquid glugged onto the ancient runner.

'Oh shit!' Anderson moaned. 'Red wine stains are a bugger

to remove. The Archbishop will nail my balls to the bloody wall if he hears I spilt wine on his precious bloody mat. Where did that bloody woman, God rest her soul, but the carpet stain remover.' Anderson staggered to his feet, flung the runner over the nearest pew, and walked unsteadily over to the church storage rooms.

Richard seized his chance. He tiptoed back to the church foyer and slipped through the porch gate.

The graveyard stretched before him.

He watched for a moment.

There was no movement.

The dead appeared to be resting quietly in the darkness. Richard walked quietly through the graves, hoping his presence would not disturb the more recently deceased. He had no desire to meet Mrs White again. She would undoubtedly find his mud-splattered appearance unChristian and most disappointing.

Richard shook the thoughts of Mrs White from his head. He had spent too long in the church. Streams of light burst through the navy clouds as the sun started its daily ascent. The songbirds began their morning chorus, only to be drowned by a shrieking cacophony, as the rooks left their roosts and circled the edge of the graveyard in a black, cawing mass.

Cold air brushed against his face. Richard wished he had brought his jacket with him. He had left it in the car in his rush to save Bethany.

The church gate was closed but unchained. Tentatively, Richard touched the black iron bars. The bars felt cold under his fingertips. He smiled with relief. The demon had moved on.

Richard hurried down the road, crossed the market square,

and disappeared into one of the narrow streets which radiated from the square. The terraced houses which lined the streets were old and haphazardly built in an array of different sizes. Some lurched to one side. Others had front doors so low to the ground, people had to bow to enter their interiors.

Illuminated beneath the pale orange glow of the scattered hooded streetlights, Richard could see several grey shadows crossing the street.

Richard stopped by a terraced cottage. An overlarge white china plate, stamped with the words 'Bishop's Nod', had been nailed to the wall, by the recessed front door, with the words 'Myrtle Cottage' sprawled across it in bright blue paint. Underneath were two overlarge, yellow flowers with long trumpeting heads. Richard was not sure what type of flora a myrtle was, but he felt sure that it probably did not look like a daffodil. However, he was not going to tell that to the rather prickly, present lodger.

The Victorian sash windows of the little cottage were small, their lower windowsills lined with clay flowerpots. The two upper windows peered out from underneath a heavy, thatched roof. Unlike the rest of the terrace, the cottage had resisted the white-washed glow, so inappropriate for countryside living. It had been painted a light mud-orange, and was camouflaged by a naked tree, its fragile twigs criss-crossing in front of the house. The strip of dirt separating the cottage from the road was filled with dwarf bushes in various stages of life. The tiny front garden was barely visible, as the shadows began to lengthen. The night air seemed to become heavier; darker and more dense.

Richard shivered as the temperature plummeted.

'I know you are there, reveal yourself, spirits,' he demanded.

A dozen ashen faces peered at him from the shadows.

'An' a good evenin' to you, Master Radcliffe.' Nathaniel Turner bowed and stepped out from the shadows.

Richard was relieved to see he had retaken his pre-death form.

'Good evening to you, Master Turner, and how can I be of service?' Richard asked with a confidence he did not possess.

There were darker, faceless shapes in the shadows too. Richard did not know who or what they were, but he wanted to appear in control of the situation, and not panic the gathering of ghosts.

'Well, we was just talkin' an' noted that a hell hole was opened last night, an' John the curate was thrown down into the *Abyss*, to suffer eternal damnation, even though 'ee never did nobody any 'arm an' you was meant to be findin' his bones an' sendin' him off up into the *Elisium*.'

A series of groans and wails came from the shadows which bulged out towards him.

Richard took a step backwards. 'Look! I'm trying my very best here. I know you want to rest in peace, but it isn't that easy. Someone summoned a demon and has held it trapped in the church for more than half a millennium. Over that time, it must have grown too strong to be held by an unsealed demon trap and has broken loose.'

'So, are you goin' to fight it an' send it back to whence it came?' Nathaniel asked.

'Er… I tried to but it was too strong. John sacrificed his

soul to save my life.'

'Judas!' said Nathaniel. 'Then all hope is truly lost.' His blue eyes stared into the distance.

'Did 'ee hear that?' Snowy appeared next to Richard. 'We are all goin' to be taken away by demons. I'll never see me Mary again, an' it's all 'ee's fault.' He lunged at Richard.

A gust of wind knocked Richard from his feet and threw him against a mud-stained car, parked with its left side wheels balancing halfway up the pavement. A high-pitched alarm screamed through the night. Dogs began to bark, and upstairs lights flashed yellow in the night.

'Behold a legion of demons is coming!' Richard Dicken's wide-eyed face appeared in the shadows, his hair waving around his head. 'Take sanctuary in St Anthony's. Tis our only hope for salvation! Make haste! Make haste!' he screamed and faded from Richard's sight.

The remaining ghosts howled in agreement.

The wind picked up the howl and spread it from the village to the outlying fields and into the woods.

The remainder of Dicken's body materialised. He ran from the shadows down the tiny road heading towards the main square and the church. The wind increased as he ran, sweeping errant leaves and discarded papers into the air and carrying them through the village.

CHAPTER NINETEEN

The rippling, dark shadow covering the front of Myrtle Cottage fractured, as the ghosts stampeded after the hysterical curate. Nathaniel pushed Richard to the ground. They crouched behind a quivering garden fence as the panicking ghosts fled. In their wake, a frozen wind howled through the village, tearing at everything in its path. Unlatched gates swung open, slammed shut again, and were thrown open once again by the next gust.

The trees dotted around the village began to groan. Their branches, caught by the increasing wind, rattled against cottage windows, as if knocking to be allowed in. Heavily swollen black clouds appeared in the early morning sky.

In the distance, the electrified sky awoke, and thunder rumbled across the moorland.

The dark blue tones of the early morning took on an eerie blood red glow.

Nathaniel glanced up at the sky. A frown crossed his boyish face. 'Judas! Come on Richard, inside with you, quickly. The sky is beatin' a funeral march, an' it can't be yours just yet!'

'Er… thanks. I think!' Richard shouted, over the screaming wind. He stood, holding onto the wooden fence for support.

One by one, the fence panels were ripped from the ground

and thrown high into the air. Richard staggered as a gust of wind pounded at his chest, sucking the air from his body. The wind tossed him against the remaining fence post and howled down the lane.

Richard held onto the post as he braced himself for the next gust.

A mechanical whir came from somewhere within the red-tinged darkness.

Hidden in the early morning light, a green four-wheel drive, its headlights dimmed, crawled to a halt in front of the cottage. Emblazoned across the driver's door was an extremely large, beaming yellow chicken.

The car doors opened, and two squat men, as wide as they were tall, climbed out. They wore identical green raincoats with a picture of a very happy chicken, drinking a pint of cider on their right breasts. Underneath, Richard could just make out the words, 'Witherleigh Scrumpy Makers Est. 1770'.

'Oh Christ!' Richard groaned as he edged nearer the cottage wall.

'Well, well… we've been looking all over for you, sunshine…' The older man lounged against the car and stared at Richard.

'Dr Ashcroft wants to 'ave a little word in your shell-like. Seems you're off yer meds and off yer 'ead. Seeing all sorts of weird shit. Disturbing the manor, as it were.'

A streak of lightning ripped across the sky and Witherleigh flashed white. A second later thunder rolled across the sky.

The younger man looked skywards. 'Bloody hell! We need to get inside. It's gonna piss down any second, Frank.'

'Do not let the squire's men take you away, for they are brigands and mean to do you grievous harm. They have the look of murder,' Nathaniel whispered in Richard's ear.

'Get 'im, Kai!' the older man ordered.

The driver's door, caught by a gust of wind flung open, creaking on its hinges, and blocked Richard's path.

Richard stepped backwards, away from the car door.

The younger man leapt from the passenger seat and ran around the car boot, looming menacingly behind Richard. The man grabbed hold of Richard's shoulder, his sausage-like fingers pressing down into the sinewy muscle.

Richard tried to pull away but was trapped between the man mountain and the open car door.

A horizontal line of blue-white light flashed across the sky and smashed into the roof of Myrtle Cottage. The chimney stack exploded, and the chimney shards rained onto the street.

A roll of thunder rumbled across the sky.

One of the fragments taken up by the wind, flew across the front of the cottage, and sliced through Frank's face. He screamed, clutching his cheek as blood poured through his fingers. Frank collapsed back into the car seat, desperately hunting through the glove pocket for anything to apply pressure to the dripping cut.

The noise distracted Kai. He loosened his hold on Richard.

Richard twisted and dropped to the ground.

The man was left holding nothing but air and swore as he tried to grab hold of Richard.

'Don't just sit there, like some drunken doxy. Get inside, now!' Nathaniel yelled and dragged Richard up by the hood of his sweatshirt.

Richard pulled on the driver's door. The door would not move. He was trapped.

'What the hell!' Kai screamed, as the chimney fragments lying on the pavement, were swept upwards into a cloud of terracotta shards, and hovered in the air just above his head.

Richard tried to squeeze between the car door and the cottage wall.

'Oh crap! Richard whispered, as he watched a veil of black mould spread across the car bonnet.

A little girl appeared, holding a Barbie doll by its matted blonde hair. Her face covered by strands of long black hair, which were caught by the wind and blew around her.

'Beat it, kid!' Frank ordered, mopping his face with a McDonald's napkin.

'I'm hungry.' The little girl stared at the man and held out her hand.

The man tutted and threw a melted Kit-Kat onto the road by her feet. 'Now scram, we're on official company business.'

'Frank… help me!' Kai whined, as the cloud of chimney shards hovering just above his head, chimed together as they began to turn in the wind.

A silver zig-zag line raced overhead and arced downwards.

The car flashed white as the lightning hit the car's antenna. Frank jolted and danced; his hands fixed to the steering wheel as several thousand volts shot through his body.

Thunder growled overhead.

Frank's hands reddened, blistering in the heat as they melted into the plastic of the wheel. His neatly centre-parted grey hair frizzled to his scalp. His flesh sagged, hanging from his face, and bloodshot eyes protruded from his skull.

His head lolled forward.

'Frank, you alright mate?' Kai whispered, his gaze caught between the twisting shard vortex hanging above his head, and the smoking car.

'I'm waiting,' said the little girl. She turned towards the younger man. The doll dangled from her fingertips.

Kai looked at the doll. Its eyes were covered in scratches and its features had melted into its face. It was not the doll of a normal child.

'Get away from me... you... you bloody monster!' he screamed.

The girl shook the hair from her face. Her eye sockets were smoky black hollows. 'You people are just so ordinary. You are not really worth killing, but I suppose I must. I do have a certain reputation to keep, you understand.'

The vortex collapsed.

A storm of jagged shards pierced Kai's chest. The force threw him backwards, pinning him against the car bonnet.

The intense heat radiating from the electrified car, burnt through his jeans and jacket. Pain soared through his body.

The demon-girl opened her mouth, too wide, to reveal a row of small, serrated teeth. She leapt onto Kai. He tried to move out of her way but was trapped. His clothes had melted onto the car by the super-heated metal.

Tiny, razor sharp teeth clamped down against his jugular. Blood spurted vertically into the air, showering everything in red. Desperately, Kai grasped at his neck. A gurgling sound came from his throat. His light blue eyes caught Richard's gaze and opened fractionally, conveying a message Richard could not understand. Kai's eyes opened wider for an instant, and then faded to grey as they stared into nothingness.

The girl giggled with delight.

Richard stood transfixed to the spot.

All outside noises seemed muted and faraway. Kai's blood dripped down his arm and plopped loudly onto the road.

Richard's chest felt cold but sweat ran down his forehead, and his legs would not move.

He watched as a white glow surrounded the two bodies. Their souls were departing the physical world.

'Do somethin' godly or they'll be trapped here like the others,' Nathaniel warned.

Richard clasped his hands together to pray for their souls, but the words had flown from his mind. Richard cursed.

'Er… I'm so sorry,' he muttered.

'May God have mercy on their wandering souls,' Nathaniel whispered as he shook his head sadly. Then he man-handled Richard inside the little cottage and shut the door.

From the living room window, Richard could see the spirits of the murdered men rise. The ghosts stood together, staring at the burning car, their disarranged faces frowning in confusion. They nodded to each other and walked down the road.

'They will be back,' Richard said grimly.

'Aye,' Nathaniel replied. 'The unblessed normally do.'

The little girl's face appeared at the window. A white apparition in the navy blue of the early dawn.

Richard almost screamed. He clutched his chest, his heart

beating through his ribcage.

Nathaniel pulled him back against the wall.

The girl banged on the window with the head of the Barbie. The glass panes rattled. The oddly smelling, coloured glass bowls of potpourri, sitting on the deep windowsills, jumped with each knock.

'Invite me inside and I will tell you where your girlfriend is,' the little girl said softly.

'What have you done with her?' Richard replied.

'Me? I've done nothing. What would I want with that whore? Not my type at all,' she smiled. Her head flopped to one side.

'Bethany, are you in here?' Richard screamed.

There was no answer.

He raced through the little room and bounded up the narrow staircase, taking two steps with each stride.

At the top of the staircase were two doors.

The bathroom door was ajar. Richard peered inside. A row of girl-type cosmetics stood in line on the narrow shelf beneath the mirror. Two fluffy white towels hung toasting over the radiator. Glass shower doors sparkled in the corner, opposite the toilet. He picked up a tiny floral china pot and unscrewed the lid. It smelt of roses and lemon. The smell that followed Bethany when she moved.

Nathaniel materialised and snatched the pot from Richard. 'Don't touch ladies' stuff. That will lead you nowhere but a heap of trouble.'

The demon-girl rattled the letterbox.

'Invite me in. You might just be in time to save your whore,'

257

she said, her grey fingertips just visible through the slit as she tapped against the metal. The sound followed them up the narrow staircase and through the house, a quiet but constant staccato tap which reverberated through Richard's brain. He felt a band of tighten around his forehead. His head began to pound.

Richard pocketed the little cream pot.

Nathaniel tutted and rolled his eyes. 'Women will cause you no amount of trouble, you mark my words. It was a wench at the Bishops Nod that done for me.'

'She's not like that, she's brave and beautiful!' Richard said.

Nathaniel half-smiled and raised one eyebrow but said nothing.

Richard opened a door marked, 'Bethany's Boudoir,' and his heart dropped.

The room was dominated by a double bed. Its red covers lay flung across the beige carpet, the sheets were a crumpled mass of cotton waves. A dark wood wardrobe stood against the far side of the room, its doors flung open, as a mountain of clothes spilled onto the carpet. All the drawers of her bedside table had been removed. Their contents dumped on the floor. The remains of a white chair and its cargo of clothes lay scattered across the bedroom.

Richard recognised the clothes as those Bethany had been wearing at Saint Anthony's.

'Oh, bloody hell! She's been taken.' Richard muttered. 'I think they've been looking for her research. They don't know that all her notes are up at Stillbone Chapel.'

Nathaniel nodded and picked up a frilly, black bra lying on

the floor. He held it for a minute and placed it solemnly on her bed.

'What are you doing?' Richard frowned.

'Just tidying up a bit,' Nathaniel whispered, then blushed, and disappeared.

The downstairs knocking stopped.

Richard was alone in the silent cottage. The silence was more deafening than the noise.

Bethany was gone but not dead. He was sure if she had passed over, he would know about it instantly and loudly. The Ashcrofts had to be behind this. They ruled the village. There was a lurking menace behind their smiles which terrified the villagers into silence.

He would have to find them and undo the damage that their ancestor's pact with the demon had caused.

Richard was about to go downstairs when he turned to check Bethany's bedroom for one last time. There sitting neatly on top of the disrupted bed was Bethany's lacy bra. He felt his cheeks burn. He dived forward, grabbed the bra by its straps, and hurled it across the room. The bra landed precariously on top of the wardrobe. One cup dangling suspiciously over the open wardrobe door.

Richard was pretty sure that Bethany would kill him, if she found out, he had touched her bra.

He fled the bedroom and ran downstairs.

The windows in the living room had cracked but were still held in place by the lead struts which divided the glass into diamonds. He picked up a green glass bowl and sniffed its dried brown contents. It smelt lemony, with a touch of peppery warmth and bitter undertones – cumin and salt. Evil could not enter this cottage, unless invited to or unless the physical barriers had been breached. Bethany certainly knew her potions. Cautiously, he opened the front door and peered into the early morning dawn.

An icy mist had rolled across the fields, covering everything in a layer of white.

The car had been left abandoned. Its bonnet covered in swirling brown stains of boiled blood, its doors wide open, and its passengers untouched. Richard shivered as he tried to circumnavigate the bodies.

Kai's corpse lay where it had fallen. His face had taken on the colourless hue of the recently dead, which contrasted vividly with the red gaping wound across his throat.

Richard thought it strange that no one in the sleeping village had noticed the altercation. He scanned the windows of the neighbouring cottages. There were black cracks in the upstairs curtains.

The street was awake and watching him.

Quickly, Richard crunched over the remains of Bethany's flowerpots and rosemary bush, which had been reduced to a scattering of twigs. Then he scurried through the village to his car, which was half-submerged by a fresh fall of browning leaves.

Richard took a thick blanket from the boot and settled into the driver's seat, wrapping the blanket over his legs as he drank a carton of orange juice and ate a selection of sweets, he had found secreted at the back of Bethany's well-stocked kitchen cupboard. He had been surprised to find that most of her food came from the Happy Chicken monopoly and had been brought in bulk. He could not think why she needed five kilograms of plain flour, but then a lot of what women did remained a mystery to him.

A heavy sounding vehicle squeaked around the bend approaching him. Richard dived sideways into the passenger seat. He tensed as he waited for the squeal of brakes as his car was spotted.

The vehicle sped by. Richard peeked through the back window and saw the jingling back end of a tow truck, its lights blaring amber towards Witherleigh.

A collection of amorphous grey buildings emerged from the grey morning mists. Occasionally, the yellow glow of an electric light, irradiated the mist.

The village had woken.

Richard finished his Twix and pondered his next move.

He had to rescue Bethany but where would she be held? He could not imagine Reverend Anderson allowing a murder at the vicarage. It would affect his standing in the community and perhaps even interfere with his nocturnal activities.

The cider mill was too close to the centre of the village for them to risk holding a prisoner there, and it had proved unsecure. Even he had managed to escape the mill.

Richard thought for a moment.

Armitage Hall was situated in the middle of nowhere, on the edge of the moor, and was therefore, an ideal location for conducting illegal activities.

'Like killing curates?' he whispered.

Richard swallowed as a feeling of panic fluttered in his

chest. He pinched the inside of his arm tightly and rummaged through the glovebox. Two rubber bands were hidden at the very back, behind a packet of melted sweets, a collection of aged maps of the south-west in the sixties, which an elderly colleague from London had forced upon him, and a grim-looking yellowing hanky, its origin unknown. He slipped the bands over his wrist. Instantly, the feelings of panic began to subside.

He breathed a sigh of relief.

'Well, what are you doing sitting in this contraption playing with yourself, when that pretty little doxy of yours has been kidnapped?'

Richard blushed.

'I'm…er… not playing with myself, I'm just planning my next move,' he stuttered.

'Aye, just like all those rotten officers I 'spect. Spent all their time drinkin' an' playin' cards an' then when the fighting started, all you could see was their hats bobbing up an' down as they chatted on their prancers at the top of the hill. While us commoners had to fight. Many the times I thought that we was fighting the wrong people,' Nathaniel winked.

'Yes, well, speaking of unhelpful parties, where did you disappear to when I was facing a demon?' Richard enquired, raising his eyebrow.

Nathaniel shrugged sheepishly and stared out of the window.

''Tis hard coming from the *Mortalis* into this world again. You can see it an' walk through it but it's like a wedding veil is covering everything. You're just a shadow on the road, wandering an' alone. You have to rip through the whiteness to walk in the living world an' only a few of us can do it. Even then, only a few people will see you. Half of those will pretend they don't. Then the loneliness hits you again… but tis a hundred times worse if you are like poor old Snowy, an' your crimes follow you each time you cross back into the *Vitare*.'

Richard frowned. 'Why hasn't he gone down into the *Abyss*?'

'He has sort of,' Nathaniel replied. 'He gets hanged everyday by the villagers in the woods. 'Tis the feeling your chest is about to explode, that's the worst, you know. He has never made it through the *Mortalis*. The whiteness blocks his way an' he dies over an' over again. Whether the righteous living burn his bones or not.' Nathaniel shook his head.

'But why are you trapped here?' Richard enquired with a frown.

'I cannot travel onwards because me bones have not been blessed. I've wandered in Witherleigh for so long that I can cross through easily enough, though the *Mortalis* always pulls me back eventually.'

He looked earnestly across at Richard.

'You need to find me bones an' give them a right good Christian send off, so I can go through an' might even get to the *Elisium*.' He grinned at Richard, his blue eyes twinkling.

'But you're a highwayman!' Richard replied.

'Aye an' you talk to demons,' Nathaniel grinned. 'Neither of us is going to be in the running for archbishop, are we?'

A siren wailed through the silence as another car whooshed around the corner. Richard threw himself across the passenger seat, diving through Nathaniel's body. His body tingled. It was the feeling of someone walking over his grave. The touch of a ghost.

Nathaniel tutted.

'Do you mind, I'm not that sort of ghost,' he winked.

'Damn,' Richard muttered as he peered over the passenger seat and saw a police car race towards the village, its lights blaring.

'They've called the police. I bet I'm being blamed for all this too,' he said.

'Aye,' Nathaniel replied solemnly. 'Well, word has it that you spent some time in Bedlam. A dose of the pox will do that to you. That being said lunatics are commonly known as being dangerous creatures, you know.'

'I do not have syphilis!' Richard exclaimed.

Nathaniel laughed. 'Don't worry, 'tis nothing to be shamed of, we've all had to go for the mercury cure.'

'Well, I am quite dangerous, you know. I have salt in my rucksack, and I will use it if you don't start being slightly more useful,' Richard replied.

Nathaniel put his hand on his heart, 'I am mortally wounded, sir.'

'Again?' Richard smiled as he started the car.

The net was closing in on him. He would only have a short time to save Bethany before he was caught and disposed of. He would have to go to Armitage Hall in broad daylight and somehow rescue Bethany. It did not seem like his greatest plan, but it was all he had.

The car spluttered to life and chugged around the corner. Richard turned to Nathaniel. The ghost had disappeared.

He checked his mirror. Nathaniel stood in the middle of the lane, waving to him. Richard stopped the car and rolled down the window.

'What happened?' he yelled

'I fell through your carriage as soon as it moved,' Nathaniel exclaimed, his arms flapping by his side.

'I will meet you at the hall… If I can…' Nathaniel added sheepishly and he disappeared.

Richard saluted the empty space where the ghost had been standing and drove into the swirling morning mist.

CHAPTER TWENTY

The fog increased rolling through the valley. The road markings and the road itself had almost disappeared beneath a thick blanket of white. Richard's knuckles whitened as he gripped the steering wheel tightly and slowed the car to a crawl. If the car wandered off the road and fell into the deep gullies which ran along the lane, he could be trapped in the wilds for hours before anyone passed by. Tall grey skeletons of trees peered out from the mist. Richard felt the car wheels lose traction slightly as they skidded over an invisible mud spill. He swerved to the right and kept driving, hoping that he was still on the road.

The road climbed higher. The mist evaporated, and the lane snaked out in front of him, cutting through dark fields lined with overgrown hedgerows. At the top of the hill, a white signpost rose from the parting mists. The sign stated 'Symmionsbath/ Exmoor 7 miles', its arm pointing leftwards down a barely visible lane, about the same width as a farm track. Cautiously, Richard turned left. He felt his tyres begin to slide over a layer of mud.

'Oh Christ!' he muttered as he ran his hand through his hair and prayed the mud would not become a quagmire. He was sure that Bethany would not be impressed if he came to rescue her on foot. A pheasant hiding in the crouching brambles, its branches spilling into the lane, made a disgruntled 'cock-cock' sound and flew off. The rustling of heavy wings lost in the mist.

A dark shadow loomed out of the mist. Richard slammed on the brakes. The car skidded in the mud. The back tyres circling around to the front, as the car lunged to the right, and jolted downwards.

'Oh crap!' Richard swore, as the car bounced precariously up and down. Gingerly, he opened the driver's door and peered down into the muddy gulley. The car rocked.

Richard closed the door.

'I think I will be on foot from here,' he muttered and slid carefully across to the passenger seat. The car bounced up and down once and then slid downwards into the ditch, landing diagonally; its left side wheels still clutching the lane.

Richard scrambled out of the car and dived onto the road. A gust of mist swirled around him. He stood up and brushed the dirt from his sweatshirt, as he searched for landmarks among the whiteness. Thick grey branches appeared and were swallowed once more by the moving mist. Richard knew he was still on the lane, by the feel of the tarmac beneath his feet. However, he could not tell which direction he had come from or where he was going.

'Oh, bloody hell!' Richard groaned. He would have to summon help.

Nathaniel had haunted Witherleigh for centuries. He should be able to navigate his way through the mists to Armitage Hall and he was still sane.

'*Venite ad me exspiravit*, come to me spirit!' Richard commanded.

An icy breeze rushed down the lane, seizing clumps of mist and twirling them into spirals, fracturing the fog bank to reveal glimpses of green and brown. Richard breathed a sigh of relief. Nathaniel was coming through.

The scene flickered.

A high-pitched scream carried across the fields.

Richard frowned. It sounded like a lost spirit. Either too new or too old and confused to understand their curse.

'I'm such an idiot,' Richard muttered to himself. He had forgotten to name the spirit he was summoning. Anybody could be coming through.

'Shit! I am really not good at this demon hunting business,' he said glumly.

London had shown him that. It had led to the deaths of the whole Pembroke family and he was still making the same careless mistakes. He pinched his wrist hard and silently prayed that old Snowy was not going to shuffle out from the mist.

Sounds of feet ran past him, brushing against the left side of his sweatshirt. A cold sensation ran up his left arm which burnt and tingled, as if touched by ice. Richard looked down at his fingers. The ones on his left hand were blue with cold. He thrust them into his pocket.

A figure ran from the mist towards him. Richard covered his face with his arms. The shape ran through him and into the small copse of twisted trees and squatting bushes which sat beside the lane. Richard stumbled forward as the ghost touched his back, sending a series of icy shocks through his spine.

Richard turned and ran back, towards the safety of his car. The car had shifted slightly, falling further onto its side in the ditch. Its left side wheels stuck out from the ditch and turned slowly in the air. Richard squatted next to the mud-drenched undercarriage and waited.

Discordant, heavy footsteps ran towards him and vanished.

The wind thundered through the mist and twisted around the trees. One of the elderly trees cracked; a gnarled branch tumbled to the ground and splintered, narrowly missing Richard's head.

The roar of the wind grew louder. Its pitch rising through the scales until it sounded like an over-lengthened scream. Richard covered his ears with his hands and searched the probing edges of the mist.

The noise stopped in mid-scream and the wind died. Several twigs and other windborne debris clattered against the road.

An icy hand touched his ankle.

Richard froze. His heart thumping through his chest as if trying to escape his body. He looked down at his leg. A black, wrinkled hand gripped his ankle. The remainder of the arm disappeared inside the road. Richard tried to pull his foot away, kicking out at the hand with his free foot. The wrist tightened its grip on Richard's ankle.

Something behind him rustled.

Richard twisted round.

A dwarfed oak tree loomed over him, its trunk sweeping backwards into the woods. Its narrowed branches stretching towards the lane. The lowest branch was missing, leaving a light jagged scar on the tree trunk.

The brown bark below the scar began to ripple.

There was a crunching sound, as the rest of his car was sucked down into the ditch and disappeared.

Richard leapt to his feet, forgetting his trapped ankle. He tripped and fell backwards onto the muddy lane. The mud rippled as blacked fingers pushed their way through the tarmac and wormed towards Richard. Smells of putrid flesh and mould filled the air and clawed at his throat.

Richard felt a knot of panic squeeze his chest as adrenalin surged through his body. The fingers grew into wrinkled black hands that grabbed hold of his legs, their sharp nails clawing into his skin, as they dragged him downwards into the road.

Richard pinched his left wrist. The pain cleared his thinking.

'I wish to speak to the spirit!' he ordered, not really wanting a reply.

A face stretched from the tree trunk, its eyes and mouth hollows against the contours of the bark. A group of white bulbous growths appeared from the tall grasses around the base of the oak. Richard squinted through the thinning drifts of mist and saw the growths enlarge and stretch upwards, their white heads bobbing. He watched as the mushrooms opened to form thick umbrellas, jostling with each other for space among the oak roots, forming a bobbling carpet of white.

The mushrooms crinkled.

The ends of the umbrellas curled inwards, and big brown spots grew over the pristine white surface. Their tops folded against the stalks, which could not hold their weight, and one by one the mushrooms crumpled, collapsing against the black earth. The remains melted to form a khaki sludge which bubbled and dissolved back into the soil, leaving behind a large brown circle of burnt, blackened mud in the dark green grass.

The muddy circle sunk into the earth to reveal a dirt-encrusted leathered head with teeth spilling from its jaw. On the righthand side of the head, was a depression with cracks radiating from it. While strands of brown hair waved in the wind.

The teeth lying scattered on top of the soil, began to jump back inside the head, and a wriggling mass of purple worms poured through its eye sockets.

Richard felt his stomach churn. He tried to shuffle away from the head, but the withered hands held him fast. Two weathered black hands gripped each leg.

Four hands meant two victims.

'Name yourself!' Richard commanded.

The face in the tree looked down at him. Its mouth pressed wide against the bark, as if trying to shout through the wood.

'H... Harry... Harry Hood,' the head wheezed. The flesh around its skull reformed, repairing itself to reveal the ruddy features of the latest lost curate. Its empty eye sockets hidden by ginger-fringed eyelids, which closed over the sockets, and gave the head the appearance of being asleep.

'H... help me, something's wrong... There's been a terrible accident. I can't see a damn thing,' Harry cried.

Richard thought back to Bethany's board of the damned.

Harry Hood was a scholar-curate who had disappeared in Elfsworthy Woods, while compiling data for a biological diversity survey of the woodland. His disappearance had been classified as an emergency recall to Oxford to take part in a two-year study into the effects of radiation on the local flora in Fukushima. Apparently, one of the research team had dropped out of the trip at the last minute due to 'family problems.'

This research opening had been a miraculous opportunity and Harry had jumped at the chance to further his post-graduate studies. He had packed up his possessions and disappeared overnight, leaving Reverend Anderson only a brief letter of explanation.

A note next to the newspaper clipping pinned to his photograph had commented in Bethany's spidery handwriting, 'Left drawers and wardrobe doors open, weird behaviour for the obsessive-compulsive nutjob. Dr Cecil Ashcroft, from the Department of Plant Sciences at Oxford University, released a statement saying that *Hood is out of contact with the university's basecamp doing fieldwork.* Claims that Hood has produced some very promising 'preliminary reports' for the department. However, none published. Bullshit coverup.'

Richard smiled. One of the many attributes of Bethany that he loved was her zero-bullshit tolerance.

'Harry, where are you?' Richard asked.

'In the woods… the bluebells…' Harry's voice became muffled as his connection to the *Vitare* faded.

The hands holding Richard tightened their grip. He felt his legs grow numb as they were dragged through the road down and into the *Mortalis*.

'Harry, release me,' Richard ordered.

Harry's head began turning from side to side. The oak began to tremble and shake its branches. Its roots ripped out of the soil as it swayed.

'Harry, you are dead!' Richard shouted. 'Release me. I promise that I will help you! I will show you the path through the *Mortalis* but first I must rescue my friend. She is in grave danger and it's all my fault. I should not have let her help.' He bit his lip and blinked tears from his eyes. He could not have yet another innocent death on his conscience.

'No, you can't go! You mustn't leave me here in the darkness!' Harry screamed in panic.

Richard swallowed. His vision was turning black. He felt his soul begin to slip down through his body. Harry was accidentally killing him.

'I'm really sorry to be so blunt but you are dead. You must have been chopped into pieces and scattered here, which is why you're trapped in this tree. You decomposed, and the mushrooms fed upon your body. The same thing happened to your colleague. You must release me. I can help you both pass through and gain eternal rest,' Richard said firmly.

The ruddy face looked down at Richard and screamed, 'Noooo!'

The soil around the skull began to heave and then collapsed, creating a large, black pit. The ground holding him vanished and Richard began to fall. He grabbed hold of a large tree root, dangling over the side of the hole. The hands gripping Richard's ankles loosened and fell into the emptiness. The root bent downwards, flattening Richard against the side of the pit. A blackened foot stuck out from the sides of the hole, inches from his face. Richard recoiled in shock; his hands slipped down the muddy root.

He screamed for help.

***

'You want help?' a quiet voice queried.

'Get me out of here!' Richard shouted.

Chef Sheng leant over the pit. His long, white ponytail dangled into the hole as he pulled on the root. The Chef's small stature belied massive upper body strength, attained through years of chopping through carcases with his meat cleaver. The cook hauled in the root and helped Richard onto the grassy mound adjacent to the tree.

'Watch out for my truffles!' Sheng commanded.

Richard lay gasping for breath and then rolled onto his front. The oak tree stood silently observing them, devoid of any faces.

'You need to watch out. Open mine works are dotted all over the woods. When the iron ran out, they just covered the pits over with debris and moved on. The soil slips, it's very dangerous.'

'Thank you for rescuing me,' Richard gasped. 'The hands in the pit were dragging me into the *Mortalis*.'

The chef shook his head.

'You are very mad. Now out of my way.' He knelt by the mound and began to scoop handfuls of leaves from the mound. Next, he took a little trowel from his bucket as he began to scrape away the soil.

'Did you see the…' Richard asked.

'I need to concentrate,' the chef interjected, not taking his eyes from the ground as he carefully removed the top layer of soil and deposited it on the grass. A shiny object lay half-buried in the soil heap. Richard waited until the chef was preoccupied with his digging, reached forward, and grabbed the object.

'Ah ha!' the chef announced. He stopped scraping and picked up a black lump which looked like a small piece of coal. 'Wild foraged truffle. Very rare and very expensive.' Sheng smiled happily.

Richard was shocked. He had never seen the chef smile before.

'How did you find it then?' Richard asked as he quickly hid the object in his sweatshirt pouch.

'The wild boar found them. Boars are very intelligent truffle gatherers and also make good stew.'

'Oh, I see,' Richard said, feeling sorry for the animals. 'Do you know who owns these woods?'

Chef Sheng nodded towards the moss-covered trunk of a willowy beech. Its remaining leaves forming crinkled amber leaf clouds on the tips of its twigs. Tied around its trunk was a metal sign. The sign was covered in green mould, but Richard could just make out the words, 'Keep Out. Happy Ch…' in thick black letters, which peered out from beneath the green.

'Is this wood owned by the Happy Chicken Company too?' Richard asked.

The chef nodded as he dropped another truffle into his bucket.

'They own everything that touches the village and everyone in it,' Sheng muttered.

'Who are the Happy Chicken Company? How do they own everyone?' Richard asked.

Chef Sheng's deep brown eyes widened momentarily. He

275

glanced over his shoulder. 'I need to get back to work, prepare the lunch service. Freshly foraged truffle shavings on roasted leg of wild boar with an edible flower garnish.'

The chef stood up and began to walk back to the road. 'You want a lift into Witherleigh?'

Richard shook his head. 'No, I'm fine thanks. I'm just out for a little stroll. It's good to get out of the village.' Richard smiled and shivered as a light fall of rain began to drip through the woods.

'Well, be careful and do not fall into anymore holes,' The chef warned as he disappeared into the wood, shaking his head, and muttering under his breath.

Richard stood and watched flashes of golden-brown pass through the naked trees as the chef's car sped away. He took the object from his pouch and began to pick the lumps of soil from the shining metal object.

It was a ring.

Richard had seen this ring before. It was in a framed picture on the mantlepiece above the fire in Bethany's cottage. It was a photograph of a smiling Reverend Bond, with his arm around Bethany's shoulders, as they ate ice creams and squinted into the camera. The calm sparkling light blue sea lay behind them.

A large silver ring with a silver cross, on an onyx black background, dominated the Reverend's right hand.

Richard looked inside the ring band. It was initialled E.B. – Ezekiel Bond. Bethany's missing father.

He had to go to Bethany, but he could not leave her father here trapped in the torment of the *Mortalis*. She would kill him.

Richard walked down the slope and came to a flattened

piece of overgrown grassland.

He dumped his rucksack on the grass and took out his folding spade. Then he knelt and began to dig a large outline of a circle. Digging a circle through the tough grass was a lot harder than it appeared. Richard sat back onto his heels, breathing heavily as he wiped the sweat from his forehead. He took a long drink of holy water from the thermos flask, secreted inside his rucksack, and pinched his wrist for good luck.

Next, Richard rummaged through his rucksack. At the very bottom, beneath his wooden cross and stake, was a hemp 'gris-gris' or spirit bag. He opened the little bag and began to pour the white powder from the bag into the outline of the circle.

'*Spirituum veniunt*, spirits come to me. *Transire in lucem*, and cross into the light,' he chanted, quietly at first.

A sudden wind whistled through the trees. He shivered as the woodland air grew colder.

They were coming. It was time.

Richard raised his arms above his head and shouted, '*Spirituum veniunt, et suscipe benedictionem accipere et transire in lucem.* Spirits come to me and cross over into the light.'

Eerie grey shadows appeared from the fading drifts of mist and were pulled towards the circle. Some moaned and wailed as they approached. These were the spirits of those who had not wanted to pass over. Those too scared to leave the known world behind. Only to become trapped in the never-ending emptiness of the world of the dead.

Other ghosts stumbled towards him in a jerky, irregular manner, their broken bodies moving clumsily through the trees. These were the ghosts Richard wanted. The ones haunted by their own violent deaths. Their bodies buried without a blessing. They would never find their way to the *Postvitum*, the place of judgement, unaided.

He made the sign of the cross and said blessings for the souls of the dead. The lingering mists evaporated. A shaft of glowing white sunlight fell from the overcast sky.

'Dear hosts of the *Elisium* hear my pray. Saint Michael the Archangel, I beg you rain down your fire, to protect the lost souls crossing into the *Postvitum*,' Richard prayed.

The shaft of sunlight touched the powder. The circle exploded into flames. One by one, the ghosts floated through the circle of fire and disappeared into the shaft of sunlight.

The blackened skull re-fleshed itself. Richard watched in amazement as the white shadowy shape of a portly curate rose from the skull and drifted towards the light.

'Bless you, Richard Radcliffe, you have freed me.' The spirit entered the shaft. Richard watched in awe as the curate ascended.

The shaft flickered as the bridge to the *Postvitum* began to disappear.

Richard smiled. He had helped trapped souls to escape their torment and enter the judgement of the *Postvitum*. Most of them were curates, so, hopefully, it would be a good day for them. Their souls would finally be able to pass through the *Gate of Judicium* and find eternal peace in the beautiful lands of eternal summer in the *Elisium*.

Perhaps it was going to be a good day after all.

Something touched his arm.

Richard shivered as the coldness of death sent electrical

pulses racing up his spine. Reverend Bond glided through his body. The Reverend's delicate face grim as he was sucked into the circle. He opened his mouth to speak but no sounds came. The spirit stuck its arm out of the shaft and gripped Richard's arm. Richard winced as the Reverend's fingernails dug into his flesh. Their eyes met for an instant.

'I will save her,' Richard promised.

The Reverend nodded and released his grip. The shaft turned grey. Richard saw the shadows of the countryside appear as Reverend Bond ascended just in time.

The shaft of sunlight vanished.

Richard looked at his throbbing arm. It was covered in a criss-cross of deep red cuts. After a few seconds, the jagged lines adjusted themselves, to form the spikey word, 'Ashcroft'. Richard stared at the words for a moment, as a cold feeling crept over his body.

CHAPTER TWENTY-ONE

Chef Sheng's car had turned right towards Witherleigh.

Richard knew the Exmoor road snaked in the opposite direction. He turned left and walked down a lane, which appeared to possess more potholes than actual road. The trees crowding the sides of the lane grew denser as it wound through Elfsworthy woods.

The early morning mists had lifted to reveal the sombre greyness of Devon, as the golds of autumn turned to the dull drudgery of winter. The naked trees that clung to the edges of the road had lost most of their twigs, taken by the winds that raged across the moor. Their trunks were wrapped in dark green ivy, which protected them against the frosted wind. The ground beneath the trees lay hidden, covered by a decaying tapestry of leaves, and fallen twigs.

Richard jogged down the lane. His bulging rucksack thumped heavily against his back with every jog, but he did not mind. Every step took him nearer to Bethany. The lane swung lethargically to the left as it avoided a copse of towering ancient trees.

A small, circular stone wall hugged the road as it turned, to prevent the speeding cars of tourists disappearing into the fields below. Richard leant against the wall for a moment, his chest pounding as he tried to catch his breath.

The topmost stones stood upwards; the builder had obviously grown bored with the horizontal grey slab monotony. Over the years, nature had used the stones as a canvas, covering the monotone grey in light green mosses and organic streaks of black and white. There was a rustling of feathers as a flock of blue tits flew from a holly tree, tweeting a warning as they flew deeper into the woods. Their red berry breakfast disturbed.

Richard crossed to the left side of the road, keeping as near to the edge of the lane as possible. His form was lost amongst the bent shapes of the weathered trees and bushes. The little lane swept majestically to the left. Richard followed the bend and found that the grey lane was straight for the next few hundred feet, a miracle in engineering for the ancient Devon roadbuilders.

Veering off from the right of the lane, was an even narrower mud track with a painted sign falling off its post, which proudly pointed the way to Lower Thorne Farm. A collection of mud-painted cars lined its entrance.

Richard crept closer to the gathering, crouched behind a prickly blackthorn bush, and listened.

Police Constable Bates stood leaning against his patrol car; its door wide open as the sounds of the police radio crackled in the background. 'So, do 'ee wants me to arrest the boy for murdering poor Frank an' Kai or don't 'ee? Them's were alright fer foreigners. The car looked like Old Blightie's cuttingroom. I'll 'ave to report it.'

'No!' Strange replied. 'That interferin' curate 'as to go quietly. There's been too many unnatural deaths these last few weeks. We can't be havin' anymore, or the townies might grow suspicious an' come an' ruin everythin'.'

'I don't take orders from you, Strange.' Bates snarled and crossed his arms, as he glared down at the diminutive shopkeeper.

'No, but you do from me.' Dr Ashcroft stepped from his spotless Range Rover. Reluctantly, Chef Sheng slid from the backseat.

A Land Rover, emblazoned with the Happy Chicken logo, pulled up opposite the farm lane. Two drawn-looking men got out from their cars and joined the others. Richard peered through the bush. One of the men, he recognised instantly as Farmer Butt. The other he realised was in fact a well-built, middle-aged woman.

'Butt... Mrs Stacy. My sincere apologies for your loss Primrose... Violet was a good woman. May she rest in peace.' Dr Ashcroft added as an afterthought. 'We need to put a lid on this now or there will be a lot more deaths.'

'But that Bond girl ain't no vicar,' Mrs Stacy argued. ''Ee won't want 'er.'

'Well, I don't know,' replied the doctor smiling slightly. 'He might find some use for her. In the meantime, Butt, Mrs Stacy... you two go to the village. Have the bodies removed and buried in the churchyard, Reverend Anderson will not give you any trouble. Tell the garage I want that car repaired like new. No trace evidence. And you...' Ashcroft nodded at Bates, 'go with Sheng, find that meddling little curate, and bring him to Armitage Hall.'

Richard crouched lower into the bush. He needed to get to Armitage Hall. However, at his rate of walking it could take at least a day, and he had to rescue Bethany before it was too late. Also, he was not exactly sure where the manor house was situated. All he really knew was that it was big and on the outskirts of Exmoor, and Exmoor was a very big moor. He ran his hand through his tousled hair as a voice inside his brain whispered, 'Why don't you just get caught?'

Butt and Mrs Stacy nodded and mutely got inside their Land Rover, turned very slowly to the left, and drove sedately around the bend, while the Ashcroft's Range Rover roared into life and headed right.

'Right then, Sheng, where did 'ee see 'im last, then?' Bates questioned.

'I told Dr Ashcroft already. I need to get back to my kitchen or lunch will be ruined,' Sheng said. His hushed voice betrayed his silent rage.

'You'll do as you are told. How is dear old Ma Sheng? Still enjoyin' that expensive nursing home, is she? Don't seem right. The good doctor lookin' after your old mum so well, an' you bein' so begrumpled, do it?' Bates stood with his legs apart, his hands on his hips, staring down at the chef. 'Now, I bain't got all day.'

'He was at the truffle patch; we should start there.' Sheng replied, as he stared at his feet and plunged his hands in his pockets.

'I see,' replied Bates. 'Well, we'll cut across the scrub an' trap 'im there.'

He took the chef by the elbow and dragged him across the lane. Moments later they were hidden amongst the entangled trees.

Richard crawled out from the bushes. He stretched his cramped legs, then reluctantly jogged back down the lane.

∗∗∗

Half an hour passed. The lazy winter sun climbed mid-way up the sky and hovered almost hidden by an array of grey clouds, as their shadows passed over the empty landscape.

'There he is!' Sheng called out as he spied the figure of Richard, sprawled facedown across a small grassy mound. A grotty blue rucksack by his side.

The policeman pushed Sheng out of the way and flipped Richard onto his back.

'Bugger me, 'ees all bloody,' Bates swore as he frowned down at Richard's face. 'I best report this.' The enormous policeman walked over to a clearing and took out his mobile.

Sheng knelt next to Richard. He put his hand over Richard's nose. The chef felt hot, moist breath on his palm. Sheng frowned. His eyes narrowed as he scrutinised Richard's face. Richard opened one eye and winked at the chef.

Sheng nodded.

'The curate is alive but very sweaty. I think he has had a heart attack… I am not giving him mouth to mouth.' The chef stood up and folded his arms.

'Damn,' Bates muttered as he scurried back. ''Ee must 'ave tripped on yon root,' he pointed to the twisting brown surface root of a gnarled Chestnut tree, 'then banged his 'ead open an' 'ad an 'eart attack. These townies ain't that strong. Proper weeds most of 'em. If he needs mouth to mouth, I'll give it to 'ee though. 'Tis my job.'

He bent over Richard's face.

'No!' shouted Sheng. 'You need to wait and see if he stops breathing first.'

The policeman tutted. 'Very well, but I ain't tonguing no corpse.'

He hauled Richard over his back.

Sheng grabbed the muddy backpack and they stalked back through the scrub.

CHAPTER TWENTY-TWO

Richard swallowed a wave of nausea, as Bates pulled his body higher onto his broad shoulders and stomped through the scrubland. After what seemed hours of being bumped and jolted, they ended up back at the clearing. Richard was unceremoniously dumped in the back of the muddy patrol car.

Something inside the boot rustled.

Richard tensed, hoping that he was not sharing the cramped space with any member of the rodentia species, a gang of which had chased him hungrily through the London sewers. It had been a bite from one of the possessed brown rats that had poisoned him and destroyed his life. The experience had also left him with severe musophobia. A fear of mice and rats which had greatly disappointed his father... among other things.

Slowly, Richard's eyes adjusted to the semidarkness. He breathed a sigh of relief. No vicious furry creatures sat glaring at him. Instead, he found himself lying on top of a year's worth of McDonald's ketchup containers, wrappers, and drink holders, which stuck to his clothes and hair. The smell of old congealing fat made him gag but at least he was not going to be eaten alive by rabid rats or wandering lost through the woods. Soon he would be with Bethany. He smiled and tightened the handkerchief bandage over the cuts across his wrist. Then he attempted to comb through his wild hair with his fingers.

After what seemed a few hours, but in reality, must have been less than one, the car slowed down and swung round to the left. Its tyres crunched over a rolling gravel driveway. Eventually, the car ground to a halt and the boot door sprung open.

'Take 'im through the kitchen an' remember, we need 'im breathin' when 'ee dies,' Bates ordered. 'I must get back to the station an' all. I've got to write a report an' investigate a crime before I goes 'ome tonight. There's a proper crime wave goin' on in the moor. Some bastard keeps stealin' clothes off washing lines. Then, I gets a call and has to investigate it. If I catch 'im, I will give thems a piece of my mind.'

'Aye, 'an tell thems to piss over t'other side of the moor,' Butt growled. 'I blame all these young'uns. I worked a twelve-hour day when I was young an' it never did me no harm. Youngsters these days are bone idle wastrels. Bring back National Service, that's what I say.'

'Very true,' a woman's voice agreed. 'Young people these days have no respect for their elders.'

'Aye 'tis so… but stop your chattin' an' come give I a hand. I've got criminals to catch an' all,' Bates whined as he grabbed Richard's sweatshirt and began to pull.

Richard closed his eyes and feigned unconsciousness as two pairs of rough hands manhandled him out of the boot.

The car sped off down the drive, showering everyone in gravel.

'Right then, we'd best get 'ee settled. Then what about a

nice cup o' tea, eh, Primrose girl?' Butt flirted as they carried Richard through the kitchen door.

A door slammed shut.

The chef appeared from the storeroom carrying a large bag of flour, which he threw down on the heavy wooden kitchen table, muttering furiously to himself about the dangers of rushed hors d'oeuvres.

A cloud of flour mushroomed around the kitchen.

'How do Sheng, why aren't you at the Nod?'

Sheng glared at him through the flour haze. He opened a drawer beneath the table, took out a cleaver, and proceeded to massacre a beef tomato garnish.

'Perhaps we'll 'ave a cup o' tea later, Primrose,' Butt said, and they quickly vacated the kitchen.

The villagers turned down a narrow corridor and went down a series of stone steps. The temperature dropped as they descended.

A heavy door groaned open, and Richard was unceremoniously dropped onto the cold stone floor. A second later, his unzipped backpack was thrown in after him. A plastic squash bottle rolled across the stone, the demon-burning communion wine sloshing from side to side as it rolled.

'How do, Bethany, enjoyin' life at thee manor, I see,' Butt jeered.

'Go to hell, Elijah!' Bethany snapped back. 'You do realise, you drink any more Bishop's Finger and your little todger will be as limp as leftover lettuce… Mind you, if what your wife says is true, she won't notice the difference!'

Butt's face went scarlet. He marched towards Bethany but

was held back by Mrs Stacy, 'Leave her, Elijah, she bain't worth it. No Godfearing woman would ever work in a tavern. She is a Jezebel. Go to the kitchen an' see if Sheng will let 'ee into the larder. We 'ave to keep our strength up. I want nothin' fancy mind you; just a couple of Cornish Farings, an' a few fresh fruit scones with cream an' jam, an' maybe a good strong cup of tea.'

'Right you are, Primrose,' said Butt. He dug his hands deep into the pockets of his brown corduroy trousers and headed towards the kitchen.

Mrs Stacy waited until the footsteps disappeared and closed the cold room door.

The gentle smile fell from her face. She walked over to Bethany, who was sitting in the corner of the cold room and slapped her hard across the face.

A trickle of blood ran from the corner of Bethany's mouth. Bethany stared up at the portly woman, her brown eyes conveying that wonderful mixture of boredom and disappointment that only a woman can.

'Oo… that hurt so much,' Bethany sneered. 'Do you like it rough then? If you want to play, I'll have to give you my safe word.'

'You filthy little harlot!' Mrs Stacy gasped in horror and fled the room.

***

The door shut. The windowless room descended into a shadowy darkness. Its only light filtered in from beneath the thick, insulated door. The temperature inside the storeroom began to fall.

Richard sat up and smiled shyly at Bethany.

'So, you're not that dead, then?' Bethany's voice cut through the silence.

'Oh, h…hello, Bethany,' Richard stammered, 'I'm absolutely fine thank you. How are you?'

'What have you done to your face? It's covered in blood,' Bethany demanded.

'Oh that… It's nothing I just smeared a bit of blood from my wrist to make me look authentically injured, so I could catch a ride,' he beamed. 'Now, let's get you out of here.'

'Hmm… clever, but how? I'm kinda chained up,' Bethany pulled on an ancient set of manacles, which were attached to a heavy ring, set into the stone wall, by a thick, rusty chain.

Richard frowned and pinched his wrist, hoping Bethany would not notice.

'Why would anyone have chains in their cold room?' Richard asked, looking at the shelves lined with preserves, pickles, and brown china pots. Small bundles of drying herbs hung from a wooden rack attached to the low ceiling by thinner chains.

'The Ashcrofts are an old, rich Devon family. The problem with those is that to keep their money in the family estate cousins tend to marry cousins and over the centuries become completely insane and do really weird shit, like use their larders as prisons. Perhaps playing dungeon master and prisoner is what keeps the spark alive in what must be a very staid marriage?' She grinned, enjoying Richard's obvious discomfort.

Bethany winked at him. 'It's ok! I will get us out of here, before anything freaky happens. I have a plan or at least the start of one.'

She shuffled on her bottom, rocking to and fro. Then grimaced as she rolled backwards, shoving her manacled wrists beneath her bottom. With a great deal of sweating and panting, she managed to slip both feet through the manacles, so that her hands were finally in front of her.

'Can you unlock these with a hairpin or something?' Bethany asked showing Richard the manacles.

'Err…' Richard frowned. He had come equipped for fighting demons and releasing confused ghosts. He had nothing to help him defeat the human kind of evil. Richard crawled over to his backpack and rummaged for a while.

'Aha!' He said triumphantly, 'I have a small Swiss army knife from scouting. Will that do?'

'Only if we want to open a tin of baked beans,' Bethany replied. 'Come over here and sit next to me. I'm freezing and don't try anything funny!'

'Hmm...' Richard blushed as he shuffled across the cold room.

***

Several hours later the cold room door opened. Strange stood in the doorway looking down at Richard. 'Well, nice to see you aren't dead yet, curate.'

He turned to the shadowy figures behind him and ordered, 'Escort the curate and the Jezebel to the orangery for refreshments.'

The sound of male laughter echoed behind him. Richard glanced at Bethany. Her face was grim.

Richard was hauled to his feet, his hands tied behind his back, and marched into the corridor. He could hear Bethany swearing and kicking at her captors as the chain dropped to the floor and she was dragged from the cold room.

Bethany fell against Richard.

An electrical charge ran up and down his body. He shivered. It was the touch of death.

'Aw, that's the problem with 'ee townies,' laughed Butt. 'Can't stand a bit of cold moor weather.'

He took Richard's arm and marched him down a long, thin corridor, which led to a small green door, recessed into the red brick wall. Strange took a heavy iron ring of keys from his jacket pocket. He selected an old-fashioned silver key with an overlarge bow, and a square blade with an uneven cross carved into it and unlocked the door.

The door slid open to reveal a tropical paradise.

The humidity of the orangery hit Richard like a furnace. Sweat began to run down the inside of his shirt.

A heavy rain began to tap against the vaulted glass ceiling and formed raindrop paths, which ran down the glass walls. Through the glass, Richard could see the afternoon sky darken to shades of flint, as the mist rolled in from the moor towards the manor.

One of the ventilation windows which ran along the top of the orangery slammed shut. The diagonal glass panes on the roof, rattled and shook. Richard looked up at the glass panes with suspicion and stooped down, so that he was slightly lower than his captives. If any fell, he hoped the glass would hit them first.

They were marched through a series of Chinese-style pots filled with ferns and exotic broad-leafed plants bearing strange, gaudy orange flowers. The light green leaves of the banana tree, which fanned across the furthest corner of the orangery; shivered and rustled. Richard looked up at the giant tree. Brown bark was falling from its green trunk as if it were unpeeling itself. A huge multi-layered bunch of plump, bright green bananas, hung from its lower branch.

Almost imperceptibly, the bananas began to swing.

Richard stared at the hanging bananas. The bananas were all moving independently of each other. Some of the bananas bent in the middle, signalling him to come nearer.

A giant terracotta pot holding the dwarf banana tree nearest him chinked, as the bark chips covering its soil, began to move.

A hard push in the back sent Richard hurtling through the potted plants. He landed on his knees in front of a decorative white metal table laid out with a silver-rimmed tea service and a matching silver three-tiered cake stand filled with mini, crustless sandwiches.

A second later, Bethany joined him as Dr and Mrs Ashcroft walked through the white double doors, surrounded by an ethereal woodland mural.

The Ashcrofts made their way towards the sandwiches. Dr Ashcroft pulled the chair from the table and once Mrs Ashcroft was seated, helped push her chair neatly under the table. Then he sat down and asked, 'Shall you be mother, my dear?'

'Certainly darling,' Mrs Ashcroft replied and raised the teapot.

'Let us go… you bloody nutters!' Bethany shouted as she

struggled to get to her feet.

Heavy hands on her shoulders forced her to remain kneeling.

'How can we let you go when you are so… needed?' Mrs Ashcroft smiled as she poured the tea.

Murmured whispers and shuffling footsteps echoed through the orangery.

Richard recognised the voices of several of the villagers as they traipsed through the servants' doorway.

Dr Ashcroft smiled to his wife as he replaced his teacup in its saucer, 'Now we are gathered, we can begin the harvest.' He walked over to the woodland mural and stood for a minute observing the scene.

Ashcroft seemed to be praying. There was a shuffling sound from behind Richard.

The villagers dropped to their knees.

'What are they doing?' Richard whispered.

Bethany shrugged. Richard saw her fingers moving as she tried to untie her rope, while everyone's attention was preoccupied with the mural.

The mural seemed out of place in the conservative understated elegance of the orangery. It showed a woodland path winding through the crowded trees which reached over, entwining with each other's branches to form a tunnel. The trees at the front of the painting were dark leafless forms, which contrasted vividly with the almost yellow light at the end of the tunnel and the vivid green leaves of the distant trees. Almost lost in the darkness of the painting, one of the leaning trees in the foreground had a black symbol scratched into its bark. Richard peered closely at the symbol. It was an elongated triangle. Below the triangle was a truncated name – *Mam.*

Richard quickly flicked through the pages of the *Liber Fieri Dæmoniorum* in his mind. There was only one demon whose name began with those three letters. It was *Mamonae*, the demon of greed. In the book, *Mamonae* had been depicted as a naked man with horns, cloven feet, and two black-ribbed wings, carrying a sack of gold over its shoulder. Richard glanced over at the kneeling villagers. He breathed a sigh of relief. *Mamonae* was not among them.

Richard tried to wriggle his fingers free from the rope. He had been right. The ghostly presences and disappearances in Witherleigh were the side effects of a demonic presence. The energy of the demon was blocking their passage through the *Mortalis*. If he exorcised the demon, the way into the afterdeath would be cleared and the ghosts would be released from their wanderings.

'*Veni adi moi* Mamoner!' Dr Ashcroft raised his arms and screamed at the mural. A huge crash echoed around the orangery as the wind slammed a topmost window against its frame. 'He is coming through. We must make ready,' the doctor commanded.

The sigils burnt into Richard's palms began to tingle.

He frowned at the doctor's back, vaguely recognising the corrupted Latin of his demon summoning.

Something felt very wrong.

Farmer Butt turned a huge white handle, situated next to the righthand door, and two heavy chains descended from one of the green metal ceiling supports. Richard and Bethany were dragged to their feet. Butt stopped turning when the chains dangled just above their heads. Strange slipped a pair of manacles through the large circles at the end of each chain and grabbed Richard's wrists. Richard kicked at the diminutive shopkeeper, who toppled backwards into a quivering aspidistra. Bates jumped from the crowd and twisted Richard's arm behind his back.

Richard let out a yelp of pain and fell to his knees.

Strange untangled himself from the plant leaves, his eyes blazing. 'Go to hell, and be damned, you bloody incomer!' He walked stiffly across to Richard and stood glaring down at him. Then the shopkeeper snarled and punched Richard in the jaw.

Richard's world went black.

CHAPTER TWENTY-THREE

Richard woke to find his ankles being licked.

He looked down and saw Spud carefully removing any traces of dirt from his boots. Richard knew the mud contained a few more unsavoury components than usual and tried to move out of the reach of the dog's tongue.

'Get that bloody hellhound away from me!' Richard said as he struggled against the chains. Four heavy hands grabbed him by the shoulders and forced him to stand in front of the Ashcrofts.

Spud eyed him reproachfully and carried on licking.

'Come by 'ere, Spud,' his owner growled. Spud slunk over to Farmer Butt's side. The farmer placed a thick pile of ten-pound notes, tied with a rubber band on the metallic white table, where Mrs Ashcroft sat nibbling on a cucumber sandwich.

''Tis all I got left after the summer rains near destroyed the 'arvest,' he muttered.

Mrs Ashcroft took the money and placed it in her handbag. 'Mamoner thanks you for the offering. He will bless you and the village.'

Farmer Butt nodded and followed the line of villagers back

through the servants' door.

The door clicked shut.

Dr Ashcroft sat back at the table, helped himself to a handful of sandwiches, and smiled at his wife. 'Well, how much did we make this year, my dear?' he asked, gazing fondly at her brown leather handbag.

'Twenty thousand in cash not including PayPal, much better than last year's offering,' she said. 'They do like it when it's a curate.'

'I know, my dear, but curates are hard to come by. Vagrants and other animals are much easier to tidy up,' he added.

'What are you going to do with us?' Bethany glared at the doctor.

'Well, make good use of my surgical rotation, for once, my dear,' Dr Ashcroft replied. 'I'm going to nail your hearts to the hollow oak tree in Elfsworthy Woods… Well, you have to keep the old village traditions alive, don't you?'

'My father will find you!' Richard shouted. 'He is coming down soon, and when he realises what you have done, he will come after you.'

Ashcroft sighed.

'Only if he thinks you are missing. A letter declaring your love for young Bethany here and your intention to make a new life together in Australia will sort that problem out. He knows you are weak and easily led astray. He will understand that my attempts to dissuade you from such a reckless course of action were futile. I might even get a special bonus from him. As to your remains, Sheng will break your carcasses down into pieces. After all, we have just bought two new terracotta urns for my wife's Manchineel seedlings and good compost costs so much these days,' the doctor stated, shaking his head.

'Hasn't anyone ever told you, people always lose when they try to make a deal with the devil?' Richard replied grimly. 'But I think you lost your soul a long time ago.'

'Oh dear.' Dr Ashcroft shook his head. 'Save your delusions for someone who's interested. I'm a general practitioner and really have no interest in your schizophrenic babblings.'

A slight movement from inside the mural caught Richard's attention. Something flickered from deep within the tunnel of branches. A small grey shape began to walk towards him.

The orangery darkened as a wave of black mould began to move across its expansive windows, blocking out the sunlight. The tropical heat of the greenhouse dropped. The hot sweat running down Richard's back turned cold against his skin.

Dr Ashcroft slipped a brown monk's habit over his head.

'You know, you really should stop watching those dreadful B-movies, boy. Old Squire Ashcroft knew exactly what he was doing when he started this little enterprise. The tithes were minimal, and the peasants needed another tax. He found out that some of his tenant farmers had been giving their money to a local cunning woman in return for her blessing on their crops. After some persuasion, the old hag agreed to share her profit with my illustrious ancestor but why share when you can have it all? Squire James hit on this marvellous scheme: get the villagers to give him as much money as they could in exchange for the blessings of a powerful demon. A sort of demon tax as it were. The irony was, after he had hanged the hag for witchcraft, he used her own sketches and illiterate scribbles to add a touch of realism to the venture. The peasants just lapped it up. Unfortunately, the ever-righteous Versey would not play along and had to be sacrificed, which actually made the demon tax even more realistic,' Ashcroft laughed.

'Your ancestor should not have used the witch's possessions or spellcraft. They were cursed by the violence of her death. He brought a real demon to Witherleigh.' Richard spoke softly, as he watched the mural.

Mrs Ashcroft's teacup clinked against the saucer. Her husband spun round.

'Please get on with it darling. The painter is coming to decorate the meditation room at 3 and I need to be there to supervise him, or god knows what he'll do,' she smiled.

Dr Ashcroft nodded and turned to face the mural, as he clasped his hands together in prayer, and began a low, whispery chant in pig Latin.

The grey figure of the little girl, with long black hair, stared at him from inside the mural. Her head flopped over onto her shoulder. She waved at Richard and grinned.

The girl climbed out from the mural and stood just behind Dr Ashcroft. She raised her head. Richard could see the dark hollows where her eyes had been.

The girl raised a grey finger to her lips.

Richard edged backwards. His chain stretched tight.

The demon-girl turned her face towards a huge terracotta pot, which dominated the right corner of the greenhouse, next to the double doors. One brown leathered hand grew from its soil and gripped the lip of the pot, its dark grey nails digging into the clay.

Black fracture lines ran across the pot.

A shrunken brown face rose from the base of a rippling palm tree, its empty eye sockets just above the soil's surface. A curtain of black hair hung across its face; one clump tied back with a straggly black ribbon.

Mrs Ashcroft scrolled through her iPhone and announced, 'The demon offering is working already. The Happy Chicken Company is increasing the prices they pay per farmer by five per cent, and a few small money hoards are being discovered around the Witherleigh area.'

'Good work, my dear,' Dr Ashcroft nodded to his wife. 'Well, let's get on with it. Shall we? We can't very well have the offering rewards being reaped before the offering actually takes place. That would really raise some eyebrows.'

He walked over to the ornate table and kissed his wife's delicate, pale hand. Mrs Ashcroft rose and walked towards Bethany, the red dot of her iPhone staring at Bethany as she began to film the offering.

'Get away from me, you bloody freak!' Bethany growled trying to kick the phone from her hand.

Mrs Ashcroft deftly stepped to one side as Bethany overbalanced and swung round on her chain.

Dr Ashcroft put the hood of the monk's habit over his head, his face lost in shadows as he approached Bethany, an ornate ruby-handled knife in his hand. He placed the point of the blade just below her ribcage, its blade pointing upwards towards her heart. A thin trickle of blood dripped down the pink of her kitten-themed pyjama top.

'O great Mamoner, demon bringer of gold, please accept

this offering. *Mamoner oncede platapusi,*' he raised the knife and lunged at Bethany's heart.

Bethany kneed him in the groin.

Dr Ashcroft squealed and dropped to his knees clutching himself. The knife clattered to the floor.

'I'm not being anyone's platypussy!' Bethany declared aiming several kicks at Dr Ashcroft's head.

'Um… I think what he meant to say, in the worst Latin I have ever heard, was that you are being offered to *Mamonae* as a sacrifice,' Richard shouted, tugging on his chains, as Mrs Ashcroft approached him with a butter knife.

'So, you hear a lot of Latin then?' Bethany asked, one sleek brown eyebrow raised.

'Er… well… don't tell me you never played speak only Latin Fridays in your house?' Richard replied panting. A cloud of dust and chipped paint wafted downwards as his chain rattled against the metal cross beam.

'Funnily enough, no… yes!' Bethany replied as one of her kicks hit Dr Ashcroft in the throat. He flew backwards and crashed against the huge terracotta pot which contained the rippling palm tree. A dark green palm leaf snapped from the tree trunk and fell onto the white floor tiles. A shrivelled brown hand reached out from the pot and grabbed the doctor by his hair. The shrunken face watching from inside the bark reanimated, its hair neatly pulled back by a black ribbon, to reveal the youthful features of Richard Dicken. His green eyes opened. The dead curate leant forward and whispered something in the doctor's ear. Ashcroft screamed and began to tear at his head with his hands.

Richard winced as he saw wriggling white maggots drop from the doctor's nose and mouth. Dicken put his hands either side of the doctor's face and squeezed. A stream of maggots gushed from the corner of the doctor's eyes.

Mrs Ashcroft ran over to her husband. 'What the hell are you doing. It's only a bit of mud for goodness sake! Get a grip.'

'That dead curate has got me!' Ashcroft screamed as he ripped the skin from his face. His eyes bulged, their blood vessels rupturing as his face grew redder. Blood began to trickle from his eyes, ears, and nose as the dead hands squeezed harder against his skull, staining the maggots red.

The demon-girl giggled, her high-pitched laughter ringing through the orangery.

There was a loud crunch. The doctor's head exploded across the double doors. An expressionist vision of angry demon in red and white.

Mrs Ashcroft screamed and ran down the path, between the stirring plants, towards the servants' exit.

The demon-girl leapt through the air, transforming into a huge raven, which dived talons first into the fleeing woman's back. The force knocked Mrs Ashcroft from her feet. She landed in some low-lying, moss-filled pots. A raven, perched on the lowest fanning leaf of the palm tree, watched her with unblinking, amber eyes. Mrs Ashcroft sat up. Her eyes darted around the orangery as she tried to locate her attacker.

The grey shape of Reverend Versey rose from behind a wall of bamboo. His black clerical robes ripped and bloodied. Open wounds on his face, hands, and torso began to bleed as he walked towards her.

303

Mrs Ashcroft covered her face with her hands and screamed. The raven swooped from the palm. It landed on her chest, its talons digging into her blouse. She grabbed the raven's body and tried to push the bird away. The bird twisted its head around and pecked through her right eye. A thin stream of blood trickled from her eye socket. She flopped back against the broken pottery. Her remaining eye stared lifelessly at the glass roof.

The raven cawed loudly and transformed back into the little girl.

The girl winked at Richard and dragged Mrs Ashcroft, by one stilettoed foot, into the leafy ferns.

'We've got to go… now!' Richard whispered to Bethany as the ghosts of Versey and Dicken appeared next to him touching and pulling at his clothes.

'I know,' hissed Bethany, 'but these bloody chains would stop a bull. We haven't pissed off any ghosts, so perhaps they will leave us alone.'

Richard looked into the blank faces of the two ghosts. Their minds had become lost in the confusion of their violent deaths and unchristian burials. 'I think we just need to be very quiet,' he whispered. 'And to be honest I am more worried about the demon.

Bethany frowned. 'What demon?' she mouthed looking round the orangery.

'The one who just dragged Mrs Ashcroft into the ferns,' Richard said, staring into the moving foliage.

'Mrs Ashcroft fell into those pots and rolled off dead.' Bethany stared at Richard. 'Don't bloody lose it now!'

Something flickered inside the greenery.

'Oh God,' Richard whispered. 'Here she comes!'

Mrs Ashcroft rose from the foliage. Her white blouse covered in blood. The right side of her face had been shredded. She stared around the orangery in confusion.

A heavy, grey rain cloud moved aside, and the sun peered through the break in the clouds, sending a shaft of white sunlight through the grey sky, hitting the white floor tiles just in front of the mural.

Richard said a prayer for Mrs Ashcroft. He hoped she would find her way into the light and enter the *Postvitum* without wandering.

The headless body of Dr Ashcroft rose and staggered blindly through the plants.

Mrs Ashcroft's face elongated, her mouth and eyes wide dark ovals, as she watched the remains of her husband stagger towards Richard.

There was a rustling of feathers as the raven grew and then disappeared in a flurry of black feathers. The feathers fell to the ground to reveal the grey shadow of a man.

Mamonae stared with satisfaction at the chaotic scene in front of him.

The demon stood over six feet tall. Its beautified, finely sculptured face was slightly too grey to be human, its eyes too black. A long, black ponytail trailed down his back. The creature wore an immaculate single-breasted, black three-piece suit with hand-stitched notched lapels and contemporary straight pockets. Its shirt was starched white and open at the collar, to reveal a triangular sigil pendant. The demon looked as if he had just stepped out of *Vogue*. Richard looked down at his own mud-splattered clothes, and instantly wished he had not. He looked more like a 'Help the Homeless' ad campaign than a respectable church worker.

He hoped Bethany had not noticed his bedraggled appearance.

The demon pointed his finger towards Dicken. Instantly, the ghost's face melted to that of his death mask. Dicken flew backwards, his body pressed against the glass, as he tried to escape the demon's gaze. Dicken's body flickered twice then disappeared, leaving only the trace of his spirit – a series of terrified, discordant screams which ran around the orangery.

PC Bates burst through the double doors.

'An' what's goin' on 'ere then?' he demanded.

An invisible force picked him up. He rose slowly into the air, his feet dangling in space as he began to turn.

'Help me!' Bates whimpered, looking down at Richard.

Richard tried to grab his boot but missed. Bates stopped turning and was tossed against the mural. A loud crunch echoed through the orangery as he fell groaning onto the floor.

His radio crackled to life.

Bates pressed the button on top of the radio and whispered, 'Save me.'

The demon raised one grey finger in the policeman's direction. Dr Ashcroft lumbered over to the fallen policeman and promptly walked through the prone body.

The demon laughed as the doctor bent down and began to search for the policeman.

Bates screamed and rolled over; his back pressed against the floor tiles as he tried to escape the doctor. The cold dampness of the mould-infested tiles sent a series of shivers through his body.

The demon's mouth twisted into a black-lipped smile. He bent down and touched the forehead of the prone figure at his feet. Bates screamed in pain clutching at his head as the veins in his eyes bulged.

'*Mamonae ab hoc loco*, demon leave this place!' Richard shouted, desperately pulling on his chain.

The demon cocked his head to one side and said, 'Swing puppet!'

Instantly, the chains began to move. Richard and Bethany flew through the air as their chains began to swing forwards and backwards, their feet swishing through the plants.

'I know your name, *Mamonae*. You must do as I will. Leave this place and go back to the darkness. *Et tu iubes*!'

'You are not strong enough, boy.' The demon laughed, plucking a fallen leaf from his jacket lapel.

The demon twisted its hand to the side and the chains broke in mid-swing. Bethany and Richard were flung against the metal rafters supporting the roof and fell.

A gust of wind caught them and lowered them to the floor.

Dicken's face appeared in front of Richard; his mouth wide as he screamed through the convergence, 'Save our souls! Do it now before we are all damned.'

Richard nodded. He had no desire to fight with the supernatural on two fronts. If he could eliminate the accidental threat posed by the ghosts, then he would be free to concentrate his energy on the smirking demon, who seemed momentarily pre-occupied with the contents of Mrs Ashcroft's designer handbag.

Richard grabbed a handful of soil. Quickly, he sprinkled the earth into the shape of a circle over the blood-stained tiles.

A shaft of sunlight appeared, casting yellow beams against the darkened windows. The mould steamed and disappeared.

Richard took a hemp bag from the pocket of his jeans and filled the outline with white powder as he whispered, '*Spirituum veniunt*, spirits come to me, and cross into the light.'

He knelt by the circle, raised his arms above his head, and shouted, '*Spirituum veniunt… et suscipe benedictionem accipere et transire in lucem*. Spirits come to me and cross into the light of God.'

The shaft of sunlight touched the powder. The ring exploded into flames.

Dr Ashcroft moved towards the sound, crossing through the circle of flames and vanished. Mrs Ashcroft ran after her husband, her ghostly body disappearing into the flames.

'No!' screamed the demon. 'You are spoiling my fun!' The demon shrunk into the body of the little girl and flew at Richard.

'*Ut auferat*, leave my charge alone!' boomed the voice of Reverend Anderson as he raised the plain wooden crucifix, which he had stolen from Stillbone Chapel, above his head. 'You have no business here! Leave us!' He threw a jar of water at the demon. The demon-girl hissed. Her body steamed as the holy water began to eat away at its form.

The demon howled with pain and vanished.

'Don't just kneel there, young man, finish the job.' Anderson shouted across to Richard, who sat staring at the Reverend in shocked surprise.

'Hurry up Richard!' Reverend Anderson called as he took a hip flask out of his inner cassock pocket and drained it.

Richard nodded.

'*Mortuorum spirituum ad me*, ghosts come to me and cross into the light,' Richard shouted, as he made the sign of the cross.

The face of Richard Dicken sailed towards the light. His ghost flickered for an instant and the curate reappeared in his pre-death form, his black hair smartly tied back, his black tunic sweeping down to his knee, his black riding boots shining and spotless. Dicken stepped into the circle and bowed. 'Thank you, Richard, Reverend Anderson, you have saved our souls. We go to join the angels.'

He held his hand out to Versey, who was hovering just outside the circle, and pulled him into the shaft of light. Both curates closed their eyes and ascended.

The shaft flickered. The bridge to the *Postvitum* was failing.

'Christ what was that?' Bethany said as she sat down next to Richard and wiped the spots of blood from her face.

'The ghosts have passed on,' Richard answered, running his hand through his hair.

'So, it's over.' Bethany beamed with relief.

'Almost,' replied Anderson. 'Richard has something for you.'

Richard glanced over to Anderson and frowned. There was more to this Reverend than he had realised. Richard took the ring from his pocket. 'Your father has passed on too. His bones are buried under the hollow oak tree at Elfsworthy Woods. He wants you to move on with your life now and be happy.'

Bethany took the ring and clasped it to her chest as she furiously blinked away tears.

'Thank you!' she muttered and kissed Richard on the cheek.

Richard went scarlet and felt the excitement rise inside him. Perhaps she did fancy him after all he thought hopefully. 'Err… perhaps we could go out and…' his voice trailed off.

'Or perhaps you can grab Sheng. He will help you find your father's bones.' Anderson interjected.

Bethany gave the vicar a hug.

The Reverend squeezed her waist. 'Now let's get out of this bloody place, shall we? We'll take the back passageway. The villagers have gathered in the parlour, so we need to go quietly.' Bethany and Richard nodded.

They crept silently from the orangery and tiptoed past the parlour, its door slightly ajar, sending wafts of basil and wormwood through the hallway. Richard peeked inside. He frowned as he recognised some of the villagers, who were kneeling with their backs to the door. In front of them was an animal skull with large horns, placed in the centre of a highly polished Georgian table. Next to the skull was an ornate black chalice. Thick black pillar candles stood either end of the table. It was like a scene from a cheap horror movie.

'Mamoner, come to us an' grant us thy blessing!' Strange chanted, wearing a small horned animal skull perched on his head. Richard assumed it had been made from an unfortunate sheep.

Strange sliced open the top of his finger with a small knife and squeezed a drop of blood into a black chalice. He passed the knife and chalice to Primrose Stacey. She stabbed herself in the palm and squeezed several drops into the chalice. Then passed the chalice to her neighbour.

'Come on,' Anderson whispered and dragged Richard down the corridor towards the kitchen.

The kitchen smelt of fresh yeast and strawberry jam. Bethany squealed and jumped into Sheng's arms. Her feet wrapped tightly around his waist.

'We know where my father is! He can have a Christian burial!' she said kissing him on the lips.

Sheng nodded. 'That's good news. We will go after the rolls have finished proving.'

'No, you must go now,' Anderson instructed the chef.

Sheng frowned and stared at the vicar's face. They both nodded, sharing a private secret.

'Of course, we go now.' Sheng smiled at Bethany. He exchanged his chef whites for a khaki green jacket and escorted her to his car.

Richard watched as Sheng opened the passenger side door of his old car and helped Bethany into the seat. She smiled up at him as he closed the door.

Richard felt his heart shudder and break in two.

The Reverend placed a heavy hand on his shoulder.

'There goes one great piece of ass,' the Reverend said following Richard's gaze, as he watched the chef's elderly car crawl down the gravel driveway.

The smile fell from Reverend Anderson's face. 'We need to finish this now, follow me.'

He locked the front door of the hall. Then Reverend Anderson rolled three large barrels of Bishop's Finger from the boot of his car and placed them next to the front door.

'What's actually in that stuff?' Richard asked.

'Always stay away from the local scrumpy, stick to spirits,' the vicar said. He reached into his pocket and took out a hipflask. Richard refused the offered tipple. Anderson shrugged and took a large sip, golden liquid spilling down his chin. The Reverend wiped his chin with the back of his hand and carefully screwed the top back on the flask before secreting it away inside his cassock.

'Best I can figure is somethings in the bottom of the vat which was blessed by the demon a long time ago. It rots your soul and opens the door to wickedness. That's why it's warm to touch.'

Richard stared at the vicar's flushed face. 'It's the bones of the little girls, isn't it?'

Anderson nodded. 'Probably… Alice Sidwell was the first child sacrifice. You walked past the Sidwell graves at Stillbone cemetery. Unfortunately, *Mamonae* later developed more ecclesiastical tastes. Probably at the command of his master.'

'So, he demanded curates instead?' Richard said.

Anderson nodded. 'It's a direct attack on the church. If you kill the next generation of vicars, the church will eventually collapse and there will be nothing left to stop the *Daemonium – princeps,* the destroyer of man crossing through a convergence and entering the *Vitare*. The land of the living.'

'But killing a few curates in Witherleigh will not cause the collapse of the entire Anglican church,' Richard replied. 'I know there is a shortage of vicars but it's not that bad!'

'Not unless this is a repeating pattern,' Anderson replied

grimly. 'Remember London. That's why you were chosen to become an *Indagator* – a hunter for the church and sent down here.'

'Chosen?' Richard pinched the inside of his wrist. 'I was told I was insane, thrown out of college, and placed in a mental institute by my own father. No one chose me for anything.'

'Yes, well, your father thought your spirit needed strengthening,' Anderson said as he hauled a petrol can from the boot of his car and poured it carefully through the front door letterbox.

Richard felt his legs tremble. He collapsed onto the grass. 'My Father knew all along and just left me to suffer? I lost everything.'

Anderson nodded. '*And whoever does not carry their cross and follow me cannot be my disciple. Luke 14:27*. We all suffer Richard.'

He struck a match and tossed it through the letterbox. The door burst into angry orange and yellow flames. The flames touched the barrels. They exploded sending sheets of fire across the front of the mansion. In a matter of seconds, the flames had spread across the lower floor of the mansion. The windows cracked under the heat and black smoke billowed out from the downstairs rooms.

The trapped villagers panicked and ran to the windows. Their screams and shouts for aid were just audible over the sounds of wood cracking as the manor began to collapse in on itself. The whole roof wobbled and cracked, falling into the second floor.

There was a series of loud explosions as the fire reached the orangery. Every glass window exploded.

The villagers tried to smash through the leaded windows of the morning room. Chairs and broken table legs bounced off the fragile glass.

Richard watched in horror as one by one, the villagers fell consumed by the smoke. Mrs Stacy banged at the window shouting at Richard, her words taken by the roar of the flames.

Richard picked up an ornamental granite rock and ran towards the window. Something grabbed his legs and he catapulted face downwards onto the lawn.

Reverend Anderson leapt onto his back, his weight pressing Richard into the damp grass. Richard desperately tried to shake him off, but the Reverend was immovable. Richard heard him take another gulp from the hipflask.

The terrified faces in the window vanished as flames poured from every window, sending a column of smoke soaring into the grey sky. In the distance, the sound of sirens raced across the moor.

Reverend Anderson stood up and said a prayer for the dead.

Richard sat back onto his ankles and watched the fire destroy everything as tears rolled down his face. 'You murdered them all. How could you?'

The Reverend lit a cigarette and shook his head. 'They were dead as soon as their ancestors signed the pact with *Mamonae*. Save your tears for the innocent. We are soldiers of Christ. Now get up, the fire will not touch the demon. It will come after us now.'

CHAPTER TWENTY-FOUR

The Range Rover skidded to a halt in front of St Anthony's, its passenger side wheels resting on the pavement. Reverend Anderson ran from the car and unlocked the heavy iron gates.

Richard sat in the car; the image of the dying villages burnt into his brain.

'Come on!' shouted the Reverend. 'We haven't got much time!'

Anderson swore and ran around the front of the car. He opened the passenger door and grabbed Richard by the shoulders. 'Don't go soft on me now, Richard. *Mamonae* will not leave quietly. Do you want another massacre like Stillbone?'

Richard shook his head and followed the vicar into the church. The Reverend lit the thick altar candles, their flames cast dark flickering shadows across the grey stone walls of the church.

Anderson knelt and crossed himself in front of the altar his hands together in prayer.

'Come on, Richard, stop dawdling!' he commanded.

'But you killed them all,' Richard murmured, his naturally pale face white with shock as he stood in the church doorway.

'Well, everyone dies, Richard, and besides as a man of God

it is my duty to save peoples souls and show them the true power of the church. Their physical bodies are a secular matter.'

'But they are all dead,' Richard whispered.

'Yes, but at least they are not worshiping demons anymore,' Anderson said as he jogged over to the broom cupboard. He reappeared moments later with a huge, ornately decorated, golden incense burner with three thick golden chains.

'Give me a hand. This thing is bloody heavy,' he shouted. Richard ran over and helped hold the incense burner as the Reverend climbed up onto the top of the altar. He hung the burner on an outstretched gold hook just above the font. Anderson lit the charcoal in the burner. Immediately, the church was filled with the essence of sage, lavender, and barbeque.

'Got to keep the good stuff hidden from the locals,' Anderson stated.

The Reverend climbed down from the altar and walked across to the nave. He pulled back the faded, T-shaped embroidered runner which ran up the centre of the nave, separating the two sides of the church, to reveal the large triangle with elongated lines trapped within a circle.

'Time to close this demon trap once and for all,' he said.

'You knew about this all along? Why didn't you tell me?' Richard stared accusingly at the Reverend.

'Well, I could of done, but then I would have had to kill you. That's the problem with secret religious orders. They have to remain secret,' Anderson said gravely.

'So, are you going to try to kill me then?' Richard asked quietly.

Anderson laughed. 'Definitely not! Your father would rip my bloody balls off! Besides which, you were born to be part of the order. Now enough questions, we have a demon trap to seal.'

'But why wasn't this sealed earlier?' Richard muttered. 'Like a couple of hundred years ago?'

Reverend Anderson sighed heavily and took a bottle of communion wine from the well-stocked church wine cupboard. He poured himself a large chaliceful of wine.

'As soon as the pattern of missing curates was found, the Archbishop called in the hunters. The demon exorcism did not go well. Stillbone hamlet was lost. Eventually, the demon was trapped in here by Reverend Goodebody, who sacrificed his life in this church, to trap the demon. After that, the Archbishop created certain precautions,' Anderson said.

He pointed to the stained glass windows, the vivid yellows, reds, and blues of the demon fighting angels. 'And the trap was created; but without the demon's name it could not be sealed *in aeternum.*'

'So... the church used me as some sort of demon bait?' Richard frowned.

'Well, you do have a way of attracting demons... and ghosts for that matter.' The vicar nodded to Snowy, who sat fidgeting on the back pew.

'Good day, Vicars, I'm just waiting for me wife, Martha,' Snowy nodded back, looking at his broken watch, and shaking his head.

The heavy church doors slammed shut.

The stacks of hymn books which had been piled neatly

on the table at the front of the church exploded, sending the books crashing into the walls of the church. A storm of torn pages fluttered over the pews.

A dark shadow crossed the church as one by one the stained glass windows turned black with mould.

The candles on the altar flickered. Their orange flames darkened and stretched upwards casting long, smoky black shadows. Their subtle waxy aroma transformed into a clawing sulphurous smell, which drifted in a grey mist from the altar, overpowering the delicate incense.

'He's coming. Do it quickly. Carve his name into the trap and bind him here for eternity. I will keep him from you for as long as possible,' Anderson said as he rummaged through the stack of magazines piled at the back of the wine cupboard.

'Yes, found them!' Anderson grinned. He took out a miniature hammer and chisel which he passed to Richard.

Richard knelt and began to tap away at the middle of the elongated triangle. The chisel slipped on the solid granite and cut into his hand. A drop of red fell into the circle. The blood soaked into the stone.

'Well, that will certainly summon him here,' Anderson tutted, shaking his head.

Richard said nothing.

He tore a strip of cotton from his shirt, wrapped it around his hand, and continued chipping away at the stone.

A loud crunching noise echoed through the church.

'Bloody hell, that didn't take him long,' Anderson swore.

Richard looked across the pews. His mouth went dry as a series of grey footprints led from the door to the nave, sinking into the stone flag floor as they walked.

The footprints stopped two feet from the clerics.

Anderson took out a heavily beaded rosary and wrapped the beads around his wrist, the ornate crucifix dangling loose. He raised the cross in front of his face and whispered, '*Abiit potest daemonium,* begone demon, you have no place in the house of the Lord.'

Richard looked up at Anderson in surprise.

'Just something I borrowed from Father Ignatius at a southwest interfaith meeting.' The flushed vicar smiled.

'Does he know you took it?' Richard asked.

'I hope not,' Anderson replied. 'He's got a bastard of a temper.'

The crucifix began to turn.

Lightning cracked and danced around the church. Every stained glass window in the church shattered.

Anderson and Richard fell to the floor, covering their heads with their hands, as glass shards rained across the church.

Somewhere in the distance thunder growled.

'Well, this is all getting rather tedious, isn't it?' a bored voice stated.

Anderson stood up and placed himself between Richard and the demon.

'I name you *Mamonae*, do as I command. *Abiit potest daemonium*, be gone demon.' He chanted over and over, as the crucifix spun faster.

The demon glared at the vicar. 'Come out from behind your little cross and let us end this charade.'

Mamonae raised a delicate grey hand and pretended to

snatch the crucifix. Anderson swivelled away from the demon. The crucifix hit the side of the front pew and became caught in the carved wood. Anderson tried to tug the cross free. The demon raised one hand and squeezed his fingers together slowly until he made a fist.

Beads of sweat sprinkled across the vicar's forehead and ran down his flushed face.

Anderson gasped for breath, as he clutched at his chest, and collapsed against a pew.

The demon rearranged the cufflinks on his shirt sleeve and smirked. 'It's just all too easy.'

Richard cast a quick glance towards the demon as he finished carving a wobbly 'M' into the circle.

Slowly, his right hand moved across to his left.

'You will have no dominion over me,' Richard said, murmuring protection prayers in Latin under his breath, as he tried to will his hand to stop moving.

His right hand stabbed the chisel into the back of his left. Richard screamed in pain. He dropped the chisel and clutched his bleeding hand to his chest.

The demon smiled and nodded towards the church wall. A grey marble plaque commemorating the village's WWI fallen, slowly cracked in two. The two halves crashed to the floor in a mushroom of dust and sandstone.

'You and your pathetic church will never win,' *Mamonae* hissed in his ear. 'You are all just too weak.'

Richard felt the imprint of a hand on his head, crushing his skull.

The demon squeezed harder.

Richard felt his eyes begin to pop from their sockets. A band of red-hot pain wrapped around his head. He screamed and fell forward across the demon trap.

Mamonae leapt onto his back. He sliced through Richard's sweatshirt and undershirt to reveal a pale, slightly toned body.

'Thank you for being so compliant,' the demon whispered in his ear. 'Your precious Christian-tinged blood will bind my contract with the villagers here… forever.'

Mamonae reached forward and took a piece of the shattered plaque. Richard closed his eyes and tensed. The demon's weight on his back shifted slightly and he felt his skull explode. Richard's vision narrowed to black as he collapsed onto the floor.

The demon tutted. 'That was so much easier than Stillbone; millennials are just such a waste of a good soul.'

In the distance, Richard heard the church door opening and the sounds of feet running towards the altar.

'Oi! I think you have slightly underestimated us!' Bethany shouted as she approached the demon.

'Run!' Richard mouthed. The blood from his head wound dripped into the lines of the triangle. The stone slab grew warm, as the circular seal began to hiss.

The demon sighed. 'Oh, a villager, how quaint… Eager to join your father I see, little girl.'

Mamonae stood up. A black shadow rose out of his body and took the form of a huge raven. The raven squawked loudly and soared towards Bethany. She covered her face with her hands and screamed, 'Now!'

A bottle of Bishop's Finger sailed through the broken

stained glass window above the altar, a rag carrying a red flash, fixed inside its neck. The bottle smashed against the stone slab inches from the demon and exploded into flames.

The raven swivelled its head, one hundred and eighty degrees. It cawed angrily. 'You cannot burn me out of here – you stupid bitch.'

The demon-bird flapped its enormous wings once and landed claws first, ripping into Bethany's arms. The impact of the bird knocked her to the ground. The bird's talons pierced her arms. Bethany screamed and tried to punch the bird away as blood began to trickle down her arms.

Another bottle exploded through the broken window. Flames flickered, running across the church pews. Moments later Sheng ran towards the demon, his big chef's cleaver in hand. The raven reared upwards, flapping its wings. An unseen force flung the chef upwards, pinning him to the church ceiling.

His cleaver clattered to the floor.

'Well, so many souls on offer. I feel a little spoilt for choice,' the demon sighed, as he transferred back to his human form, 'but I'll take the curate first.'

Mamonae kicked Bethany in the ribs. He laughed as she groaned and tried to grab his foot. He kicked her again. His foot meeting the softness of her stomach. She curled in a ball, gasping for breath. 'Then, I'll rip your heart out and suck it dry, while your darling chef just hangs up there and watches. I like it when people watch me perform,' the demon whispered in Bethany's ear, 'It gives me such an adrenaline rush.'

The demon picked up the cleaver and walked towards Richard.

Anderson held out one shaky arm to try to block the demon's path. *Mamonae* waved a grey hand in the air and Anderson flew across the church. 'Just die old man,' he hissed.

The demon knelt by the prostrate body of Richard.

'Not yet dead I see, there is a God!' He laughed and grabbed Richard's hair, pulling him from the floor. 'I'm going to enjoy playing with your soul,' *Mamonae* whispered. He pressed the cleaver against Richard's throat.

Richard closed his eyes, and his body went limp. The demon roared in delight.

'I am going to kill everyone here and there is nothing your blessed church can do about it!' the demon laughed.

The blood running through the circular seal began to smoke. Then the seal exploded as a glowing bright white light burnt the demon trap into the granite.

The demon looked down in confusion.

Richard's hand opened. The chisel fell from his grasp to reveal the word '*Mamonae*' scratched into the centre of the sigil.

The demon's pact was sealed.

The demon screamed with rage as he was sucked into the trap. The sides of the seal spun upwards creating a spiralling, translucent column which touched the church rafters.

'I will return and kill you all!' he screamed, beating his fists against the column.

The flagstones beneath his feet began to crumble away to reveal a deep pit beneath the church. The demon tried to cling to the sides of the column as the last of the flagstones fell into the darkness of the pit.

The vortex spiralled downwards.

The demon lost his handholds as he was sucked into the pit. His screams faded to nothing. The flagstones mended themselves.

'Good job,' Anderson whispered as he staggered towards Richard.

Sheng crashed down onto the pews below. Richard rolled onto his back and smiled up at the vicar. 'He talked way too much!'

Anderson pulled Richard to his feet and they hobbled down the nave.

Sun streamed through the broken window above the blazing altar.

***

Outside the church, Farmer Butler was standing over Bethany, flapping a frayed grey handkerchief at her blood-stained face. Sheng hobbled over and sat next to her. Butler handed him a mug of steaming tea from a daisy-covered thermos flask.

Butler nodded at the vicar. 'So, I'll be taking down the demon lines then, shall I vicar?'

Anderson nodded, his arm around Richard's shoulder as he half-dragged him to the road.

Richard's eyes met Bethany's for a moment. She nodded and then beamed as Sheng whispered something in her ear. Richard smiled at the couple, the heavy weight of heartbreak crushing his chest.

'Thank you for your help with all this.' Richard waved a bloodied hand towards the broken church. 'And for believing in me.'

Bethany stood up and hugged him. 'Well... if you can't trust a curate, who can you trust?'

'But I'm not a...' Richard began. He was stopped by a quick but painful punch in the arm.

'Well, you are in our books,' she grinned.

Sheng came over and solemnly shook Richard by the hand. 'If you ever come down to Devon again, please visit us, but only if you are free from ghosts and bad spirits.'

'Er... of course,' Richard muttered, as he watched Snowy walk out of the church, carrying the incense burner under his arm.

An engine purred quietly as a highly conspicuous white Rolls-Royce drew up outside St Anthony's. Everyone stared at the car as the driver's window slid down.

'See, I told you we'd take good care of him,' Anderson said as he hobbled over to the car and shook the driver's hand.

'Well, he's not as rough-looking as I've seen him in the past,' Reverend Radcliffe replied.

He opened the door and went to greet his son. 'I always knew you had it in you Richard. It just needed prising out. Too much of your mother in you for your own good.'

Anderson nodded. 'She is an extremely attractive woman.'

Radcliffe eyed him suspiciously. Richard waved goodbye to Bethany and Sheng.

He shook Anderson's hand. 'Thank you for saving my life, Reverend,' he said.

'Well, that's what we do.' Anderson smiled and drained the last drips of gin from his hipflask.

Richard settled into the back of the Rolls.

'When were you going to tell me?' Richard asked, sinking into the leather seat and closing his eyes.

'When you were ready,' Reverend Radcliffe replied as he drove smoothly through the village, stopping to let a stream of emergency vehicles pass.

'Welcome to the hunt, Richard, and may God help you,' he muttered, frowning as a grey shadow crossed his mirror.

The Wall of Honour

The Witherleigh Puzzle provides clues to an object in North Devon. If you are one of the elite few who solve the puzzle, send in a photo with you holding this book by the object described.

To enter the puzzle please fill in the online form at-pjreedwriting.wixsite.com/horror/the-witherleigh-puzzle

If you can solve The Witherleigh Puzzle correctly, your name and photograph will be added to the Wall of Honour. You will also receive the Witherleigh Puzzle winner's badge.

A Glossary of Legion Terminology

Abyss   A land of choking firepits and ashfalls,
                   where those judged unworthy are doomed
                   to wander for eternity.

Cold Spots   Cold Spots occur when something is
                   passing from the Mortalis to the Vitare, the
                   plane of the living.

Convergence   A convergence occurs in places where
                   the walls of the Mortalis and the Vitare
                   are very thin and allow things to pass
                   between the two.

Covensteads   A generic term for a gathering of demon
                   followers. Each covenstead worships their
                   own nominated demon.

Daemonium   Asmodeus, the leader of the demons,
– princeps   General of the Legion of Solise. He was
                   cast from the Elisium into the Abyss, after
                   his defeat in the Six Thousand Year War.

Demon lines   A form of demonic and spirit protection.
                   A protective perimeter is created using
                   a rope. Sharp metallic objects are hung
                   from the rope. If a spirit or demon tries to
                   pass through the perimeter, the rope will
                   move and the metallic objects turn, cutting
                   the air and ripping the convergence. The
                   convergence will collapse, and they will be
                   drawn back into the Mortalis.

Demon trap	A sigil trap for a demon. The demon is trapped by the sigil and a vortex between the Vitare and the Abyss is opened. A demon caught in a demon trap is cast into the Abyss.
Divus	The Creator of Worlds and Keeper of the Scales of good and evil.
Elisium	The land of eternal plenty, where those judged as deserving spend eternity.
Gate of Judicium	The gate of judgement. The gateway to the Elisium.
Indagator	A member of the Legion of St. Michael, specialising in demon hunting and exorcisms.
Mamonae	The greed demon.
Mortalis	The 'Afterdeath' an empty void where the spirits who cannot move on exist. It is the home of the fallen and other creatures, who have escaped the horrors of the Abyss. Occasionally, where the walls of the Mortalis touch those of the Vitare, the spirits and the fallen can cross over to the land of the living but only for short periods of time, because the walls between the two spaces are constantly moving.
Postvitum	The afterlife, the world next to the Mortalis, where spirits go to be judged. After judgement they are either sent up into the Elisium or down into the Abyss. Either way the judgement is eternal.

Resonare	A re-enactment of a crime that was so terrible it caused a wound in the wall of the living world. When the scar is disturbed the memory replays itself.
Sigil	A carved magical symbol which can be used for good or evil.
Solise	One of the legions of angels. Alone among the angels, the Solise possessed freewill, so they could be advisers to Divus, the creator. However, with freewill comes desire and they fought with the other legions as they desired sole control of the Earth. A great war was fought for six thousand years and human life almost perished. When the legion of Solise were finally defeated they were cast out of the Elisium and sent into the Abyss as eternal punishment. Over the millennia, the Solise became disfigured and corrupted in the acidic, firelands of the Abyss. However, they endured, their one goal being to escape their prison and have dominium over the Vitare.
Vitare	The land of the living.

Liber Fieri Dæmoniorum

An extract from the *daemonium compendium*

Demon	Character and Appearance
Mamonae – The Demon of Greed.	*Mamonae* appeareth to the congregation in the form of a man. He wore no cloth but was naked. The demon was identified by the *Indagor* as *Mamonae* for it possessed two horns, cloven feet, and two black-ribbed wings. Over its shoulder it carried a sack of gold. The demon may takest the form of a master, small maiden, or bird.
Se Irim – The Reaper of Death	*Se Irim* takest the form of a monk wearest he a brown habit and hood that coverest his face. He appears stooped and leans on a knotted staff. He is plague. He is death.

A Devon Dictionary

Dialect	Standard English
alrite me luvver	'Alright my lover,' a traditional friendly Devonian greeting.
an'	and
ark at ee	listen to him
backalong	something that happened in the past
bain't	have not
cow dog	A farm dog used for herding cows. Usually quite murky. Often found sitting in the back of an ATV (All Terrain Vehicle).
ee	him or it
ees	he is
'em	them
'er	her
'ere	here or 'did you know'
dimpsey	the falling of dusk
gert	large
grockle	a slightly derogatory term for an outsider or holidaymaker
'im's	he has
proper job	a job well done
raymes	skeleton

shippen	a milking parlour, where the cows go to be milked.
'tis	it is
townie	An outsider. Anyone who lives in a town outside the village.
up north	anything north of the somerset border
yer tis	here it is

References

1. (2016) English Bible, England
2. Matthew Hopkins (1672) Triangulum, England
3. Michah of Canterbury (1505) Liber Fieri Dæmoniorum, England

Printed in Great Britain
by Amazon